Critical acclaim for A Little Death*:*

'Remarkably skilled first novel, told through three narrators flashing back from the 1950s to the First World War. Works as both a locked-room mystery and a nugget of social history. Great promise' Mike Ripley, *Daily Telegraph*

'Laura Wilson weaves a spellbinding and atmospheric tale that re-creates vivid pictures of period living. And with the ventriloquist skill of the truly imaginative writer, she gets under the skin of her narrators to produce a haunting tragedy of damaged and distorted lives'
Val McDermid, *Manchester Evening News*

'I urge everyone towards an offbeat, literate, wonderfully imagined novel . . . Tightly written, completely true to period, quietly horrifying' *Poisoned Pen*

'An accomplished first novel . . . an evocative picture of a past era with a childhood death which remains unexplained until the final pages. A very promising debut'
Susanna Yager, *Daily Telegraph*

'. . . winds up the intrigue so that the book is difficult to put down. Written in a deceptively sedate style, it nevertheless had me galloping through the pages to see what the characters would get up to in the next chapter. *A Little Death* provides a strong sense of time and place, it is understated, witty and sharply observed, building a multi-layered, seductive and spell-binding mystery' *Crime Time*

Laura Wilson was brought up in London and has degrees in English Literature from Somerville College, Oxford, and University College London. She has worked briefly and ingloriously as a teacher, and more successfully as an editor of non-fiction books. She has written history books for children and is interested in history, particularly of the recent past, painting and sculpture, uninhabited buildings, underground structures, cemeteries and time capsules. Her first three novels were critically acclaimed, and the first, *A Little Death*, was shortlisted for both the CWA Historical Dagger and the Anthony Award for Best Paperback Original. She lives in London.

By Laura Wilson

Hello Bunny Alice
My Best Friend
Dying Voices
A Little Death

A Little Death

Laura Wilson

An Orion paperback

First published in Great Britain in 1999
by Oriel
This paperback edition published in 2000
by Orion Books Ltd,
Orion House, 5 Upper St Martin's Lane,
London WC2H 9EA

Third impression
Reissued 2003

A CIP catalogue record for this book is available
from the British Library.

ISBN 0 75283 477 0

Printed and bound in Great Britain by
Clays Ltd, St Ives plc

To my parents, June and William Wilson,
and to the memory of Liz Rimmer (1970–1997)

I am very grateful to Judith Amanthis, Paula Breslich, Harriet Brittain, Tony Colwell, Claire Foster, Jane Gregory, Lisanne Radice, Janet Ravens-croft, Michael Rimmer, Paul Sidey, Selina Walker, Jane Wood, Catriona Woodburn and Cathy Wood-man for their encouragement, advice and support.

FRIDAY 11 NOVEMBER 1994

Obituaries

Louisa, Lady Kellway, CBE, died in hospital after a short illness on November 6 aged 104. She was born on 20 July 1890.

When Louisa, Lady Kellway died last week, the final hope of solving two of the most celebrated British murder mysteries of the century died with her. Born Louisa Lomax in the Victorian twilight of 1890, Lady Kellway was one of a generation who believed that a lady's name should appear in the newspapers only at birth, marriage and death. Daughter of a country squire, she came from a family whose values were rooted in the certainty of an immutable class system and an empire upon which the sun would never set. In 1920 she married David, Lord Kellway, a war hero and the owner of a stately home, a magnificent Italianate garden and several hundred acres of Wiltshire, now administered by the National Trust. It was a happy marriage and there was one child, Caroline, born in 1921. Lady Kellway's was a worthy life, including service as a JP and as the chairwoman of the local WI. As she herself said in a radio interview in 1977, it was all about 'being sensible and getting on with it – no fuss or divorces or anything like that'.

This was true as far as her own life went, but Lady Kellway knew all about scandal. She was the first cousin of Georgina Gresham, without whose name no true-crime collection would be complete, and it is for her connection with this enigmatic woman that she will be remembered. A water-colour of the two girls by a long-forgotten RA shows two classic profiles with dazzling complexions and alabaster shoulders rising out of clouds of tulle. The portrait gives no clue that although Georgina Gresham, née Lomax, came from the same four-square county background as her cousin, she stood trial in 1928 for the murder of her husband, millionaire James Gresham, and was acquitted to howls of public fury. In 1955, Georgina's body was discovered in her London home, together with those of her brother, Edmund Lomax, and their housekeeper, Ada Pepper. All three had died from gunshot wounds and the police concluded that one of the trio must have shot the others before committing suicide. Despite a lengthy investigation, however, which one and why was never established.

Photographs of Georgina reveal little more than the portrait. One, dating from 1926, shows her arm in arm with her alleged lover, the Hon. Edward 'Teddy' Booth, now Lord Tranmere, watching the cars at the Brooklands motor-racing circuit. Others, taken during her trial, picture her being escorted in and out of the Old Bailey, and one depicts her leaving court after her acquittal, cloche hat pulled down over haughty, heavy-lidded eyes, one gloved hand holding the collar of her fur coat tightly round her neck. Louisa and Georgina's brother Edmund stand on either side of her, fringed by journalists with out-thrust notebooks and flash-bulbs.

The last known photograph of Georgina Gresham was taken in 1952, three years before her death. She is in London's Cromwell Road, with the Natural History Museum in the background. In what looks like the same fur coat, she has a large number of coloured scarves tied round her head and is wearing white ankle socks. At 62, her skin has the stretched, parchment look of someone far older and the surprising lengths of bare arm and leg sticking out of either end of the mangy fur are needle thin.

The questions raised when Georgina's name first appeared in the newspapers almost seventy years ago remain unanswered today. Her husband, James Gresham, died from a massive overdose of sedatives and the prosecution asserted that Georgina had administered them to him, possibly with Edward Booth's connivance, because Gresham refused to grant her a divorce. In other words, it was a *crime passionnel*, scarcely different from the case of Edith Thompson and Frederick Bywaters in 1922, which resulted in the hanging of both – except in two respects: first, the complete absence of love letters or any other physical evidence to tie Georgina and Booth to each other and second, class. The gloss of his father Lord Tranmere had clearly rubbed off on Mr Booth, at least so far as the judge, Mr Justice Cudlip, was concerned; twice during the summing up he referred to Booth as Lord Tranmere. Although the newspapers of the day promised mouth-watering revelations of how the other half committed adultery, no evidence ever materialised. Both Georgina and Booth insisted that they had never had 'improper relations' and the judge consistently refused to allow the prosecution lawyers to challenge this denial. Booth's word as a gentleman, the judge said, was enough, adding bizarrely that 'no decent man would expect a lady to admit to such a thing, even if it were true'. He may also have been influenced by the appearance of Edward Booth. Portly, ruddy-faced and 54 years old, he seemed an unlikely paramour for chic, beautiful Georgina Gresham.

The public, however, were not convinced, especially when the jury reached a verdict of not guilty. It was ironic, given the mutterings of 'one law for the rich . . .' in the weeks following the trial, that as soon as her husband died, Georgina abruptly ceased to be one of their number. The Greshams had no children and although James Gresham left a small amount of money to his brother-in-law, the bulk of his fortune went not to his wife, but to a distant cousin, Leo Gresham, who sailed from Canada, claimed his inheritance and turned Georgina out of the Hampstead mansion she and her husband had shared.

Although Lady Kellway, Edward Booth and Edmund Lomax had all stated, on oath, that the Greshams were on good terms, Georgina's replies, when asked about her feelings for her husband, were oddly equivocal and unaffectionate. A court reporter recalled that she had a 'shower-bath coldness' which made her unsympathetic. 'All the time, she seemed to be saying "you people cannot judge me".' When Georgina was asked why she thought her husband might have committed suicide, she replied, 'He made a mistake.'

The death of James Gresham and his wife's conduct during her trial remain as much of a mystery today as they were in 1928. So, too, does Georgina's own death, twenty-seven years later. After Leo Gresham had taken possession of the Hampstead mansion, Georgina and her brother Edmund moved to 83 Thurloe Street, a small terraced house in South Kensington. This was where her body, together with those of Edmund and their housekeeper, was discovered by the milkman, Ernest Sharpe, on the morning of 16 August 1955. Unable to get a response to his knocking, Mr Sharpe peered through the front-door letter-box and saw the body of the housekeeper, Ada Pepper. 'The very first thing I saw was her eyes,' Sharpe said. 'They were staring straight at me, right on a level with mine. She was only a couple of feet away, sat on the floor with her legs stuck out in front and blood all down her overall.'

Mr Sharpe fetched the police. The front door of no. 83 was

locked and bolted on the inside, so Constables Robert Hartley and Harry Rowse smashed a pane of glass in the basement door and went down the corridor and up the steps that led to the main part of the house. However, before they could get into the hall, they had first to open the door at the top of the basement steps. This door opened outwards and Miss Pepper's body was leaning against it. Not realising the nature of the obstruction, the two men forced open the door, dislodging the housekeeper's body, which fell on to its side on the hall carpet where, due to rigor mortis, it remained in its L-shaped sitting position. Although Miss Pepper was wearing her overall, her face was heavily powdered, there were several silk flowers in her hair and she was wearing a pair of white gloves.

The next thing the two constables saw was the body of Georgina's brother, Edmund Lomax, in the doorway of the sitting-room they shared. Mr Lomax, dressed in pyjamas and slippers, was lying on his side. He had massive injuries to his face and the skirting boards and the lower parts of the sitting-room door were splashed with blood.

There was a lot of blood on the tiled floor of the hall and the end of the threadbare strip of carpet where Ada Pepper's body had been seated was saturated with it. By the time the two policemen had stepped over Miss Pepper's body and around Edmund Lomax's to open the front door, they had added a number of bloody footprints to the original stains, and the sergeant they let in must also have contributed his share as the three officers doubled back and entered the sitting-room. Seated in an armchair in the corner was the body of Georgina Gresham. She was wearing a georgette evening gown of pre-war design and matching gloves. The back of her head was missing from just above the hairline and the wall behind the chair was covered with blood and brain tissue.

Although all three bodies had gunshot wounds, there was

no gun in sight. The only thing which could possibly have been described as a weapon was a heavy kitchen mincer which lay on the floor under Georgina's chair, but this was ruled out because, although it was spattered with blood, there was no forensic evidence to suggest that it had been used to hit anyone.

The house was in a filthy condition and most of the rooms were so cluttered that they were impossible to enter. Eight chandeliers were found packed away in pieces, along with three sets of golf clubs, thirty-eight clocks, forty-three cigarette cases, a four-foot-high electro-plated nickel table centrepiece in the shape of a palm tree and an enormous box of cutlery which had obviously been pilfered from hotels with names like the Metropole and the Grand. There was a collection of women's clothes from designers like Mainbocher, Schiaparelli and Jean Patou, and dozens of boxes of gloves, fans and hair ornaments, plus a trunk of linen with the perfectly mummified body of a cat lying on top of the sheets. When the contents of the house were eventually taken into storage, a total of 614 crates was removed. What was missing was a single clue, either to the deaths of Georgina and Edmund Lomax and their housekeeper Ada Pepper, or to that of James Gresham twenty-seven years earlier. The police did, however, discover a revolver wedged behind a stack of newspapers under the hall table. Unfortunately, it was too heavily blood-stained to yield any fingerprints. Ernest Sharpe remembered seeing 'something that might have been a gun' on the floor near Miss Pepper's left hand when he looked through the letter box, so it is possible that the weapon was dislodged when the two constables opened the basement door, knocking over her body. In the weeks that followed the discovery of the bodies, there was much speculation as to whose hand had been nearest the gun – the housekeeper's or Edmund Lomax's.

Lady Kellway was called to give evidence at the inquest into the deaths, although she had been at her Wiltshire home on the night of the shootings. When she was asked if she knew of any reason why her cousins would have killed each other or committed suicide, she replied that they were becoming depressed because their health was failing. Pestered by journalists, she issued a statement saying that she had nothing further to add. Like Edward Booth, she was to maintain her silence until she died.

It is, of course, possible that Lady Kellway had nothing further to add. But it could also be that this tweedy, matronly figure, with her common-sense Christianity and *noblesse oblige*, knew a good deal more about her cousin than she was prepared to divulge. The hallmarks of the Gresham trial – the bland testimony of Georgina Gresham's friends, the loyalty of her servants, the deferential attitude of the judge and the fact that the defendant herself seemed to expect all this as of right – are those of a different age.

It is too late now to discover the truth. The horses have not been frightened, the boat remains unrocked.

Lady Kellway is survived by her daughter, Caroline Cornford.

⇸ PART ONE ⇷

83 Thurloe Street, SW
July 1955

ADA

It was my birthday last week. Lovely flowers from Master Edmund, beautiful. He always remembers, but Miss Georgina doesn't pay attention to those sorts of things and I don't expect it. Anyway, birthdays aren't important when you get to my age. But this afternoon when I was having my rest, I heard her go thump-thump on the floor with the broom for me to go up there. I told her, 'Don't you go summoning me up here again in a hurry, my knees are poorly.'

She said, 'Sit down, Greymalkin.' That's what she calls me at present, though I don't know what it means. Six months ago she was calling me Brunhilde, and before that it was something else just as daft. But I don't take any notice, it's just her games. I took Master Edmund's chair next to hers in the window where she sits all day and looks out. Then she says, 'Really, Ada, you make such a *fuss* about everything. I'm not asking you to charge into the valley of death with the six hundred. I only asked you to come up because I've got a present for you,' and she wallops down a box of chocolates on my worst knee. The doctor says I'm diabetic now, so I can't have chocolates and sweets, and she'd know that if she ever bothered to think, which she doesn't. It was on the tip of my tongue to say, 'Very nice, I don't think,' but I kept mum, so of course she said, 'Well, don't I deserve a thank you?'

'It's very kind of you, Miss Georgina, I'm sure.' That's typical, making me look ungrateful like that.

I don't know what I'm supposed to do with these blasted

chocolates. They had to go straight into the back of the cupboard, so I wouldn't be wanting to eat them, and then of course I had to go and drop a tin of peas on my foot doing that, so now that's something else that hurts along with the knee. I'll have a sit-down and look out into the yard. It used to be a nice view from my little kitchen when Master Edmund got me the tubs of flowers, but they didn't thrive; there's not enough light for them down here.

Master Edmund calls us his two guardsmen. Me and Miss Georgina, he means. One guards the front and the other the back. Although what there is to guard in this basement I don't know.

Miss Georgina never goes outside any more. She stopped getting the people coming up to her a long time ago, so it isn't that. I think she's lost interest in what goes on, apart from the papers. As long she can have a read and do her crossword, that's all she cares about, really. This wasn't the house where it happened, of course, nothing like it, but we moved up here straight after, while it was all still in the papers, and we did get the odd one or two sniffing around. Not reporters, just normal people. I caught a couple of them on the front porch once. Two women. I'd come out the basement door and I looked up and there they were. Broad daylight and one of them was peering through the letter-box. The other one's stood behind her, going, 'Can you see anything, then?' But that was nothing to what went before. Miss Georgina used to get people shouting at her, nasty letters, all kinds of things. It was always women who did it; you don't get men doing that sort of thing, do you?

It's all forgotten now, of course, but there was a terrible to-do about it at the time. It's not surprising – Mr James was rich, he knew a lot of important people: politicians, in the world of business, that sort of people. A *cause célèbre*, that's what you'd call it. And Miss Georgina was so lovely, they couldn't take enough pictures. I thought at the time, it's a good job they never found out what happened to Miss Georgina's brother Freddie, how he died, or goodness knows what sort of wicked things they'd have made up. Because there were plenty who thought she'd got away with murder as it was, without dragging all that into it as well. I thought there might be some trouble with the neighbours when we moved here afterwards, but they're all nice people, and Master Edmund is so well liked they have plenty of friends. If Miss Georgina wants to see people, Master Edmund only has to telephone and they all come to play bridge. I think Miss Georgina gets just as much of a kick from hearing Master Edmund talking on that telephone as she does from the company: 'Doo telephone,' she says. 'Dooo telephone, Edmund', and then she always has to have the door open so she can hear him out in the hall. But it does make me laugh; to see him touch that telephone, you'd think it was going to explode at any moment. He picks it up and says, 'Are you there?' – it sounds as if he's shouting into the mouth of a cave. Sometimes, if she's talking to him and she thinks he's not listening, she puts on a voice and says, 'Are you there?'

Miss Louisa comes here every week to see them. She's Lady Kellway, really, by her marriage to Lord Kellway that's dead. Master Edmund's very fond of her – his face lights up like Christmas whenever she comes. Miss Georgina doesn't like it, but Miss Louisa's been a good friend to her and she knows it, though she'd never admit it. Miss Louisa's daughter, Miss Caroline, or Mrs Cornford I should say, she comes to visit too, sometimes. He's Cornford's pickles. They repeat on me, but of course I wouldn't ever say that to Miss Caroline. But somebody must eat them, because he's got money coming in hand over fist.

We were here all during the war, right on this spot. I said to Miss Georgina, 'Why don't you go as a paying guest?' because there was plenty in the country taking them at the time. Well, she wouldn't hear of it. I told her, 'Don't worry, I'll be here to keep it nice for when you come back,' but would she listen? Not on your nelly. Not that I was surprised, mind you. I might as well be a lump of coal for all the notice she takes of me. 'I'll sleep in my own bed and if Hitler wants to bomb me, that's his look out.' That's what she said. Of course, where Miss Georgina goes, Master Edmund goes, so there was me, sat down here all alone, under the stairs, night after night, worried sick. One night there was a huge bang right on top of us and all the plaster coming down, and I thought that's done it, I only hope Master Edmund's got his teeth in. I wouldn't like him to be found without his teeth in . . . and then I heard this thin little voice: 'Ada, Ada, where are you?' And I looked up and there they were, covered in dust and plaster, and looking like ghosts, Master Edmund in his pyjamas and tin hat, one arm all over blood, and her in a satin night-gown and his old tweed coat with a shawl wrapped round. What a pair they looked! But Master Edmund is a card, he made me laugh, even then. I'd done some washing, and of course the rack had come down with the bang and it was all over the floor. Master Edmund looked down and said, 'Has the clothes-horse bolted?'

It turned out the damage wasn't too much, it was the house behind us that got the worst of it, and all we had was windows gone and a bit of mess, so it was fixed up soon enough. Master Edmund and Miss Georgina'd been told over and over to sleep downstairs – and that time the ARP man sat Miss Georgina down and said, 'You'll be stopping downstairs from now on, won't you?'

'Oh, yes,' she said. But I knew she wouldn't and sure enough, the next night: back upstairs.

I've known Miss Georgina from when she was a little girl. Me? Well, I wasn't a little girl, exactly, because I was thirteen when I went into service with the family. I missed my mother so much, when I first came away from home, I used to start crying if I even thought of her. But I soon grew out of it. Miss Georgina, she lost her mother when she was ever so young. I was there when it happened. I never even knew she was ill. We were all in the same house, but it was like another world, the way they lived, and nobody talked about those sorts of things, certainly not to their servants.

The day she died, it was perishing. November. I was out there at six in the morning, scrubbing down the front steps. I'll bet they can't get anyone to do that now. But it had to be done every morning and I was the one to do it, because I was the under-housemaid and that was that. In those days, you couldn't go to your trade union and say, 'I won't do this and such at six in the morning,' because there wasn't nothing like that. I'm sure that's how I got my trouble with my knees. I've had a habit, over the years, same as my mother, of saying, 'Oh dear, oh dear,' if something hurts. When I was a girl I said to my mother, 'Why do you say that?' and she said, 'Because it makes me feel better.' And I don't know why, but it does.

After the steps, I'd got my fires to do. That was what I hated most, the fires. Kneeling in front of those grates full of cold ash, I always felt like I was the only one in the world who wasn't tucked up in a warm bed. I couldn't even stop to enjoy the fire once I had it lit, because there were five others to do before I could even think about breakfast. I was half-way through when the housekeeper came and told me I had to take a can of hot water upstairs for the mistress. I went for the water and I never thought anything about it until I got to the landing outside Mrs Lomax's room. I thought her own maid would come out and take it from me, but she never, and I didn't know what I was supposed to do. The can was heavy and I wanted to put it down before I spilled the lot. I knocked, 'Ma'am? Ma'am? I've come with the water,' but no one answered, so I thought: Oh, she can't be in there. I gave the door a push, ever such a little one, and it came open.

Mrs Lomax was in there lying in the bed, with her hair all spread out on the pillow. She'd got her eyes closed and her face – I tell you what it reminded me of: once me and my brother Charlie stopped to watch the watermen drag up a corpse out of the river. They said it had been a week floating in the water and it was grey-white like a fish, with the mouth gone blue. And when I looked again, I thought, she's dead . . . I didn't know what to do. I put my can by the fire and ran for it. I was so confused I went down the wrong stairs, the proper ones, and I almost crashed into the housekeeper and the doctor coming up. I thought, now I'm for it, but the doctor said, 'Wait!' He wanted things bringing, water and linen, so I was up and down with that. I never went in the room, I put the things down at the door and knocked, and he came out and took them. Then he said to me, 'Fetch the bath.' I thought, what does he want with the bath? But I went and got it. I knocked a lump of paint off the doorway getting it and I was worried in case someone noticed, but there was no one to see and anyway they were all too het up about Mrs Lomax to bother with that. I asked one of the others afterwards and she said there was a baby, though I don't know how she knew. When I heard that, I got it into my head that the doctor put the baby into the bath. I don't know why I thought that, but I used to dream about it, the dead baby lying in the tin bath, that someone gave it to me and I had to keep it in my room, and I didn't want it.

I don't know why I was so upset over it. After all, I'd seen a baby dead before, several times. My mother used to have a baby every year or so. She'd tell us children, 'You go and see your Auntie Vida, and when you come back, there'll be a little baby brother for you, or a sister.' The babies usually died after a few days, but there was a lovely one, a boy, that lived for longer – about a month, I think. Every morning I'd ask my mother, 'Can we keep this one?' and she'd say, 'No, Ada, not this time.' I could never understand how she could be so cruel. Because for a long time I thought my mother was the one deciding if they could live or die and I wanted to ask her why she couldn't let this one stay alive, but I thought if I did that she might change her mind about *me* and then I'd have to go too!

Miss Georgina can't have been more than six or seven when her mother died and Master Edmund two years older. They were lovely children, beautiful. Took after their mother: black hair, big dark eyes that glowed out of their faces, skin like cream. To see them together, it was like a mirror with a boy on one side and a girl on the other. Poor Master Alfred, that they called Freddie, he was the youngest and the odd one out. Didn't look like he belonged in the family at all, with his hair like carrots. But he was a dear little thing, ever so bright. I remember seeing him at Dennys – that was the Lomaxes' country house – picking up handfuls of grass for the horses, even when they were standing in a field full of the stuff, and he was far too small to reach them even though he stood on tiptoe with his little hand stretched out, and of course the horse gave one sneeze and it all blew away.

Not that I saw them much, not then. They were always with the nurse. It was always 'nurse', never 'nanny'. She was a very religious woman – a Christian, but a different sort to the rest of us. The older servants were very suspicious of her, because she kept telling them, 'I'd never touch one drop of drink, not if it was poured in a golden cup.' Not that I ever noticed any of them drinking either, but they thought she was making herself out to be superior because of her religion and they didn't like that. To be honest, I was more than a little bit frightened of her.

Master Edmund was sent off to school soon after Mrs Lomax died and Miss Georgina and Master Freddie went to live at Dennys for good. Mr Lomax was to stay on in London. The London house was half shut up and I was afraid I'd lose my place, but the housekeeper told me I was to go to Dennys with them, because they needed an extra pair of hands for the cleaning, so I was thrilled with that. I went down there on the train: 'Third Class and Servants'. The nurse took off and left me with the bags, and I got in a terrible muddle and couldn't find a porter. But the house! I loved that house. It was made of pale bricks, with a green veranda running all round the bottom and a porch with flowers and a wooden seat. It had decorations all up the wall in shiny bricks, with lovely flowers and leaves carved in a sort of frieze, and a beautiful stained-glass window. And there was grass! I'd grown up in a city and I felt as if I was escaping, except I wasn't going for the fresh air, I was going to work, and I knew I'd be lucky to stick my nose out of the scullery door once a week, never mind country walks. But still, it was all there outside, even if you could only see it through the windows.

I was ever so nervous the first time I opened up the big kitchen door at Dennys. Inside it was all steam and noise, and everyone seemed to be in a tearing hurry. I didn't know what to do, so I just stood quiet against the wall and wondered if anyone would notice I was there. That was when I met Ellen. She come straight up to me: 'Hello, I'm Ellen.'

I said, 'I'm Ada. Am I meant to come in here?' because they were all so busy I thought I must be in the way. She said, 'That's where the door is, isn't it?' in the cheeky way she had and grabbed hold of my trunk. 'I've to take you up to my room. You're sharing with me.' The minute I set eyes on Ellen I knew I was going to like her. She always looked a mess. Always cheeky and always a mess. She had yellow hair that flopped about and big round blue eyes. Her cap was always shoved on to the back of her head with great hanks of hair hanging down, and even if she was told to go and tidy it up it would be all over the place again in five minutes. Well, she took me up to her room and they'd got a sort of camp-bed thing fixed up for me to sleep on because it was the only space there was. The room was so small you couldn't open the door all the way, you just had to take one step in and you'd fall right on to the bed.

But I was glad to have a friend. That's what I'd missed in the house in London. There were plenty of people, other servants I mean, but they were all older; they didn't want to be friends with the lowest one. I had two brothers and three sisters at home, and we'd all shared a room together with a curtain hung down the middle to separate the boys from the girls, and then I came away to work and had to stay in that tiny attic room and I hated it, being on my own.

Ellen could talk the hind leg off a donkey, she had so many stories to tell. The first night I was there I hardly had a wink of sleep, we were talking and laughing away, but I didn't care, I was so happy. The next morning, though! I felt terrible, and Ellen and I were up and down ladders, lugging pails about, brushing the wallpaper, cleaning the paint, unstringing the blinds, you name it. It's a miracle no one sent us up a chimney. When I had the charge of my own staff, if I'd had two like me and Ellen I'd never have had them together working, not on your nelly. Never get anything done in a hurry with two like we were. But we were always put together, and of course it suited us down to the ground. We were up in one of the back bedrooms where you could see into the yard and Ellen was chat, chat, chatting away to me, when she suddenly stopped and grabbed my arm, 'Ooh, look, Ada! There's William!' Well, I thought *oh-ho*, because this was a name that hadn't cropped up before, and sure enough, Ellen turned red: 'I think he likes me, Ada. He works for Mr Vincent.' Mr Vincent was the butler. Then she said, 'He always stops to talk to me and he's ever so handsome.'

I said, 'Oh, get on with you,' but she fair pulled my arm off.

'Quick, Ada, come on, let's go and change our water, then you can see him.' My water wasn't any more dirty than hers was, but of course I followed her like a ninny.

Ellen was looking round for William, but I thought: I'm down here, I may as well change my water, so I went to the tap. I shut my eyes for a moment to enjoy the little bit of sun and when I opened them, there was this man standing there as if he'd just fallen out of the sky or something, looking right at me. I don't think I've ever felt such a fool in my life, being caught standing there asleep on my feet like a horse, and it was worse because he was handsome, just like Ellen said. He looked more foreign than English, with black hair and a browny sort of skin. He said 'How do you do?' to me, and stuck out his hand to shake. I was so confused I didn't know where to put myself. Ellen goes, 'This is William,' as if I couldn't have guessed it from the daft way she was looking at him.

Then he said to me, 'Your bucket's run over the top.' There was water everywhere and I hadn't noticed. Then of course I had to stand there beside him while Ellen filled up her bucket. He said, 'Ellen has told me all about you. You're a very important person.'

I could feel myself going scarlet. 'I never said that!'

Then he said, 'Ellen seems to think so. She seems to like you very much.' Looking at me like it was beyond him to see why anyone would like me at all, never mind very much. I thought, who does he think he is? He certainly thought he was clever. He was nineteen or twenty, I suppose, and he must have had all the girls he met go mad for him, looking the way he did. I thought: Well, he needn't think I'm going to go spooney over him. But Ellen was, trying to look out for her water and us at the same time, chattering away nineteen to the dozen.

All I could think of was how silly the pair of us must look and I wasn't half glad when William went off back to his work. But then Ellen started up: 'Ooh, he's so handsome, isn't he handsome, Ada?' She couldn't leave the subject alone for five minutes. She got sillier and sillier about it – she told Mary and a couple of the others: 'I think William's taken a fancy to me,' and instead of telling her to pull herself together like they should have, they were all ears, listening to her nonsense and joshing her about having a young man. Telling her it was true, even. I thought: I hope William doesn't get to hear of it, he's got enough opinion of himself already – but of course the true reason was because I didn't want him to think I had anything to do with a lot of silliness.

One day, we had a stack of sheets to turn sides to middle and of course Ellen wasn't lifting a finger; she had her nose glued to the window in case you-know-who should come along. Yammering away as usual, but I wasn't paying any attention. She was like the wireless, was Ellen. It's company, but you don't take in all what they're saying. William frightened the life out of me, tapping on the glass, and of course Ellen couldn't contain herself. She would have bashed her brains out getting the window up if I hadn't helped her. William had this lovely silver tray that he'd filched from the dining-room and he put it in the window, so we could see there were two beautiful red roses on it. He said 'Good-morning, ladies' as if we were a pair of duchesses sat there sewing.

Ellen goes in feet first: 'Ooh, William, aren't they beautiful? Is it for me?' I just sat there, I wasn't going to jump up and down for him.

But he held out the flower towards me. 'Won't you take your rose, Miss Ada?' Miss Ada! I thought: I don't want the stupid thing, specially not if it was pinched, which I thought it must be.

Ellen took it and practically threw it at me, 'Here you are, take it!' so she could talk to William. I never touched it, just left it in my lap and went on with my sewing, but I could see William's face over Ellen's shoulder and I knew he was putting on a show for me. She was gushing away; 'Oo, William it's ever so sweet.'

Then he said to her, 'Aren't you going to give me a little bit of something nice for it?' I couldn't believe it! He was looking straight at me when he said it, his eyes were laughing, but of course she was too taken in to notice.

I thought, that's not fair, even someone as daft as Ellen doesn't deserve that, so then I said, 'I can hear someone coming,' and that got him moving pretty sharply. Ellen slammed down the window hard enough to break the glass and stuffed the rose down the side of the chair.

Of course, no one came and she went all suspicious: 'You never heard no one, Ada, so why say you did?'

I said, 'I thought I heard Mrs Mattie,' because that was the housekeeper's name.

Ellen said, 'No you never. You're jealous, Ada. I never thought I'd see that from you.' I didn't know what to say. I couldn't say the truth, which was that William didn't care that! about Ellen, nor ever would. I was glad when it was time for me to go up with the tea-tray, I've never wanted to get out of a room so much. So off I ran as fast as I could, and I fell right over Jenny in the passageway and nearly broke my neck. In big houses like those, there was always some poor mite that did all the roughest work and at Dennys it was Jenny. She was a mental defective, but harmless enough. She was tiny, with such a skinny little neck it looked as if her head would just go wibble-wobble and fall right off, and her arms were like two sticks. Every time I looked at her I'd count my blessings. Mind you, she had a better situation than most of her kind – at least, she did until what happened to Master Freddie.

Anyway, I'd come a real cropper and I was busy putting myself right again when I saw William down the corridor. He was just lounging about, leaning against the wall, looking like he owned the place when he shouldn't even have been there. Well, I had to walk past him to get to the kitchen anyway, so I thought, right! And I marched straight up to him: 'I want to talk to you.'

Well, he just couldn't resist it: 'To what do I owe this honour, Miss Ada?' He'd just watched me tumble down – I noticed he never offered to help me up – and there he was, hands in his pockets, looking like he thought he could break my heart with one snap of his fingers. That look of his!

It made me furious, and I said, 'Why don't you save that for Ellen? She likes it, I don't. And don't call me Miss Ada. Why do you have to do all that?'

I thought: That's told him, but he said: 'All what?'

'Giving Ellen a rose and carrying on like that.'

This is William: 'Like what?'

I blurted out: 'Like you was her fancy man!' I didn't know what a fancy man was, not really. I thought, suppose it's something dreadful, but I've said it now; I can't take it back.

William said, 'But I gave you a rose as well, didn't I?'

I said, 'You only did that because you want to get round Ellen.'

'No, I didn't. You're worth ten of Ellen, anyone can see that.' And he levered himself away from the wall and was off. 'You're worth ten of Ellen.' I still can hear him saying it. Well, I didn't know what to think. No, I tell a lie, I was pleased. Of course I was pleased. I felt guilty because it was Ellen and she was my friend, but I never asked him to say it and if he liked me, well, it wasn't my fault, was it? He'd looked straight at me and said it, and I thought it was wonderful.

I went to the window and had a quick look in the glass to see if I'd changed at all. I don't know who I thought I was going to see, the Queen of Sheba, but it was still the same old Ada. I haven't told you what I looked like, have I? A fish, that's what I thought I looked like. A lot of people with red hair have that look, especially if they have a big mouth. Big pale mouth and pale eyes, that's what does it. My hair was nice, chestnut, but I've never had any eyelashes to speak of and I'm all over freckles. I look as if someone flicked a brush full of brown paint at me and forgot to wipe it off after. So I wasn't going to win any prizes, but I felt like I could after William said that. If he'd said, 'Oh, Ada, you're so beautiful,' well, I wasn't stupid, I'd have known it was flannel. But he didn't and it was the way he looked at me, that was what mattered. And there I'd been, saying to myself, 'I won't take any nonsense from him.'

After that I couldn't bear it when Ellen started on 'William this' and 'William that'. I'd be listening to it, all her nonsense, but inside I was thinking, stop it, stop it. I think I would have told her, but she'd never have believed me, and nor would any of the others if I'd told them.

It was right after that, poor Master Freddie died. It was just – well, it was beyond anything you could think, really. Because who could do that to a little child? That's what I could never understand. It was a lovely summer day, I'll never forget it. I was working in the scullery when I heard the scream. I was up to my elbows in dirty cloths, but I rushed straight out into the passage to see who it was. Miss Louisa and Master Roland were staying at Dennys, and her governess come tearing round the corner and smack! into the opposite wall, just as if she was blind. I can see her now, she had a grey skirt and a white blouse; she was blundering from side to side in the passage, hips bumping against the walls, beating her hands on them, almost falling, screaming and screaming as if she was possessed. I called out to her, 'Are you hurt? Shall I fetch Mrs Mattie?' but she just went on as if I wasn't there at all. I didn't know what to do. I was afraid to go up to her because my hands were wet from the washing and I thought: Even if she has gone mad, she won't like me to get her nice clothes all dirty. She ran through the door and into the yard, and I was going to follow her in case she did herself a mischief, but Mrs Mattie suddenly came up behind me and grabbed me by the arm. She was only a little mouse of a woman, but she had quite a force when she wanted to – you should have seen the bruise I had, it was like a chimney-sweep's handprint on my arm. I said to her, 'I was just going to see about the noise, Mrs Mattie,' because I didn't want her to think I was the one screaming and shouting, but she wasn't having any of it.

She got hold of my shoulders and spun me right round, 'You're going back in the scullery. Now!' and pushed me in the chest. Well, I just stood there gawping at her. Just then, Ellen and some of the other maids came dashing round the corner to see what the noise was, because honestly, you could have heard it a mile off, the racket Miss Louisa's governess was making. Well, there was Mrs Mattie and I in the middle of the passage, about five steps away from the back door, and Mrs Mattie took one look at all these girls and she went and stood in front of that door like a policeman, yanking me by the collar so I didn't have no choice but to go with her. I heard my frock rip, which was just as well because she was holding me so tight I was choking. The others stopped dead when they saw us barring the door like that. To be honest, at any other time it would have been funny, because they were all standing there in their brown-and-white uniforms boggling at us, it was like a herd of cows had got into the house. Mrs Mattie was holding me in front of her so I couldn't see her face, but I could feel her eyes all right, burning into Ellen and the rest of them. 'Stop! Get back to your work, all of you. There's no need for this rumpus.'

Well, for a minute they all stared back at her and I thought, they're going to charge at us, but then Miss Louisa's governess suddenly appeared at one of the windows, screaming and pounding on the glass with her fists: 'Help me, somebody help me!' It was right next to where Ellen was standing and she leaped clear into the air from the shock of it, and then just for a moment we all stood quite still and stared at this horrible face, all pink from crying and blurred against the window like her skin wasn't made in fast colours, going, 'For the love of God, somebody please help me!' Then one of her hands smashed right through the glass and she slid down, crying and howling, until all we could see were her ten fingers holding on to the sill, covered in threads of blood and bits of broken glass.

Mrs Mattie roared, 'Into the scullery, all of you, *now*!' like a lion. Then she let go my collar and rushed towards the girls, and shooed them all in there and shut the door. Then she dashed past me and out of the back door and into the yard. I was seeing everything a bit fuzzy, so I sat down with my head between my knees and tried to get my breath back.

Ellen came out of the scullery after a few minutes. 'You don't half look peculiar. Are you all right?'

'I should think I'll live. What's happening?'

'I don't know. I thought you did. Wait a minute, though . . .' and she went over to the broken window and looked out into the yard. 'Mrs Mattie and Miss What'shername just went behind the hedge, there's something going on . . . Ada! There's a man there, one of the grooms, he's got Master Freddie in his arms, he's carrying him like a baby. Master Freddie's got a handkerchief wrapped round his head, there's blood . . . It must be an accident, Master Freddie's had an accident! Oh my Lord, they're coming back to the house. Quick, Ada, get up! Whatever it is, we'd better make ourselves scarce or we'll catch it.' We got back to the scullery in the nick of time.

Mrs Mattie came in. She looked very serious and said, 'I'm afraid there's been an accident and Master Freddie's been hurt. Now, I don't want a lot of talk and fuss, because that won't help poor Master Freddie, will it? I want you to do what you're told as quick as you can and we'll soon have things put in order.' Then she started telling us we had to scrub floors and sweep the yard. We weren't best pleased about having to do such rough work, which, as I say, we didn't normally.

Someone said, 'Where's Jenny?' because those were her jobs by rights.

But Mrs Mattie fairly bit her head off: 'Never you mind about Jenny. If you want to keep your place, you'll stop asking questions and get on with your work.'

Well, of course we all wanted to know what was going on – we were only human – but that got us working in a flash. Ellen and I were put to scrubbing down the passage, which didn't make us very happy, but that was how come we knew a policeman had been called, because him and Mrs Mattie were outside in the yard and we could hear them talking through the broken window. The two of us were right underneath it on our hands and knees, trying to hear what was going on. 'Perhaps you could show me where it happened?' That was the policeman.

Ellen whispered, 'Whatever does she want with a copper?'

'I don't know.' I put my head up a bit so I could see. 'Oh, it's only the bobby from the village.'

'Well, he won't do much, he'll be too frightened of Mr Lomax.'

That was true enough, because he wasn't doing anything that I could see, just saying, 'Oh, it's a bad business, a terrible business,' over and over again. They walked out of sight behind the hedge for a moment and we couldn't hear, but when they came back, Mrs Mattie was saying something about would he like to speak to the doctor and the policeman said, 'Has he finished examining the body?'

Ellen's eyes were like saucers. 'What body?' Then we heard the back door go and we scrambled back to our places and scrubbed for all we were worth while Mrs Mattie and the policeman came past. The moment they'd gone, down went our brushes. Ellen's face was stark white, like chalk. 'There's been an accident and Master Freddie's been killed,' she said. 'Oh, Ada, isn't that the most terrible thing in the whole world?'

GEORGINA

Mr Victor Mishcon, a solicitor, yesterday visited Holloway Prison, London, and saw Mrs Ruth Ellis, who is due to be hanged today for the murder of David Blakely. The Home Secretary on Monday decided not to recommend a reprieve. I'm not at all surprised. Little tart. Who else has died? *Dr Kenneth Macleod, who collected many traditional Hebridean airs and songs and composed the well-known 'Road to the Isles'* . . . Probably bored himself to death. But then Ascot – I wish I were there. It looks *so* . . . but it's probably not worth going, nowadays. Princess Margaret in a dreadful hat. And the Queen wrapped in a herbaceous border. Or perhaps they're fried eggs. Well, they could be.

Sussex, glorious view, handy for Tunbridge Wells . . . Mains water and electricity, septic tank drainage, heated hen-house. In all about three acres. Auctioneers Harrods Ltd, Kensington 1490. Heart of Kent, 15th-century residence . . . An all electric house in the luxury class . . . 3 staff bedrooms . . . hard court . . . Only £9000 freehold . . . Only! Not on your nelly, as Ada would say. What have we got today? One Across: *The field marshal turns back to the commanding officer and it ends.* So *it* ends the word. Need capital letters . . . FM and CO . . . field marshal turns back – MF. How many? Six. CO–MF–IT. So, then. *In the matter of tongues it started at Babel, starting with a C.* Well, that's confusion, that's simple enough. *Claims in the manner of two degrees* . . . have to think about that.

Who's this coming past the window? Looks rather like

Vivienne Wyatt. She was as mad as a hatter. Had an imaginary dog she used to take for walks in the square. She was dreadfully upset when they came and took all the railings away for the war effort. 'Poor darling Poopsie, he's bound to run away and get lost in the black-out, and he's so *dreadfully* afraid of the dark, poor little lamb.' They took the railings from the square, but for some reason they left the gates, and the man who looks after the square carried on locking them every night and unlocking them in the morning. He said to Edmund, 'It may be daft to you, but it's my job and I'm going to carry on doing it until somebody tells me to stop.'

Degrees . . . could be university degrees. BA, MA. *Claims. In the manner of. A la* . . . Alabama . . . Very clever this morning. I'd show Edmund, except that he's gone upstairs, which is most irritating of him. We usually do the crossword together, it's much more fun. He said he didn't feel well and was going upstairs for a 'lie-down'. His word, not mine. He's been spending too much time with Ada again or he wouldn't be using words like that. 'Lie-down!' It's got Ada written all over it. And it's monstrous of him because he knows I can't go after him, it takes too long. But when you're as fond of someone as I am of Edmund, a little selfishness here and there doesn't matter. Because we're inseparable, Edmund and I. We'll die together. It's the only way. Oh, I've thought about it very often. It's no good to have one of us hanging about for years after the other one's gone. For the one that was left, it would be like dragging a carcass around. What's next? *Darwin sailed in this hound.* Oh, for heaven's sake, *The Beagle.* Who sets this thing? The typist?

The loony-doctor at my trial said he'd examined me and found me to be a moral primitive. I was very offended. He made me sound like one of those hideous African wood carvings all the artists pretend to like so much. My lawyer hit the nail on the head – he gave me a piece of advice I'll never forget: 'Try to look as if you've got a lovely garden.' I knew exactly what he meant, which was why I asked Louisa to choose my clothes for me. Because even an African wood carver would take one look at my cousin Louisa and say, 'I'm sure she's got a lovely garden.' Meaning, of course, another dowdy Englishwoman with no dress sense. I should have been *French*. But of course everyone – including the twelve assorted butchers, bakers and candlestick makers on the jury – knows that moral primitives don't have lovely gardens . . . like poor Ruth Ellis. It was obvious from the start that she didn't give two hoots about herbaceous borders.

We've lived in this house for over twenty-five years, Edmund and Ada and I. Ada's seventy-three and we're not much younger. As long as we can manage for ourselves, it's better than being left to die in one of those places full of shuffling ghouls staining their drawers. Ada's devoted. In love with Edmund, of course. But that's a breed that'll soon be as dead as the dodo. Everything's turning upside down nowadays. You used to know where you were with people; now you don't. Ada's sound enough. She's a terrible spy, of course; all servants are. Always listening at doors. She thinks she owns us. I say to her, 'Heard enough, Ada?'

'Oh, Miss Georgina, I'm sure I don't know what you mean.' Always the same. Like one of those long-playing records with the needle stuck. But I'm sure she's got plenty to say for herself. Most of it pure imagination, of course, but her life has hardly been the most thrilling, so let her live through us if she wants. But I wish she wouldn't make vulgar insinuations about my brother and my cousin Louisa. It was Edmund who introduced Louisa to Davy Kellway in the first place and he'd hardly have done that if he was in love with her himself, would he? So you see it's all rubbish. In any case, Louisa looks like a

Bedlington terrier. Edmund could only love a *beautiful* woman. Besides, if he were in love with her, or with anybody, I would know. But truth isn't as important to that class as it is to ours.

The first thing I can remember with any clarity is the death of my mother. Everybody tiptoeing about – 'don't tell the children anything' – I'm sure they wouldn't even have told us our mother was *dead* if they could have managed without. Our nurse told us she'd gone to be with Jesus. Edmund was nine when she died and I was seven. Which I suppose means that our younger brother Freddie must have been about three. The worst thing was the mourning: one day I had rows and rows of pretty dresses in the most gorgeous colours; then they took them all away and they came back black. I wouldn't exactly say I missed my mother; in fact, if it hadn't been for the black dresses I think I would have forgotten about her almost immediately.

Our nurse was one of these excessively religious women. I've always thought it must have been some sort of nonconformist establishment that she belonged to and Edmund says he remembers her reading a Baptist newspaper. I've got a feeling that the church was called something to do with sheep, like the Flock of the Shepherd or the Brethren of the Lamb. I imagine that it was rather like Little Bethel in *The Old Curiosity Shop*, the part when Kit has to go and fetch his mother away from the church and all the people are rolling around and waving their legs in the air and being saved. Being saved evidently didn't agree with Nurse because she always came back from her church in a frightful temper. She used to see everything as a sign: the pattern on the wallpaper, the way you walked downstairs, something was always a sign. But all the signs meant the same thing: 'You'll come to a bad end.' Everything meant I'd come to a bad end. The nursery was a miserable place after my mother died, everything black: rocking horse, pictures, dolls, the whole lot wrapped in black material. And it was worse because Edmund went off to school. I remember being absolutely distraught about that, a hundred times more upset than over my mother's death, because I had no one to talk to if Edmund wasn't there. I didn't really know my mother, you see. I thought she was beautiful and I used to love seeing her dressed up in her lovely clothes, but she was like a beautiful butterfly, or a fairy . . . you wouldn't expect a fairy to bath you, would you? I don't remember her holding me or playing games or anything, just that she would brush her lips against our faces to say good-night. A kiss so soft you could hardly feel it.

I forgot her face very quickly and that made me sad. Of course, there were photographs, but they never made her look very beautiful and I'm sure she was. I suppose I could have looked in the glass to refresh my memory – when she was alive, my father used to call me his pocket edition. But if I looked in the glass now, I'd see an old woman and my mother didn't live to be an old woman, so what's the point?

Freddie I do remember very clearly, which is just as well because I've never been able to find a single photograph of him. I remember once, when I was very young, looking through a photograph album with my father. He was telling me stories about the people in the pictures and there was a picture of him and Uncle Jack with their parents, when they were boys. My grandmother was sitting in front of them on a chair with a baby in her lap and father and Uncle Jack and my grandfather were standing behind her. They all looked very cross except for the baby, who was smiling. I said, 'Look, the baby's smiling.'

My father said, 'The baby's not smiling, Georgina. It's dead.'

I looked again, carefully, but you wouldn't have known it was dead unless someone had told you. It just looked happy.

When they'd cleaned all the blood off Freddie and put fresh clothes on him, I thought perhaps someone might want to take a photograph of the two of us with my father, but there was no camera and no one to use it. Edmund says he can barely remember what Freddie looked like, but that isn't surprising because he was sent off to school when our mother died and he hardly saw Freddie at all after that. People always asked if Edmund and I were twins because we were so alike, but Freddie didn't look like us. He was fat, and he had freckles and lots of stiff little orange curls like springs. The more I think about him – and I have thought about him a great deal over the years, a *very* great deal – the more I can see that he didn't really 'fit'. We looked like our mother, but Freddie didn't look like anyone, certainly not my father, who was very handsome as a young man. I don't think Freddie would have made a handsome man. He would have been petulant looking and that's horrid. And he had the most strange eyes. They were swimmy and milky, and he never seemed to look directly at anything. I don't think he could see very well, because he was always bumping into things and tripping over – in fact that's how I remember him best, sitting on the floor bawling when he'd just taken a tumble. I asked our nurse about it once and she said, 'First cast the beam out of thine own eye,' which was absolute Greek to me. But Freddie was her favourite. I came a very poor second.

I have actually considered whether Freddie might not have been somebody else's child. Somebody other than my father, that is. I don't have anything that one could call evidence – just the lack of photographs, I suppose, and the way he looked . . . I don't say my father knew this or suspected it, although he may have done, but it has crossed my mind on more than one occasion. Because of what happened, you see, what happened later . . . People are very stupid on the whole, they want to have black and white, everything to be black and white. That's good, that's bad, that's right, that's wrong, you love someone or you hate them. But you can't, you can't turn it on and off like a tap. You continue to love, even though you know it's wrong or you have been harmed by that person – one goes on loving because one simply can't help it. I don't think my father could have stopped loving my mother, whatever happened, any more than I could have stopped loving him.

Edmund thinks our father was an ogre, but I don't agree. It was simply that he loved my mother very much, far more than he loved us. I think he had very extreme emotions and what he felt for her was a sort of worship. It was unfortunate that we – Edmund and I – both looked very like her and I think that was why he sent us away. Edmund would have gone off to school in any event, but there I was and worse, of course, being a girl . . . which is why I was parcelled up and sent off to Dennys, and Freddie with me. The servants told us that father was working dreadfully hard and that was why he could never come to see us, but I think the truth was that he couldn't bear to have us near him.

I often wonder, if things had been different, would my life have been happy like Louisa's? One can't help but admire that certainty – well, there's got to be something and you can hardly expect me to say I admire her dress sense. But that firmness, that steadfastness . . . That's what we're meant to have, people like us, that's what makes us happy. But of course the more one knows, or suspects, the less likely one is to have happiness. Only ignorant people can be happy. I suppose that is why I have never discussed my doubts about Freddie with Edmund. Or our father. And I have never spoken to Edmund about our father, either. I didn't want to make him unhappy. Besides, there's no point in sitting here wondering about it all. It's too late now. Far too late.

This is why I say people are stupid, they could never understand this: when I was young, to please my father was the most important thing in my entire life. Because I adored him, you see. My mother had his love, but she didn't have to do anything except be herself; and I wasn't her, I couldn't become her. My father was a very big man: big body, loud voice and a loud laugh. Always greeting people, kissing cheeks and shaking hands. Black hair on his hands, on his wrists. Once I kissed the palm of his hand. I remember to this day how it looked: short fingers and his palm was square. It was warm. He was a superb horseman, completely fearless, and he wanted all his children to be good riders. I enjoyed the lessons on the pony, but Edmund hated them. Father was always shouting at him, 'What do you think your legs are for? Use them!' Our pony knew jolly well that Edmund was afraid of it; it used to cart him off to the nearest hedge and stand there eating up all the leaves until the man came to rescue them. And then Father would say, 'If you can't use your legs to ride, you can use them to walk,' and send him back to the house in disgrace. But I loved riding. It was a good way of stealing a march on Nurse, because she was frightened of horses and that was seen as a great weakness in my family, fear of animals or not being sensible about them. Of course, nowadays they'd say it was all to do with sex – you love the horse because you're too young for a man. And perhaps they're right. Perhaps I should have stuck with horses. Can't imagine anyone murdering a horse, can you? Not a *crime passionnel*, at any rate. Unless it came last in the 3.30 at Doncaster with your shirt on it. Anyway, I've always preferred car racing.

We fought in silence for the most part, Nurse and I. She was rough with me, clumsy, putting on my clothes. Tugging, yanking, twisting, cramming, and I would be as uncooperative as I possibly could. Teddy Booth said to me once: 'You're the only woman I've ever met who can be an irresistible force and an immovable object at the same time.' He wasn't trying to get my clothes *on*, of course. Nurse used to brush my hair and wrench it back so hard she turned me into a Chinaman. I used to watch our reflections in the looking glass, fighting each other, and I would feel as if it wasn't me at all, but a scene I was watching for amusement, like a Punch and Judy show. Oh, yes it is; oh, no, it isn't.

She never spoke to me, always to Freddie. 'We're going for a walk now, Master Alfred,' or something like that, so I'd know that it was time to fetch my coat. And really, the day was so much regulated, always the same thing at the same time, breakfast or bath or whatever it was, there didn't need to be a lot of conversation about it. Freddie was really too young to talk to properly, but when Edmund was home from school I would speak to him. I rather got into the way of speaking to people through Edmund – we used to roam around by ourselves and if we went into the village or one of the farms, I'd say, 'Ask the farmer if we can look at the lambs,' or whatever it was I wanted to do, and he always would.

We did go to the village sometimes, but we were very much 'the big house'. I don't recall playing with any of the local children or anything like that; I don't think it occurred to us that there was even that possibility. Or to them, probably. But Edmund knew far more of the villagers than I did. I suppose being a boy he went about more and he was interested in the cricket – there used to be a big cricket match every summer and we'd go, and they'd always give us the best place to sit and bring out lemonade. When Edmund was older – fifteen, sixteen – he played himself, but I never saw him. I'd stopped going out by then, I never went anywhere because my clothes were so queer and I didn't want people to stare at me.

Whenever I think of Dennys, it's in the cricket season. Summer. Even going back to Dennys as we did after so many years, when it was all in ruins, couldn't destroy that memory. To this day, I can almost feel the heat of the sun and I can see us all, sitting on the grass, laughing. Edmund, Freddie and I, and my two cousins, Roland and Louisa. Uncle Jack's children. Uncle Jack and my father never really hit it off, something to do with Uncle Jack thinking my father wasn't running the business properly. I suspect that Uncle Jack was one of those people who think they could run the world perfectly if only someone would put them in charge of it. I don't think he had as much money as my father did and certainly no country house, which was why Roland and Louisa always came to stay with us for the summer. Until my father started drinking, that is. Uncle Jack wouldn't let them near us after that, even though Roland and Edmund were at the same school.

Roland and Louisa both had fair hair and blue eyes like Aunt Sophia, but Roland was quite extraordinarily handsome, even as a young boy. He had those sort of blazing good looks one only sees in story-book heroes: golden hair, bright-blue eyes and his skin was a beautiful honey colour. His face never turned pink in the sun as Louisa's did, it sunburned in a way that made him glow. Of course, Louisa was perfectly reasonable looking, rather nice if you happen to like women who look like Bedlington terriers, but you didn't look at her, you just looked at Roland. He was a year older than Edmund and we all admired him tremendously, although he wasn't particularly funny or clever. He was kind, though. I don't remember him ever saying a bad thing about anybody and even when we were very young I thought he lived in a different world from mine, not complicated and everybody nice to him.

Rather like Louisa. I don't suppose he ever imagined it could be otherwise. I suspect he hadn't much imagination at all, really. He didn't come to my wedding: 'Too difficult,' or that's what he told Edmund. Louisa did, though, and she came to stay with us afterwards, too, in spite of Uncle Jack disapproving. That's what I meant about firmness. It's the extraordinary thing about Louisa. She looks, and she certainly dresses, as if she wouldn't say boo to a goose, but if she thinks something's right, she'll stick to it, no matter what. If you didn't know her you'd have her down as the type of woman who'll agree with any man, no matter what asinine thing he says, just because he *is* a man. But you'd be quite wrong. Louisa's as stubborn as a mule if she's convinced about something: you can say what you like, she won't budge an inch. After my trial, she insisted on parading me through every single shop in London. I'd say to her: 'What's the point in my going shopping? I've got no money.'

'You mustn't hide yourself, Georgie. It's not fair. You have as much right to go about as anyone.' It was all very well for her, she wasn't the one providing the freak show. One woman actually spat at me. Middle-class woman, quite drab. Fur coat looked as if had been trodden on by a dray horse. She came right up to me and spat. In the middle of Liberty's. Louisa was furious: 'How rude, how vulgar' and so on and so on. I only just managed to stop her going after this woman and remonstrating with her. Of course, everyone in the shop saw it. They'd all realised who I was and were practically baying for blood. All women, of course. Superannuated old haddocks.

When Louisa was staying with us during the Great War, Roland came to visit her a couple of times. Of course, the uniform was the perfect thing for him, it made him more handsome than ever. I could invent a delightful romance between the two of us, but it never happened. It's quite funny, really, now I come to think about it, because Roland would have been a far more plausible lover for me than poor old Teddy, but of course he was dead by the time I needed him. I love my love with an 'I' because he is *I*mplausible. Not implausible to Jimmy, of course, only to the judge, old Mr Justice What'sit. Because poor old Teddy wasn't the co-respondent type at all. Too fat, for one thing. For quite a number of things, now I think about it. I was fond of him, though. Jimmy, too. It was said at my trial that I didn't care about Jimmy, but that wasn't true. They said I married him for his money, but I cared more about him than all those others who were friendly to his face, but called him a Johnny-come-lately the moment his back was turned because his money wasn't inherited. When Jimmy was away and Teddy gave parties at our house, those people would all turn up. You see, Teddy's father had a title, so they would come, even though they knew it was Jimmy's house and I was Jimmy's wife. They would laugh at the house because he'd designed it himself out of history books – 'Oh darling, what a *divine* staircase, it's all *perfectly outré*' – but they'd drink the place dry and burn his furniture with their cigarettes. Jimmy was worth ten of any of them. Society is a great fraud, it's all rubbish, and society people are rubbish. All except Teddy. Teddy saved me. He saved us all. Except poor Jimmy, of course.

But I remember Roland at Dennys so clearly – always in the summer. I suppose that as one gets older one always imagines that the weather was better in one's childhood, but whenever I think back there's one particular summer I remember, because the weather was blazingly hot. It was such a happy time. At the beginning, I should say. A happy time at the beginning. Before it happened. Because it was that summer, you see. The summer when Freddie was killed.

Edmund had gone off on a jaunt with some of the boys

from his school, so I had Roland and Louisa to myself. Freddie was there too, of course. There are parts of that day – when he died – that I remember vividly: sensations, the sunshine and the smell of the earth in the wood . . . but other things . . . afterwards, I tried and tried, I wanted to have a record in my mind of the whole day, to keep it, but they were just . . . lost. We'd been in the woods, you see, playing hide-and-seek, and Freddie was with us then, for some of the time. I saw him running through the trees. I was crouching or kneeling down in the middle of some bushes. I realised I'd chosen a bad place to hide, a small space with all the branches digging into me. I was trying to work out how I could escape without being seen, when he suddenly ran past me. Then he tripped over a stick or something. I was angry with him because he started howling and I thought the noise would make the others come and then they'd find me. I didn't move. I knew he hadn't seen me. After a while he picked himself up and I thought he must have gone off to find Nurse. That was the last I saw of him, the blur of his hair through the trees.

We carried on playing for a while and Freddie can't have come back, because when we came out through the shrubbery it was just the three of us, Roland and Louisa and I. I can't remember anyone saying 'Where's Freddie?' or 'Shouldn't Freddie be here?' or anything like that. I was glad the others hadn't asked where he was, because I thought I should have helped him, and instead I'd stayed hidden because I didn't want to spoil the game. We sat on the lawn and we were waiting for one of the maids to bring lemonade. I lay down flat on my back on the grass, and I was looking up at the sky and imagining I was in it, surrounded by blue with pillows of cloud underneath me to float me along. I remember I said: 'It feels like flying.'

Roland said, 'How do you know? You can't fly.'

I said, 'I can,' and of course it started a row. We all lay down flat on our backs in a line and there we were, squinting up into the sky and arguing, when suddenly someone screamed. The scream went on and on, and I could hear footsteps coming across the grass, nearer and nearer, and a big dark shape appeared over us and we couldn't see because it was blocking out all the sun. I think the others must have got up, but I was still lying there and when I turned my head sideways all I could see was this enormous boot, standing on my hair. I shouted out and started tugging at my pigtail, but I couldn't get it free. I kept on shouting, but this great big body up above me was flapping its arms up and down and twisting on one spot like a scarecrow, and screaming so loudly that no one could hear me. The others were pulling at me, all their heads and hands and knees swarming all over me until I thought I was going to choke. They pulled so hard I thought my head was going to fall off. I heard Roland shouting, 'Off! Get off!' and then we were all yelling, the noise was quite deafening, and I had absolutely no idea who this giant was who was treading on my hair and wouldn't move.

There was the hem of a skirt, very dirty, my head got stuck right under it and I remember looking up and thinking it must be a woman and how queer that she hadn't got any drawers on, and the next thing – well, she must have kicked me, because everything started spinning round and round, and I thought I was going to be sick. I could hear Louisa whispering to me, 'Quick, get up,' and I got to my knees. The first thing I saw was Miss Childers – that was Louisa's governess – trying to hold on to Jenny, the half-witted servant. Jenny's arms were doing a sort of mad semaphore and Miss Childers was trying to catch hold of them. 'What are you thinking of?' she was shouting. 'Control yourself!' She tried to give Jenny a slap, but she missed. Jenny kept shouting 'Come! Youcomewithme!

Comewithme!' Her words were sticking together like dates, and spit was flying out of the corners of her mouth. Some of it hit Miss Childers's bosom and I remember thinking it looked like a little brooch. When she embraced me later, I noticed a small dark patch where the spittle had soaked into the material.

My head hurt and I felt sick. I shut my eyes and put my hands up to my ears to blot out the noise, but it didn't seem to make any difference. Then one of Jenny's hands struck down like a snake on my arm. 'Yougetup, youcomehere,' and she dragged me with her across the grass and through the yard. I fell over on the stones, but she scooped me up and sort of wedged me under her arm, and we went round the corner behind the hedge where the servant's privy was. It was a little shed, covered in creeper, behind a thick privet hedge and designed so that you couldn't see it from the yard, and no stranger could have known it was there. Jenny panted, 'Look – you look,' and pushed me round the side of it. I looked straight ahead and didn't see anything, and then I looked down and there was Freddie, lying face down in a patch of mud. He was wearing a sailor suit, with his legs straight and his arms by his sides, like a toy soldier – or sailor, I suppose. He looked like a big doll dropped by a child and forgotten. That was my thought, that I'd forgotten him, and I think I said it out loud. On the top of his head the blood on his orange hair made it look like marmalade, sticky orange lumps, and the flies were landing on it, patting their legs up and down in the way flies do. Jenny kept her hand on my arm, she kept on screaming 'Look! look! look!' and pushing me towards Freddie.

She shoved me from behind and tried to make me touch his head where the blood was. I pulled back as hard as I could, but my fingers were getting closer and closer to the – *mess* – on his head. I didn't want to touch it but I did touch his back, I couldn't help it. I'm sure that Freddie was still alive at that moment, still breathing . . . I had my fingers on him for just a second, but I'm sure I could feel the movement . . . After that, the others came rushing up and Jenny let go of me. Roland was the first. For some reason he had a bamboo stick, a cane from the garden, and he poked it at Freddie's head where the flies were and made them buzz and fly out so that we all jumped backwards, and then Miss Childers pushed past us and took hold of the big collar of Freddie's sailor suit and pulled it and Freddie's head came up backwards and all the flies flew up and hit her face and her mouth, which was open, and she screamed and let go and ran away. Then Jenny fell down in a fit behind us. There was blood on her mouth and she was grunting like a pig and rolling about on the ground. We were watching her when I heard people coming up behind us and then Mrs Mattie's voice: 'Quickly – get the children inside. What are you staring at! Hurry!'

A man took hold of my arm and pulled me towards the house. I tried to fight him off, but someone else grabbed me round the waist and lifted me into the air. Then I remember being pushed along the corridor to the kitchen and vomiting on the flagstones, and I recollect feeling ashamed because it was in front of the servants. We were all put into chairs around the wooden kitchen table. Louisa was crying and there was some food on the table, plates of bread with jam. I said, 'It's too big,' because the slices were great big slabs and I didn't want to eat it because it wasn't thin bread like the nursery tea.

Freddie's life must have ended while we were sitting around the table. I don't know if the others knew, but some of the servants must have done because they kept coming in and out, and whispering to each other. They were waiting for him to die. I was worried about the flies on his head, that they were eating him, or rather drinking him. I thought that they would drink up all his blood and kill him. We all ran away from him, not just the children, but all of us, the servants as well. They could have covered him up with a blanket if they didn't want to look at him, but they shouldn't have just run inside and shut the door. Someone, just one, should have stayed with him while he died to keep him company. They were all afraid to go near him and he was only a little boy.

ADA

It was so hard to believe what had happened. Master Freddie was always running round the house and I used to go about my work thinking any minute now I'll hear him running down the corridor, or he'll come rushing round the corner, or he'll be laughing . . . a few times I thought I heard his laugh, but then I'd remember. Even when we saw the little white coffin going out – the weather was all wrong for it. Scorching hot and the sky was the brightest blue you ever saw, not a cloud anywhere. I don't remember if I cried. Ellen and the others were in floods, but once the coffin was gone we all had to get back to our work.

Everyone wanted to know what happened, but all we got from Mrs Mattie was that Master Freddie was killed in an accident. That night every one of us girls was too upset for talking, but the next night me and Ellen sat up in our room with another girl called Mary and tried to make sense of what happened, but we couldn't. Ellen knew the most, because she was quite shameless about gossip and listening to other people's conversations. 'William told me that Jenny was out there with Master Freddie, she had a funny turn and had to be locked in her room, that was how come she wasn't there when you asked, Mary.'

'What was *she* doing out there? She can't have been the one who found the poor little mite or she'd have told Mrs Mattie.'

I said, 'That was Miss Louisa's governess found Master Freddie, must have been.'

Ellen said, 'What, that Miss Childers? She didn't half go barmy. I got ever such a fright when her hand come up through the window like that.'

'Well, what do you expect? I heard that Jenny found him first and showed Miss Childers, and then she fell down in a fit.'

'Where was he?'

'Only out by the privy. We saw them going behind the hedge, didn't we, Ellen?'

'What was he doing there?'

Ellen said, 'I don't know. It was that nurse's fault. She wants to watch those children, not let them go wandering off getting killed.'

'Well, I've heard that she was in her room at the very time Master Freddie was killed, saying her prayers. Didn't do Master Freddie any good, though, did it?'

'You want to watch it, saying things like that, Mary Spencer, or you'll be in trouble.'

'What trouble? Anyway, I've heard she just sits up there in the nursery and sings hymns and won't come out. Won't let Miss Georgina out, neither.'

'Poor Miss Georgina,' said Ellen. 'They saw Master Freddie too, you know, the children.'

I said, 'Where'd you hear that?' and Mary said, 'They never! How?'

'They were with Miss Childers.'

'Oh, I don't believe you.'

'Well, it's true, they were out playing and when Jenny fetched Miss Childers, they all saw. One of the gardeners told me he'd taken Miss Georgina indoors himself.'

'But we'd have seen them.'

'No, we wouldn't. They went the other way, past the boot room. It was when we were all in the scullery.'

'I still don't believe it. Whoever it was told you, Ellen, he was having you on.'

'All the same, it was a funny sort of accident if you ask me, Master Freddie falling down and hitting his head like that.'

'Perhaps he had a turn, like Jenny.'

'Don't talk daft.'

But there were plenty saying that: how could it be an accident? And the ones that weren't saying it were thinking it. There was a great deal of talk about Miss Georgina's and Master Freddie's nurse too, because there was a lot of feeling against her. I heard one of the older ones call her a whited sepulchre, which I thought was a bit hard, but it's true to say that she did develop a sort of religious mania after Master Freddie was killed and wouldn't say a word to a soul, just kept on praying all the time. But it was poor Jenny I felt sorry for, when they all started on her. I think it was the policeman, really, that set it all off. Whether Mrs Mattie gave him a nudge in that direction I don't know, but he decided Master Freddie's death was her doing. When I say policeman, I don't mean him from the village, because a proper policeman came down to do an investigation. When he came along, we all had to go and sit down in rows in front of him as if we were at school, and listen to his little speech – Mrs Mattie even got me to put a little vase of flowers on the table for him – and then we all had to leave the room and come back one by one so he could ask us questions. Of course, everyone was going, 'Well, if it was an accident like they're saying, what's he want to ask questions for?' It was horrible, we felt like we were being accused of something. I think that's why some of them turned against Jenny. I'm not saying they'd done something bad to Master Freddie and put the blame on her or anything like that, but once you got in there with the policeman, he kept on and on asking the same things, and if you said you'd got nothing to tell, he didn't believe you. I was one of the last to see him, because they took us by the alphabet. He kept asking me if I'd heard people in the passageway when I was in the scullery washing out the cloths. I said, 'Of course I did,' because you could hear them coming and going. Not that I took much notice; I had my work to be getting on with. This policeman said, 'Was the door to the passage open?'

'Oh, yes, it was always open.' Well, it had to be, people coming in and out all the time with great big trays – they'd have dropped the lot if they'd tried to open the door.

'Were you facing the door?' Because there were two sinks, one looking towards the door and one the other way, and I was at the one facing.

'Yes.'

'So you could see who was going past?'

'If I looked up I could see.'

Then he said, 'Well, who did you see?'

I said, 'I can't remember,' because I couldn't, not really, you don't take notice of things like that unless you've a special reason, do you? The policeman asked, if he said their names, would that jog my memory, and he started off: Ellen, Mary, Dora, Doris and so on like that. Well, one or two I thought I could remember and I told him, and then he said, 'Did you see Jenny?'

'Well,' I said. 'I don't rightly know.'

'Are you sure?'

'I don't think I saw her.'

'You'd remember Jenny, wouldn't you? She's different from the others.'

'Yes, she is. But I can't remember if I saw her.'

'Think carefully,' he said. 'You don't have to hurry.'

Well, I'm not so daft I couldn't tell that he wanted me to say, yes, I'd seen her. 'Some of the others said they'd seen her go down to the back door,' he said. 'So she must have come past you.'

I said, 'She might have done,' because that was true, she might have. The thing was, I could see Jenny coming along the passage in my mind, ever so clear, but I couldn't remember if it was that day or another one, and it seemed so important to this policeman that I felt I mustn't get it wrong. Well, he kept going over and over it, and he seemed so certain that in the end I thought, well, it must be me that isn't remembering right, and I said, 'Yes, I suppose I must have seen her.'

'Good girl,' he said. 'Well done.' And then he clapped his notebook shut and that was the end of it.

Well, Ellen had gone in before me because her name was Corrigan, so that night we had a talk about it. I told her I didn't feel right. I thought the policeman had made me say something against Jenny, even though I didn't see how it could be, really, because five or six at least must have gone past while I was in the scullery and they weren't all going to do something bad to hurt poor Master Freddie, were they? I said to Ellen, 'I think it's barmy, all these questions. Who'd want to hurt a child like Master Freddie?' Because that was the part we couldn't understand, either of us. I said, 'I'm so worried I've got Jenny into trouble, saying what I said.'

Ellen said, 'Well, if she did do something, I'm sure she never meant to do wrong.'

Poor Jenny. When the policemen took her away, the other servants stoned the carriage. I heard people say she'd gone mad and killed poor Master Freddie, and took the other children round to see the body out of malice. Soon everyone was saying it, even Ellen. I was embarrassed to say anything in disagreement, because when had I ever had a kind word to say to the poor girl? I should have stood up for her, but I never, because I thought then they'd think I was like she was. But I noticed William wasn't paying any mind to all the gossip and that made me like him all the more.

They never charged Jenny with anything. They took her away and locked her up in a loony asylum. She did go berserk after she saw the body, and the police told Mrs Mattie it had sent her barmy for good. Most of them at Dennys thought she'd done it. 'Why didn't they charge her?' that's what they were saying. 'Hanging's too good.' Some people thought the police never charged her because Mr Lomax went and asked them not to, but I never saw how that could be, myself. More likely they couldn't because she was too crazy for them to get any sense out of her. As I say, I can't be high and mighty over that; there'd been plenty of times before Master Freddie died when I felt I should go and say something to Jenny, just something a bit friendly, but I thought: If the others see me talking to her, they'll think I'm the same as her and I won't get on. So I ignored her, same as the rest of them. But we were ignorant, we didn't understand. And to be honest, I thought if you were mad then it was all funny turns and hide the carving knife. It's not, though, and I know that now.

But it didn't make no sense to me. Because if Jenny never did it, who did? To tell you the truth, I didn't want to think about it too much, what happened, so I finished up saying to myself, well, it must have been an accident. But I suppose it was daft, really, because how could a thing like that be an accident? Even if something had fallen out of the sky – there were no big trees anywhere near, but I suppose it could have come off the top of the privy, a stone or something – and hit Master Freddie on the head, why didn't they find it there with him, whatever it was? One thing which I did think was that there might have been something there, but Mrs Mattie took it away or had it cleared off or something. Not that I'm saying she would have done that, but just that she might have moved something, perhaps because she didn't know, or . . . I don't know. It was a long time ago and it wasn't all fingerprints and detectives in those days, not like now. I don't know what the family thought of it. To this day, I've never heard Miss Georgina speak one word about it. My thought is that she's never talked about it to anyone, not even Master Edmund. But what's the good of he and she talking about it? It's not going to bring Master Freddie back, is it?

It was different at Dennys after that. It had been a happy house, but it all began to go down and bad after Master Freddie died. Mr Lomax arrived the day after and we were all lined up in the drive for him, same as usual. I don't think I've ever seen anyone look so unhappy as he did that day. When me and Ellen were upstairs in our little room that night she said to me, 'He's taken to drink.'

I was horrified; 'That's a terrible thing to say!'

'I can see it, it's like a hand that's laid hold of him.'

I said, 'You want to stop reading silly books,' because it was so fanciful I thought she must have got it out of a book, not that I ever saw her read one. Well, that was just the start of it, the two of us falling out. We were like cat and dog all summer after that. That particular summer it was *so* hot, and what with our dresses and stockings and stays, and you had all your heavy hair nailed up on your head with great steel pins, nothing felt right. You were just sticky and pricky all day long. And where me and Ellen had to sleep, the room was just under the roof and it was like the fiery furnace. But being in service wasn't a rest-cure, like it is nowadays, and you had to do your day's work even if you never got one wink of sleep because you were being boiled in your bed.

It made me feel wicked to hear Ellen going on about William, so I used to pretend to be asleep. Ellen used to say to me, 'I don't know how you do it, Ada. When you get into bed, you just die.' The hot weather went on well into October – this would have been, oh, four, five months after Master Freddie died and we were getting back to normal. If you want to call it normal, because it wasn't.

Anyway, there was one day, mid-October, when we had to wash the china and glass. Not the stuff they used for eating and drinking, this was all the fancy things from the big cabinets. A lot of wealthy people had that sort of thing in those days and they were so valuable they had to be taken out one at a time to be washed. Well, William had to bring them to me, I washed them, and then I gave them to Ellen and she made them shine. We were in the scullery with the door wide open and I had my hands in the sink – which was nice for me, to have my hands in the cool water – and Ellen kept going over and whooshing the back door to and fro to give us a bit of a draught. Trouble was, there was all these wasps that kept coming in as well. I think there must have been a nest somewhere. The kitchen maid put out all these traps for them, glass jars and bowls with water in and a scrape of honey, so the wasp would go in after it and drown. I was standing there, washing away, surrounded by all these horrible things buzzing and dying, keeping my arms right in to my sides so I wouldn't get near them. We worked away until we had a lot of china clean and we were waiting for William to come and take it all back. Ellen said, 'There's no room here, I'm going to start taking them back,' hoping she'd run into William, of course. Well, there wasn't any room, so off she went.

I wasn't going to give up the chance of a rest, so I was standing there with my eyes shut and my hands in the water, when I heard William come in. I had my back to the kitchen door, but I still knew who it was. I wasn't going to look round, not for anything, so I grabbed hold of this big porcelain thing and starting washing it; it only needed a splash of water, but I was going at it so hard I must have come close to rubbing off the colour. I could *feel* him standing there behind me. I thought: What's the matter, why doesn't he say something? But he never spoke, he just came right beside me and leaned up against the draining board. He was next to me, looking straight at me in complete silence. I can remember it as if it was yesterday – probably better than yesterday, my memory nowadays – but I can tell you this: in all my life I've never felt so uncomfortable as I did at that moment.

To be honest, I was scared to move. I had this great heavy ornament in my hands, for all I knew it was worth hundreds of pounds, even one chip against the stone sink would ruin it. I wasn't going to move towards him, but there were all those wasps on the other side of me, so I didn't know what to do. Still he never said anything, but then I felt his hand come out and touch the back of my neck and the shock of it made me give a little jump. Oh! like that. I didn't know if I liked it or not, all I could think was, whatever he does, I must not drop this vase. If I hadn't been so silly I'd have let it down gently, but I was flustered, I got sort of fixed on it, if you know what I mean. Then William kissed the back of my neck, just under my hair.

I thought my wrists were going to snap. The only thing in my mind was, I've got to put this vase down if it's the last thing I do. I said to him, 'Excuse me,' but it came out like a whisper.

He said, 'You'll have to do better than that,' so I tried again, but it didn't come out no better. Then, quick as a flash, he had the vase out of my hands, put it down on the side and gave me a kiss, a real kiss, on the mouth, with his arms round, the lot. Well, I just stood there, I didn't kiss him back, didn't know how to. The first time I saw them do that at the pictures, he bent her right back, they had all the music and everything, and

I noticed, oh look, she's got her eyes closed. I thought, well, I got that wrong, I never had mine closed. Because I was staring at all the wooden racks for the plates to dry on, that were behind William's head, I remember that.

Then we heard Ellen in the corridor, so he let go of me and shot out the back and off down the yard. Ellen said, 'I never saw William, did he come in here?' I just stared at her like I was feeble-minded. 'Ada, close your mouth, you'll catch a fly.'

William gave me more than one kiss when no one was about, after that. It was amazing we got away with it, considering how they treated us. If anyone had seen, they'd have said I was leading him on – well, I wasn't exactly trying hard to stop him, was I? No more than what's normal, anyway. I should think they'd sooner have shot all us girls than let the menservants come up to our rooms. But I never invited him, don't think I did that.

I'd only gone up to my room in the first place because I felt sick from something I ate. In that weather, food goes rotten as soon as you look at it, especially meat – it was the middle of the afternoon, but Mrs Mattie told me to go and lie down: 'You might as well, you're not doing us any good down here.' To this day I don't know how William knew where I was – or how he had the nerve, come to that – and I certainly don't know how he found out which was my room and Ellen's, but he did. It did cross my mind afterwards that he might have been up there before, not for Ellen, but for somebody else, I mean, I think that probably was true, but of course I never asked him.

I've never told this to a single soul, but who's to care if I tell it now? Isn't it funny how something can matter so much and then not at all? Well, I'd seen my brothers running around, of course, and I knew boys were made different from girls in certain places, but I'd never seen a grown man before and

I had no idea . . . I shut my eyes quick enough, I can tell you! I should have found it out the proper way, in marriage. But it made me think no woman would get married if they knew that was in store for them – so perhaps it's as well they don't know, or there'd be no children born.

There I was, lying down on the bed – Ellen's bed, as it happened – when I heard the door open. I couldn't believe it when I saw William standing there. He hadn't so much as tapped on the door, and there he was right next to the bed like a magic trick. That room was so small that once you opened the door you almost did fall on to the bed, so he was very close to me. I huddled myself up quick the furthest I could from him: 'What did you come up here for?'

'Keep your voice down, someone'll hear you.'

'And it'll be my job gone if they do. What are you doing here?'

'I must say, Miss Ada, you don't seem very pleased to see me.'

'I'm not! Did anyone see you going up the stairs?'

'Not a soul. You have a charming room.' Trying to talk all smart, like that. 'Well, now I'm here, aren't you going to offer me a seat?'

Well, I was so scared of someone coming up and finding us, I couldn't think straight. As I say, it was more than my life was worth if he got caught in my room. I suppose if I'd been more calm about it, if I'd told him to go . . . Maybe I did tell him to go, I don't really remember, just that I was petrified at the thought of Mrs Mattie coming up and finding him there. But I never offered myself to him, nothing like that. I didn't even know what it meant, offering yourself to a man. He came and sat down on the bed. I don't think he said anything, just started kissing me. I was so frantic for him to leave I'd have agreed to anything he wanted, only it wasn't really a matter of that because I didn't know what he was doing. Well, when he was finished doing it, I said to him, 'Don't you ever come up here again, I'm not having that again.'

But he wasn't listening, he was fussing with his clothes: 'I'd better go, it wouldn't do for anyone to see me.'

I said, 'You should have thought of that before you come up here. If anyone sees you, say you came up to fetch something. Don't say anything about me, whatever you do.'

When he'd gone, I just lay there – it all happened so fast, I wouldn't have believed it, except it felt sore where he'd been and the tops of my legs were sticky. I remember wondering if it would be a liberty to take off my dress and stays – I still had everything on, neither of us took any of our clothes off. Better with your boots on, that's what they used to say, didn't they? It was funny, I never thought how daft it was to worry about taking my dress off when a man had been doing *that* to me not five minutes earlier. But in the end I thought: I'm going to suffocate if I don't do something, so I took everything off down to my petticoat, then I got the drop of water we had left in the ewer and lay down and tipped it over my face and neck. And I just lay there looking up at my and Ellen's little bit of sky. It made me feel wicked, lying there with only my underclothes on. I thought: I'm doing this because I'm a bad girl now. Otherwise I wouldn't be lying here like this.

EDMUND

How *do* flies manage to walk upside down on the ceiling? That's the only place they *can* walk in this house. It's all the space that's left.

Other chaps' sisters were different. I used to watch them with their sisters, the other chaps. Most girls seemed to be chaps' sisters, that was how you met them, on the whole. Sometimes they put the fellow down in company, embarrassed him by talking about some childhood thing when he'd forgotten it, or wished he had. Georgina never did that. No, it wasn't that, too much the other way, if anything. Like looking into a magic looking glass that reflected you the way you wanted to be, rather than the way you were. There, that's used up my stock of clever talk; I'm no good at that, things being like other things. Except that I've often thought that my sister's mind is rather like one of Heath Robinson's machines: you pull a string and expect a bucket of coal, but instead you get a boiled egg or a whack on the head with a shovel. A miracle of jerry-building. All the bits work after a fashion, but you never quite know what's coming next.

Going out with Georgie was always an adventure. I remember the first time we ever went anywhere in London together, it would have been just after she was married, we took a trip on the Underground and they'd just installed an escalator at Earl's Court, it was the first one they'd built. No one had ever seen moving stairs before, so there was quite a crowd. There was a man with a wooden leg riding on them, all by himself, he'd go up and then walk down, then back up again on the escalator, and Georgie took one look at him and said, 'Do you suppose it's eaten his leg?' And of course no one wanted to ride on it after that, so we had it all to ourselves, we went up and down a few times until we got the knack of stepping on and off. It turned out the man with the wooden leg was employed by the railway company; they thought people would be afraid of a moving staircase so they hired this man to ride on it to show people how easy it was. But all this is whitewash, you know, the old whitewash on the wall. That was a song they sang in the First War: *Wash me in the water that you wash your dirty daughter in, and I shall be whiter than the whitewash on the wall.*

I've always admired courage in others and Georgie has great courage. I still admire her for it, in spite of everything. At night I pray to God to make me brave, but each morning I wake up with the same feeling of dread like a stone inside my stomach. I'm not sure, any longer, why I pray. Habit, partly. But I suppose if one is praying, one is making some sort of effort . . . but then again, why on earth should God listen to the prayers of a man like me?

GEORGINA

Isn't that the most extraordinary thing? There's a certain type of woman – they're usually servants, like that cook at Dennys – who will respond to absolutely any crisis by dishing out tea and sandwiches. Ada got into a frightful habit of that during the last war. It was bad enough being woken up night after night by Hitler, without Ada thrusting piles of beige bread under our noses at three a.m. Edmund used to keep the gin bottle under his bed, because Ada makes quite the filthiest tea you can possibly imagine. Edmund always says that any mouse who tried to trot on it would end up full fathoms five before it had time to shake its tail.

Roland and Louisa and I sat round that kitchen table and stared at those lumps of bread and jam for hours – perhaps it wasn't hours, but certainly it felt like a lifetime. The kitchen maid shut up all the doors and windows, and pulled the blinds so that we couldn't see what was happening outside. The half-light made the bread and jam look grey. I thought perhaps it was going to be some kind of *test*, to see if we were able to eat it or not. Roland and Louisa were sitting opposite me, and they had servants standing behind their chairs, and when I looked round, there was someone behind my chair. I could hear Louisa crying, but no one spoke to her. The servants didn't look at us. They were all looking at the floor so I did, too.

Nurse came to my chair and bent down, and mopped my

knee where I'd fallen over and put a bandage on it. She tilted up my head to see the bruise on the side of my face where mad Jenny had kicked me, but she didn't put anything on that. Then she said, 'Open your mouth,' and gave me something to drink. I didn't want it because it tasted vile and she pinched my jaw open with her hand as they do to horses when they want them to take medicine. Louisa and Roland had it as well. I think it was something soporific, because they fell asleep in their chairs and I think I must have done too, because I don't remember anything after that.

There is a dream I have had, many, many times, always the same. We're sitting at the kitchen table, but I get up and leave the room. The servants try to stop me – they stand in my way, but they can't touch me, I can move through them as if they don't exist. I go outside to the privy, except it isn't really the privy any more, but another part of the garden with flowers and proper grass, and Freddie's there, but there's no blood on him. He's wearing white clothes, like his sailor suit, but all white, and his hair is bright and clean, and he's smiling at me. And I feel happy. But then I wake up and it's gone.

The next morning I asked Mrs Mattie if I could see Freddie. She said she would go and see about it – she went off and it was the first time I'd been left on my own to get dressed. I didn't know if I could do it, so I said to myself, 'If I can tie my laces, Freddie won't be dead; if I can do up all my buttons, he won't be dead; if I can tie my hair-ribbon he won't be dead,' and so on. By the time I'd finished, I was convinced I'd done so well that Freddie would be fine, just a bump on the head or something. But then Mrs Mattie came back and said I could see him, and she took me and, of course, when I saw him he was dead.

He did look quite lifelike, because they'd washed the blood off and put on clean clothes. 'Doesn't he look happy?' I asked

Mrs Mattie. I remembered the dead baby in the photograph my father had shown me. 'It must be nice to be dead. Dead people always look happy.'

'You should go to your room now, Miss Georgina.'

'Yes, but may I see the photographer?'

'Photographer?'

'So we can put Freddie's picture in the album, with the other one.'

'There isn't going to be any photographer, Miss Georgina.'

'Then may I see Roland?'

'Miss Louisa and Master Roland have gone home. Now come back to your room and don't upset yourself.'

I didn't go to Freddie's funeral, nor did Edmund. Edmund didn't come home at all that summer. He told me afterwards that our father had written and had him sent straight back to school. Father came to live at Dennys permanently and at first I hoped that he might come up to the nursery to see me, but he never did and Nurse wouldn't let me go downstairs. They used to leave our meals outside the door – big mice with big feet, coming and going, but I never saw them. I remember trying to hide lumps of mutton under my dolly's skirt, but Nurse was always watching and of course it went straight back on to the plate. Mrs Mattie came up eventually. It was a very hot summer and perhaps one of the maids told her about the bad smell. She pushed the door wide open and made all the plates topple over. Nurse didn't stay long after that. When Mrs Mattie saw us I knew that she would be sent away, so I got up from the table and lay down on the bed in my room and she didn't try to stop me. I stayed there for a week and the other servants looked after me, and then Nurse came in to tell me that she was leaving. She said she had 'gladsome tidings', except I thought she said 'gladsome tidyings'. I only remembered that a few weeks ago and I told Edmund about it. He was tickled pink. He said, 'That must be what Ada does when she's happy.' Nurse told me she was going to the Belgian Congo or somewhere, to be a missionary for her church. I hope they were cannibals and put her in the pot.

I was ill for a long time after that and I don't remember much about it, except the dream I kept having about Freddie. The doctor gave me sleeping medicines, which I think were stronger in those days, so that one would sleep longer and have more dreams. I never get the chance to dream nowadays because the wretched sleeping pills don't give me more than a couple of hours most nights. But since I've taken them all my life, they've probably stopped having any effect. I take handfuls of the things, but they never work properly. I said to Edmund, 'Give me a whack with the fire tongs, that'll put me to sleep!' He went downstairs and told Ada to make me a cup of cocoa instead.

But I don't mind the not sleeping any more, not really. I don't need much of anything now – not much sleep, not much food – only cocktails. A cocktail for breakfast, lunch, tea and dinner, that's what I need. But at that time . . . well, I wanted to be asleep. It was because I thought I must be wicked. When I was awake, I was wicked.

I remember Father arriving very clearly. From the nursery window, I could just see one corner of the carriage and the top of his hat. I thought, now he will come up and visit me, but he didn't. Every day I asked God to make him come and visit me, but he never did. I tried to make explanations to myself about why he didn't come – they were excuses, really, I was trying to make excuses for him. Because it may be different now, but in those days fathers didn't come into nurseries, not in families like ours. I think there were one or two occasions when my mother was alive, but we were usually taken downstairs to see him. Years later, Edmund told me that Father's visits to the nursery reminded him of Queen Victoria inspecting a tribal delegation from a very remote and insignificant colony. Anyway, I told myself all sorts of nonsense – Father hardly ever came to the nursery so he wouldn't know the way, that sort of thing. I suppose this carried on for two or three weeks and then he suddenly appeared.

I was asleep when he came into the room, so I don't remember that part of it. But he stood at the end of the bed and looked down at me. His shoulders were folded up the way angels' and birds' are before they spread their wings, and he had his hands folded over the brass bed rail. His head was bowed as if he was saying a prayer. It made me think of the poem about the angels who stand around the child's bed, one to watch and one to pray and one to bear my soul away. I couldn't see his face properly because the room was quite dark, but for some reason I did have this sort of wild, stupid hope that he'd come to give me a blessing. You know, 'Father, give me thy blessing . . .' I suppose these sorts of ludicrous misunderstandings must be part of everybody's childhood.

Father stood there for a long time without speaking. Then he walked around the bed and stood beside me. His expression was the most . . . well, to put it bluntly he looked disgusted, as if he was seeing some excrement or some vile thing and not me at all. He said, 'You know why I have come to see you.'

'No, I don't know.' Immediately I knew it was something I had done, but I couldn't think of anything.

'You know what you have done.' His hands were shaking. My mind was whirling round like a speeded-up clock, trying to think of what it might be. I didn't know if he wanted me to answer him or not. I don't think he knew himself.

I said, 'Is it about Nurse?'

'Don't try to trick me by blaming other people. You can't expect the servants to be responsible. You are responsible.' I felt as if my mouth had been locked. 'You allowed this to happen. You deserted your brother.' His anger encircled my chest like an iron band and I couldn't breathe. It was Freddie, something to do with Freddie.

Then he said, 'I am not going to say any more. There is nothing I can do, but I will not come back. I will not see you.'

He left the room. I couldn't move or speak. His anger made the air shake, and I saw again and again the flash of Freddie's red hair between the branches of the trees while I crouched silently amongst the brambles . . . I watched him go. I couldn't change it. Father thought I was being cunning, but I wasn't. Freddie died because I didn't go after him and Father hated me.

Edmund came to see me, of course. I sometimes think that he is the only person in the world to whom I haven't been a disappointment. I never told him what Father had said – how could I? I knew Father wanted him, but I had to keep him for mine. I suppose you could say I made him choose sides. But that wasn't difficult, because Edmund had always been rather afraid of Father, certainly more than I had, and I don't think Father ever knew how to make him feel at ease. But the two of us had the most gorgeous times when he was on holiday from school. Apart from my mornings with Miss Blacker – she was a retired schoolmistress from the village my father engaged to teach me, but I don't suppose she'd been much of a teacher even in her heyday and I certainly didn't learn a great deal – Edmund and I spent every moment together. I made Ada help me pin up some sheets to make a sort of tent in my room, and we sat inside it and played games. I remember my bed used to get terrifically uncomfortable, counters and cards and crumbs all over it, more bumps and lumps every time you turned over. Ada used to come up in the evening to say good-night and shoo Edmund off to his room, but he'd always come creeping back when she'd gone.

In the beginning, we used to walk down to the village, but I stopped doing that after a while because there were too many people. I preferred it when it was just us. Edmund had a funny way of speaking at that time, I suppose they all did it at school: everything was either jolly awful or awfully jolly. I used to tease him about it, but he never minded. Every evening at eight o'clock he used to go downstairs to have dinner with my father in the dining-room. I love twilight in the summer, it's the time when I used to stand at my bedroom window and wait for Edmund to finish his dinner and come back up to me. I used to watch the shadows growing longer and longer across the grass, and the wood getting darker and darker until you couldn't make out the individual trees any more, all the different greens greying in the dusk and then black. I must say you don't get *quite* the same effect looking down the Exhibition Road, but it's still my favourite time of day. On summer evenings I make Edmund wait until the sun's gone right down before he switches on the electric light.

Edmund came up to my room one night after dinner and explained to me that our father was a drunkard. Ada must have known about it, but she didn't tell me. She wasn't a tale-bearer in those days. Quite right too. Really, that woman's character has deteriorated beyond belief. Edmund was just about to go up to university and he'd been in London all week having a terrific lot of hoopla with lawyers about money. That night, he said to me, 'You'll have to go away from here.'

I thought he'd gone mad. 'Don't be silly, where would I go?'

'Georgie, you can't stay here. Father drinks. There are bottles all over his study. That's why he never lets Ada go in there. Besides, he hates us.'

'He hates everyone, doesn't he?'

'He likes Thomas.' Thomas was the gardener, the only servant we had left apart from Ada.

'Why would he like Thomas and not you?'

'Simple. I'm alive – we're alive – and Mother and Freddie are dead.'

'Thomas is alive.'

'Yes, but he doesn't count. And Father drinking brandy all the time makes it much worse. He'll never be cured of it, he doesn't want to be. He trusts Thomas. He thinks everyone else is against him. And now, Thomas is going and he blames us for that.'

'Well, it's true. About me, anyway. Thomas seems to hate me almost as much as Father does.'

'That's why you've got to go. You can't just be stuck away here for ever or you'll end up like someone's mad old aunt.'

'I'll just have to be a mad old aunt then, because I haven't got any choice.'

'You could get married.'

'How on earth am I supposed to do that?'

'Honestly, Georgie, all you'd have to do is meet someone. You're beautiful, even I can see that.'

I was completely taken aback when he said that. I didn't *feel* beautiful and nobody had ever told me I was. Well, how could they? Nobody ever saw me and anyway, my clothes were an absolute fright. I remember thinking if I am beautiful, perhaps I can make a man fall in love with me. Then he'll buy me lovely dresses and emeralds and diamonds, and I'll be like the ladies in the fashion plates.

'Look, Georgie, it can't be that difficult, other people manage it.'

'Yes, but we aren't other people, Edmund. Well, you nearly are because of going to school, but I'm not.'

'You can learn. You just watch the other people and what

they do, and then you do it. I did it at school, it's easy. Everyone does it.'

'But even if I could, the only men I know are you and Father. I can't marry you, so who I am going to have for a husband?'

Well, of course, Edmund had no answer to that, but he was right; I did have to get away from Father and marriage was the only way to do it. And, much to my surprise, I found that it was really rather easy.

ADA

If someone had told me that that was how a woman came to have a baby I'd have said they were having me on. Anyway, how would you begin to describe something like that, there weren't any words – well, I suppose I knew there must be some words somewhere, but I certainly didn't know what they were. I thought: that must be the cause of babies and of course I started to worry in case I suddenly got one. I kept looking in the mirror to see if I was getting fatter, because that was the only way I knew to tell. It scared me, because they'd put you away if you had a baby and no husband. That used to happen all the time and with some of them, they never let them out again. The way they treated those girls, as if they were dirt – which a lot of them were, I don't deny it. But not me. Yet there I was, one of the good girls at school – that was before my father took me out of it to put me to work – worrying that I might have a baby from a man who'd never said so much as one word about marrying me! I was far too scared to say anything to William. It sounds daft now, but I was more embarrassed about saying it to him than I was scared of the baby coming. William left Dennys within a couple of weeks. He'd been polite enough after, but nothing special, no more kisses when no one was looking. And I wasn't going to go making up to him, not likely!

Well, that was that and I didn't think any more of it. I was too busy worrying in case a baby came. I thought it took about six months before you had the baby, so I kept checking, but my waist got thinner, not fatter, and in the end I said to myself this can't be right, so I didn't bother with it after that. I had no idea there were other signs. If I'd known *that*, I could have put myself out of my misery in a couple of weeks. It might seem funny enough now, but it wasn't at the time. But there was William, all prepared to go off to his new situation, baby or not, or so I thought at the time. The last thing he said to me was, 'You're a pal, Ada.' And I thought, well, thank you so kindly, I don't think.

When he left, that was the time when they found out that Miss Georgina's nurse wasn't looking after her like she should, so she was sent away. Miss Georgina was very ill after that; for a time they thought she wouldn't live, but she's always been stronger than she looks.

Ellen and I weren't getting on at all. She'd cried her eyes out when William left, but I never tried to comfort her – I had enough troubles of my own. So then she used to say, 'You don't care, Ada, you're glad he's gone,' and 'You were always jealous,' and that sort of thing. It got on my nerves. There'd be times when I'd nearly burst out and say something, but then think better of it and stop myself; and she'd start up again and it was like that day after day, the moment we were alone she'd start up saying these things. I felt so needled with it I didn't know what to do and, of course, one night it had to come out. I was so tired I'd barely managed to drag myself up the stairs and as soon as I'd shut the door she started with William this, William that, William the other, sitting there with her hair all over her shoulders looking like a tragedy queen. Well, I just turned to her and said, 'Don't talk nonsense. William wasn't ever gone on you, you dreamed it all up by yourself.' The moment it was out of my mouth I wished I'd never said it, but it was too late.

She never said a word, just blew out the candle and got into bed. Then she said 'I know' and I heard her give a little gulp, like she was crying.

I felt like such a devil, I leaned over and patted her shoulder and said, 'I'm sorry, I didn't mean that.'

She was turned away from me, but she said, 'No. I wanted it to be true about William, but it wasn't. So don't say you didn't mean it when you did.' I didn't know what else to say and after a minute she said, 'Get back in bed, Ada. Go to sleep.' Not in a nasty way, but like she was suddenly dead tired. Of course I never had a wink; I was turning it over and over all night, whether she'd ever speak to me again.

But I needn't have worried because the next night we had a good old talk, the first we'd had for months. I felt bad because I didn't need to say what I had. If she wanted to believe William liked her, where was the harm? It was pride that made me say it, because really I wanted her to know that William was keen on me. But I was too much of a coward to tell her that, so I said the other thing. Ellen told me, 'I'm not going to stay here much longer.'

I couldn't think what she meant. 'Why, where are you going?'

'I'm leaving here. My mother's written and told me she's poorly so I'm going home to look after her.'

I said, 'Oh, that's terrible.' I didn't know much about Ellen's family, except that she had a lot of brothers and sisters, more than I did.

She said, 'I'm glad I'm not staying here.'

I said, 'Is it because of William?'

'No, it's because of Mr Lomax. Drinking.' Because Ellen had spotted it right away and at first I thought she was making up a story, but when it turned out to be true she never once said 'I told you so', which she could have, easy.

So that night I asked her, 'How did you know about Mr Lomax before anybody else could see it?'

She said, 'Because my father was a drinker.' You could have knocked me down with a feather – I'd never heard anyone say such a thing before, a secret thing about themself or their family. I felt it was a great honour for me that she was telling me about it, because with those things, nobody ever talked about them. Ellen said, 'He used to come rolling home every night and clobber my mother, and if any of us young ones got in the way or made a noise, we'd get it too. When I sent my wages home I used to pretend it was something else, because if he got to it before my mother did, it would be straight off to the pub and she wouldn't see a penny.' Then she said, 'I was so frightened when I saw him hit my mother, but I knew if I did anything he'd start on me. When he died I was glad, because he couldn't hit her no more. Honestly, Ada, I've seen too much of that, drinking, and I wouldn't stay here if you offered me double the wages.' And she meant it. 'I may not be much, but I won't stand for that.' To this day, I remember her saying that. Because – and this may sound queer – that was the first time I'd ever heard someone talking as if they had a *choice.* I mean someone like me, not some important person. I mean, for people like me, working people, well, you went where you were put and if you didn't like it you could lump it. I don't know if Ellen married, or what sort of man it was, but I'm sure it wasn't a drinker like her father.

I said, 'I'll miss you' and I meant it. She was my best friend, and I never saw her again.

I'd never come across any drinking before, but it wasn't long before I got my first experience. It was the little things at first with Mr Lomax, slurring the speech, seeing the extra brandy and wine on the side every night, on the tray, well, even the slowest could put two and two together. Then there was the business of serving dinner. Mr Lomax had been home a couple of weeks and some of the girls said to me, 'Oh, you've got to go in and serve the dinner.'

I said, 'But I don't know what to do.'

'Oh, don't worry, in you go.'

Well, I'd never served the dinner, it wasn't my job and no one ever showed me how. The other girls brought all the dishes and things, and one of them gave me a shove through the dining-room door. Well, I suppose I should have guessed why none of them wanted to do it. Mr Lomax was sitting on his own at the end of this great long table and his eyes were glazed from drinking. The fire was glowing out behind him and I thought he looked like the devil, sitting there in his big chair like a throne. It was just him and me in the room, no one else. I was shaking, frightened I'd drop something or do it wrong and, of course, that made me shake even more. There was no one to help me and Mr Lomax looked as if he might go roaring out at me any moment. I nearly turned round and ran straight out again, but I thought: I can't do that. I knew the others were waiting outside and I was sure they'd report it.

I put the food down on the table. I was tiptoeing about, trying not to knock anything, but he didn't seem to know I was there. To be honest, I don't suppose he would have noticed if an elephant had come and passed him the dishes with its trunk, he was in such a state, poor man. He never even took a mouthful, just reached out his hand – to get his glass I suppose, but he knocked all the drink into his plate. I rushed forward to mop it up and he barked at me, 'No!' Then he said, 'Take it away, I shan't want any more. Go on, get out!' The plate was swimming in brandy, all over the meat, and he hadn't even eaten one mouthful. My hands were shaking so much that when I took the plate the liquid was shooting out everywhere, on the cloth, on me, on him. I never dared ask if he wanted anything else, I thought he'd just shout at me again. I fairly ran out of that room and I said to them outside, 'I'm not going back in there, so don't you say nothing.' They didn't, they knew they couldn't make me. I kept well out of the way after that, but I saw the food come back to the kitchen every night, barely touched, and the bottles always empty.

Well, you can't stop people talking and there was a fair bit of gossip in the village about Mr Lomax. One or two even suggested he'd killed Master Freddie himself in an accident when he was drunk, but it was sheer malice because Mr Lomax wasn't even at Dennys when it happened. Some of them said, 'Oh, he should marry again,' thinking that would cure him of his drinking. He never did marry again. I don't know why, but he grew to hate women with all his heart. If he saw something in a newspaper against women, even if it was just a joke or a comic drawing with some little remark, he would tear it out and save it up in a big box in his study. I suppose it was harmless enough, but seeing a whole box full of stuff about how bad women are, it wasn't very nice. I never used to lift it up or touch it, I just got the cloth and dusted round. In any case, he'd roar and shout if you moved anything. Because he'd got so he wouldn't throw anything away – Miss Georgina has that from him, hoarding. None of us girls dared go into his study when he was there, we'd be on our tiptoes outside. 'Is he in there? Can you see him in there?' It was like that all the time. Then, if the coast was clear, we'd rush in and out again, it was dreadful.

Miss Georgina lay upstairs for five whole months with her illness. She was so sick and bad that no one thought she'd live above a month, but Mr Lomax never went near her. Some of them – the servants – said it was because he was only fond of the bottle and didn't care about his daughter, but I could never believe that. I used to think, he's lost his wife, he's lost his youngest child, if Miss Georgina dies, it'll break his heart. I thought that was why he never went to her, that he couldn't bear to see her because he thought she was dying, but I don't know if it was true. Let's just say that Mr Lomax was a very unhappy man, because there's no doubting that and, in any case, Miss Georgina was so poorly she probably didn't know who was in the room. In all my life I never heard her mention her father once, except for a conversation we had during one of the air raids. It was a very nasty one, and she and Master Edmund had come down to the basement to sit it out. We were in my little sitting-room and Master Edmund had a bottle of gin, but he never brought the proper glasses. He wouldn't let me go upstairs to fetch them, so we were sitting there drinking it out of teacups. Well, I don't know if it was the gin or the raid or what it was, but I started telling her about my father, how he never took me on his knee or cuddled me as I saw other fathers do with their children. Then I saw her face and I thought, oh, I shouldn't have said that. She stared into her cup for a moment and then she said, 'At least he didn't break your heart. My father broke my heart.' Then she said, 'Perhaps I deserved it.'

Well, I looked at Master Edmund, but he was asleep, which was a mercy. 'That's a terrible thing to say, Miss Georgina. You mustn't say things like that.'

She laughed it off. 'Well, I always think children are like dogs, wanting to be stroked all the time. Can you imagine anything more tedious?' Typical! She's never said another word about it, at least not in my hearing. But I think it was very hard for her, because she was always his favourite when she was small and then he turned right away from her when he started his drinking. She married Mr James to get away from him, I'm sure of that.

If you were taking up a tray for Miss Georgina, you always

had to make sure Mr Lomax never saw you. You could slip up the stairs with no trouble, but then it had to be got across the landing. You'd try to be ever so quiet, but there was always a floor-board that creaked and he'd just appear from nowhere: 'Where are you taking that?' You had to make an excuse and not let on it was for Miss Georgina. Nobody told us to do this that I recall, we all just understood that we must do it, because Mr Lomax didn't want to hear anything about Miss Georgina. Well, no one wanted to put up with that sort of treatment and quite a few started talking about getting another place.

Then Mr Lomax accused the butler, Mr Vincent, of stealing his brandy. He was shouting it out in front of some of them and Mr Vincent couldn't have that, especially with his staff there to hear it. So he left and three or four went with him, and a couple of others soon after. Mrs Mattie couldn't do anything, but she didn't begrudge them. They got a good character, provided they deserved it, of course, and within the year they were all gone except the two of us, Mrs Mattie and me. We did our best, but we couldn't keep up the old standards. I used to miss Ellen so much. I'd got used to having somebody to talk to, even if it was just to say 'good-night', and our little room felt ever so lonely. I thought, well, she's gone now and I'd better make the best of it. I'll have a decent bed for a change, because hers was more comfortable than mine. I used to lie down on that bed so tired I thought I'd never get up again, and sometimes William would come into my mind. I never thought about him when I was worried about the baby coming, only afterwards, because I didn't want to remember all that nasty stuff. But once I knew I was safe from that, well, I wasn't *trying* to think about him, he just came into my mind, and it was nice to remember his face and the things he said. I didn't expect ever to see him again.

But most of the time I was too busy to think about William.

I was trying to do five people's work. I thought: I'll go on working like this until I drop down dead. I could have just said 'enough's enough', but it never occurred to me. Perhaps it was because I'd been so happy at Dennys before that, I couldn't imagine leaving. But that's when my aches and pains started, from that time, and I wasn't twenty-two. Mrs Mattie begged Mr Lomax to let her take on more staff, even one, but he wouldn't have new people in the house, said he couldn't trust them and she'd have to do without. I suppose I stayed as much for her as for anyone. She'd worked her way up to be housekeeper and now she was back cleaning up, sweeping up, things that no housekeeper would dream of doing in a place that was half-way decent, but she had that much loyalty . . . I couldn't leave her to run the whole house by herself. And you could say she took me under her wing, really. I can picture Mrs Mattie stood at the kitchen table, making pastry with the big range behind her. It's not quite dark outside, the sun is nearly gone, but you can still see the tops of the trees above the hedge and the room is so bright, with a lovely smell of cooking. I used to sit by her and have my cup of tea and a piece of bread and dripping. I'm not saying she was like a mother to me, or anything like that; she was still very much the housekeeper even though it was this queer situation we were in. But she did used to talk to me – mostly it was about how to run a house and look after things, and I learned more cooking from watching her and what she told me than I ever did from my mother. Looking back, I know it was done on purpose . . . I said, I wouldn't have left her, but of course it was her left me in the end.

Remember what I said about Ellen talking like she had a choice? Well, that's what I mean, because it wasn't a matter of whether I decided to stay with Miss Georgina and her father, it was decided for me when Mrs Mattie retired and went to live with her married sister in Plymouth. She wasn't married herself, but it was always 'Mrs' for the housekeeper and for the cook. She wrote to me once, and reading between the lines I'd say the two of them didn't get on; but she was like me, she never had any choice. There she was – fifty-five, sixty – and Dennys had been her whole life; she'd been there since she was a girl. She should have been able to look back and be proud of a position like that, because it was quite something to have been the housekeeper in a place like Dennys, but how could she, poor woman? And she never approved of Miss Georgina, the way she was just left to run wild. Miss Georgina was always tearing around and leaping out of corners, as if she thought she was a fairy – perhaps that's what she did think. I've never known what goes on in her mind. I didn't know then and I don't know now. Nor should I want to, I might add. Mrs Mattie used to watch after Miss Georgina when she was running around and the look on her face! She'd squeeze all her mouth up like the top of a duffel bag when the string's pulled and she'd go, 'Oooh . . . Oooh, I don't know what's going to become of her.' Lucky for her she never lived to see, I say, because that would have broken her heart even if the other didn't.

The night before she left, we were sat up in the kitchen with our cocoa and Mrs Mattie said to me, 'I'll tell you something, Ada. When I saw those children standing round Master Freddie and him bleeding on the ground like that, my first thought was it was a game gone wrong. Even when Miss Childers told me how they'd come there, I still thought they must have run away and left him, and only come back after, when Jenny fetched them. I didn't know what to do . . . and the things Miss Georgina said to me.' I asked her what they were, but she wouldn't tell me, only that Miss Georgina said queer things. She said, 'I never suspected it was Jenny till the policeman said it must be. Because it wasn't like her, Ada. She was a gentle little soul.' That was it, really, what she said. But I thought: Well, then, I wasn't the only one.

Anyway, there I was, all on my own. Holding the baby, as they say. Mrs Mattie said, 'You're a good girl, Ada, mind you take care of yourself.' She looked across at the study window, where Mr Lomax was, and she said, 'There's nothing to do for him, poor man, he's beyond saving, but you look after Miss Georgina. She's never had a chance, poor lamb.' She said it like it was her own family, not her employer: 'You look after her, Ada.' We were both stood in the driveway with her trunk, waiting for the station cart and I was thinking: Oh, please don't cry, whatever you do, don't cry, because she was looking up at the house and I could see her eyes were a little bit pink. I knew that if she cried I wouldn't be able to stop myself. When the cart come, she reached out and touched my hand: 'God bless you, Ada.'

I was blinking to stop the tears coming. It was a sunny day, so I told her, 'The sun's gone in my eyes.'

Then the horse started up and off she went to the station. I stood there till I couldn't see the cart any more and then I took myself back to the kitchen. I sat down beside a short little cupboard and rested my head and arms on the marble top because it was cool. That's when I thought: I won't ever get married. I knew it in my heart. I was only twenty-three. Not that I had time to sit and think about that or anything else, there was too much to do to try and look after the two of them. But don't go thinking, oh, she sacrificed herself, or anything like that, because there wasn't no Prince Charming knocking on my door. There were thousands during the Great War who lost the boys they were going to marry and they were the ones who made sacrifices, not me. I felt sorry for those poor girls, but by the time the war broke out I wasn't a girl any more. My brother Charlie was killed on the Somme. He was twenty-nine and I'm five years older, almost to the day. Very young for a man to die, but a woman in her thirties, if she hadn't got herself a husband by then, she was well and truly on the shelf and no chance that any man would take her off it, especially not in those times.

Anyway, you don't want to go getting sentimental about me. But I swear it, you wouldn't think it was possible that two people could live in the same house and never meet, yet that's what happened with Mr Lomax and Miss Georgina. She must have been fifteen years old when Mrs Mattie left and I never saw her from one day's end to the next. She wouldn't come near the kitchen, so I used to take her meals upstairs on a tray. Half the time she wasn't in her room, either, so I'd just leave the food there. She'd put the dishes back outside her door when she was done and I'd take them down with me when I went up with the next lot. She was like a wild thing, really, just left on her own apart from a woman that came in to give her a few lessons. Even when Master Edmund was home on his holidays Miss Georgina never came downstairs much. If there was something she wanted, it was always, 'My sister says, please would you be kind enough . . .' Master Edmund was a perfect gentleman, even then. He used to come and talk to me, I used to ask him about his school and he'd tell me stories about what they got up to. I enjoyed that. He had a very nice way with him, never made you feel uncomfortable. Unlike his sister. It's a shame she couldn't have been sent away to school too, but she might as well have been a cat for all the thought her father gave her.

But Miss Georgina was bound to get some funny ideas, really, living at Dennys all the time and scarcely meeting a soul from the outside world. I used to think: whatever will become of her? She did used to get the odd letter from time to time, from Miss Louisa, but she never saw either of her cousins – their father wouldn't let them come, even though Master Edmund and Master Roland went to the same school. In fact, I used to wonder if perhaps Miss Louisa sent Miss Georgina those letters in secret, without her father knowing. As for me, well, I'd have had a little chat with Miss Georgina every now and then, if she'd wanted it. But when I took the trays up to her I often had the idea that she was standing in the next room, waiting for me to leave. I didn't have time for playing hide-and-seek so I never looked, but I'm sure that's what she was up to.

Although I've known Miss Georgina almost all her life, I'd never say I *knew* her, if you see what I mean. Some people are just more open – I don't mean they tell you all their business, but . . . sometimes when you're with them, well, the best way I can put it is: you can see into their heart. I'll tell you who's like that – Miss Louisa. Anyone can see what a good person she is and I'm sure that's why Master Edmund loves her like he does. But Miss Georgina, I don't believe even Master Edmund knows what she's really like, not right inside. And Mr James, he didn't know her at all. Because she keeps everything locked away, all the secrets she's got shut up inside, she won't let nobody see. And she's very clever when it comes to getting her own way, there's no denying that. That's why you don't want to believe everything she says. She's as cunning as a barrel-load of monkeys. She knew she could count on me, long before I knew it myself. She knew it and she used it, too, else why would I be sat here in this dingy old basement after all these years?

After Mrs Mattie went, Mr Lomax told me to make up a bed in the study for him and he never again went back upstairs. He was all taken up with the idea that he was being cheated in his business. He never stirred from his study and of course there was no telephone then, only letters, but he brooded and brooded, and he read every newspaper he could get his hands on. He was sure that there would be something in the papers about the cheating, but there never was. He sold the London house and we never had any visitors, only folk from the village, delivering. So it was just him and Miss Georgina, and Master Edmund when he came home for the holidays. And then there was me, and I had to do for all of them.

That was when Miss Georgina started to play her little games with the furniture, after Mrs Mattie left. She must have known that Mrs Mattie wouldn't have stood for it. What would happen was I'd go upstairs and I'd see a chair in the corridor outside Miss Georgina's room, and I'd think, 'Where did that come from?' Because it hadn't been there that morning. Her trick was to go round all the upstairs rooms, which were shut up with the dust sheets over, and anything that caught her eye, she'd have it out of there and put it in her room. She was like a magpie, the things she'd got hoarded up. I'd keep finding doors ajar where they shouldn't be and I'd stick my head round, and sure enough, there were all the dust sheets pulled off in a heap and the pillows gone from the bed more than likely. Miss Georgina's always liked pillows. Pillows and cushions, all over the floor, and she had bedspreads and shawls as well, draped all over the place. When I saw that film with Rudolph Valentino, *The Sheikh*, it reminded me of Miss Georgina's room how it looked then. It was downright dangerous, all that stuff lying there on the floor. If you didn't break your neck on the shawls, you'd trip over a pile of books and come down wallop. But there was nothing I could do. She was in a fair way to being a young lady by that time and I didn't have charge of her – Mr Lomax had never said one word to me about her. Mind you, Mr Lomax never said one word to me at all, not unless he wanted something, and then he'd just go roaring out, scaring me half to death.

When Mr Lomax got really bad, he started to wear a silk scarf around his nose and mouth – it looked how they have it in films when they're going to rob a train only of course they didn't have the films then. First time I saw it, I said, 'Is there anything wrong, Sir?' because I thought it must be the drains or something, but he started waving me away, and shouting about infections and all sorts. 'Get away from me!' That's what he kept saying: 'Get away, I know your tricks. I know what you're up to – keep away from me!' Well, I don't know what he was talking about, but it was all part of his hating women the way he did, I'm sure of that, and the alcohol made it worse, made him imagine all sorts of things that weren't there. I suppose he must have thought an infection would come through his breathing, that was why he was wearing the scarf. After that, he always had the scarf round his neck and he used to put it over his face if he saw me. But I never said nothing. What could I say?

He'd never let me have this scarf off to wash it – oh, it was the most filthy old thing you've ever seen. You wouldn't have used it to wrap a dead rat in. I don't know why he bothered with it, because the two of them were so busy barricading themselves in with jumble that you could hardly get from one end of the house to the other. Things, things, things, everywhere! It was like a great river of rubbish flowing through the house, through the rooms, down the stairs . . . they both used to put things on the stairs. On the ends of the treads it started, next to the wall. Books, plates, trinkets, papers, bottles, gloves, letters, and I wasn't let to move any of it. It drove me nearly mad, I can tell you! I think it was Miss Georgina started it, but then Mr Lomax would do it too; some was his and some was hers. Then, of course, there'd be such a great pile grown up that something would slip and the whole lot would come sliding down and crash into the hall. That's why I say it was like a river, more and more was added, so it had to burst out somewhere, like a flood.

It was like a parlour game for Miss Georgina – she'd even go lifting stuff from my room and adding it to one of her collections if I didn't watch her. When Mrs Mattie left, I had moved downstairs into the housekeeper's room, which was a hundred times better than my old room. But what was bad was that Miss Georgina knew where it was and she'd sneak in there while I was working. Sometimes I'd miss my hairbrush or something and then I'd find it perched on the top of a pile somewhere. Well, if I just took it back, she'd spot immediately that it was missing, goodness knows how, and she didn't like that. She'd get upset and stop eating, or she wouldn't dress herself properly, so I used to take the brush and show her, and say, 'Please may I have it back?' and that was all right – until the next time. Lucky for me I didn't have a lot to miss. Odds and ends from the kitchen would go as well and that was worse, because I'd be cooking and put my hand out for a pan and – gone! I wish I had a penny for every time the food got spoiled while I went looking for one of the pots. Not that either of them ate anything. Miss Georgina's never been what you'd call a big eater, she just picks, which is what comes of not having anyone to make her eat up.

Well, I soldiered on, but I can't say I was happy, and I got into a bad habit of talking to myself, because I was lonely. You know, I used to think: I'm fed up with this, I'm leaving, but then I'd think, how can I? If I go, what becomes of them? Then I'd think of poor Mrs Mattie and I'd stay. But I suppose I was just dreaming about leaving, if I'm honest, because I wouldn't have known where to go or what to do. So I used to pray that Miss Georgina would get married. We never had any gentleman visitors – or any other sort come to that – but I used to pray that somebody would come along. When Mr James came, I thought that God had answered my prayers. But I tell you straight: if I'd known what would happen to poor Mr James I'd have kept those prayers to myself.

EDMUND

The troops used to call it Plug Street. There was a village and a wood, the proper name was Ploegsteert, not Plug Street at all, but no one could pronounce the foreign names. It was near Messines, near Wipers. One of our mines went off there this morning – thirty-eight years too late, imagine it! The 7th of June 1917. That's when it should have gone. Twenty-one mine shafts they dug, stuffed with high explosive, dug right under the German lines. Took a year to dig. They were miners from Durham, and a lot of poor devils from the infantry carried out the earth they dug and got shelled for their pains. All the mines were detonated at once. They told us to evacuate our dug-outs in case they collapsed; I was with some other men and we stood outside to watch. There was a great roar as the mines went up. The earth shook and shrugged, as if it was trying to throw us off its back, and several of our chaps were knocked off their feet. The Messines ridge started to heave as if it was coming to life and great lumps of earth the size of cottages were flung up in the air; fire was spewing out, and pillars of smoke went up and rolled outwards at the top, like umbrellas opening, and spread across the whole sky. Then every single gun opened up and the noise was solid; it seemed to fill the whole world. I remember being surprised that the Boche were shelling us back, which they were a bit, but most of them were caught up in the conflagration, poor devils, so they never had a chance and those that weren't were taken prisoner.

That was the first time I saw a tank. I'd read about them and heard about them, but I'd never seen one. Nowadays, everyone knows what a tank looks like, but it was marvellous to me to see this thing in action. I thought it looked like a giant tortoise. It would go for a bit, stop for a bit, and then the head would peer out and look around. What impressed me most was the way it would roll over everything in its path. Mud, ditches, wire, the lot, that was wonderful to me. Tanks were a great invention, a new weapon that was going to win us the war. The Germans hadn't got any, that was the great thing about tanks, but they did in this last one, they had tanks then – *It's no bloody good.* It's the old whitewash again, I'm not thinking about the tanks at all, I'm thinking about Roland. Roland Arthur Lomax. I used to say that – repeat it – to myself. Roland Arthur Lomax. As if it was a magic spell. When I think about the Great War – about Roland – of course then one thinks about oneself, can't keep away from it. And now all this time has passed and instead of thinking about it less, I think about it more. Think about all of it more.

When we were at school, he – Roland – knew all about my family. You didn't talk about your people as a rule, but he could have really let me in for a ragging if he'd told the other chaps about mine. Never said a word, though. Of course, he was far more popular at school than I was. To hear my sister talk you'd think I could have played cricket for England, but I was never much good on the playing field and that was where it counted; it was no good simply being clever at lessons. But I never minded school – one had to go through it and besides, it kept my father at a safe distance. I suppose I must have been a selfish little swine, because I never thought what it must have been like for Georgie, stuck at home with him day in, day out. She made the holidays bearable, yet I don't think I ever wondered how she got along when I wasn't there. Because she and my father didn't speak, you see, and she wasn't allowed down for meals even when she was old enough. Not that she wanted to come down – and I always longed to have mine upstairs in the nursery with her, instead of downstairs with him. Every night, it was an ordeal. It started when I came back from school the Christmas after Freddie died. I must have been ten or eleven, still far too young to eat downstairs, but he insisted. The relief when I could leave the table was indescribable, but then the next morning the dread would grow and and grow inside me until, the hour before dinner, my mind was so filled up with the meeting with my father that there wasn't room for anything else. Sometimes I used to wish that something would happen to him, that he would die and then I'd never have to go downstairs any more.

He sat in his great chair at the end of the long table, with the fire behind him. He never allowed Ada to turn up the gas, and the darkness and the glow of the fire made him look like a huge black hulk. That was how I thought of him, not as a human being at all, but as a giant, an ogre. 'Boy' he used to call me. Never my name, always 'boy'. 'Cat got your tongue, boy? Why don't you speak?' Pushing his plate away, reaching out for his glass. Grabbing it with those great big hands of his, thick, hairy fingers like a giant or a demon king. 'Say something, damn you!' Ada would serve the meal as fast as she could. I knew she hated it as much as I did, but I had a terrible feeling of despair when I watched her slipping away round the door, because then I was alone, trapped. It always began gradually: 'So, what have you been getting up to?' He would never mention Georgie and I understood that I wasn't to either. I'd stumble out a few sentences about what we'd done, saying 'I' instead of 'we'. I couldn't say half the things we did because you couldn't do them on your own and I was scared of slipping up – if I mentioned the games we played he might notice it was something you couldn't do by yourself and then he'd get angry. And always, when I tried to speak, there'd be this awful feeling that I was about to cry, and I had to stop and look down at the plate until it passed off, and that would make him angry too: 'Stop whimpering! What's wrong with you?' I felt as if I'd been struck dumb. I used to rehearse things to myself during the day. If I went for a walk through the woods with Georgie, which was where we usually went because she didn't like people to see her, I'd make a plan about what I was going to tell him, about seeing squirrels and things. Sometimes I made things up, but it was never enough, he always wanted me to tell him more. There was a measurement he was making about me, a judgement, but I never understood what it was.

He frightened me from the time when I was a small child, when my mother was alive. I was going to say, that was before he started drinking, but even in my earliest memories he always has a glass in his hand. When we were taken downstairs to see him, he had a drink and a cigar, sitting in his chair by the fire, with Georgie and me standing to attention in front of him and marching up and down while he roared with laughter, and Mother sitting across the room, watching and saying nothing. I think his whole character probably came from inside a bottle.

I can't remember my mother ever touching me and I was too shy to stare at her, although I wanted to, very much. I've never understood how she came to be married to such a coarse man as my father. I've often wondered if she wasn't pushed into it by her parents, because that happened a great deal more in those days than it does now. It must have been terrible for her to endure his company, and she wouldn't have died if he hadn't been drunk and forced himself on her.

But I knew I was safe from him in Georgie's room. Even if

you couldn't see him in the rest of the house, you could sense him and there was always a risk that he might suddenly appear, but not in her room. The whole nursery wing seemed to be part of a different building altogether. There was a door at the end of the nursery corridor that led to the big landing and opening it was like crossing the Rubicon. It always made me think of *Pilgrim's Progress*; the hall was like the Valley of the Shadow of Death, but if one succeeded in crossing it, one could climb back up the stairs and through the door to the Celestial City and be safe from harm. When I was fourteen, fifteen, sixteen, I'd come home for the holidays and wonderful things would appear in my room, things I'd never seen before, things Georgie had found hidden away in the house. She's always been rather a magpie and I suppose that was when she started it. Really it was all old junk, but it was the way she used to arrange the things that made them special. She had muslin draped over her bed and so many white pillows piled up and eiderdowns and lace that I imagined it as a tent hanging in the sky. I always had to do something in order to be allowed to enter, a trick, or to give her something I'd taken from another part of the house, and there was a different password every day. We used to spend hours lying on the bed, playing games. Georgie read a lot, and if some description took her fancy she would try to imitate it. I remember once coming home and she'd picked handfuls of lavender and thrown it all over the floor, because she'd been reading about how they put herbs everywhere in medieval times. I'm not sure if lavender was what they actually used, but I suppose it was the nearest she could get. There was another time when she took a helmet and a pair of gauntlet gloves from a suit of armour she'd found in the cellar. I suppose it was from our grandfather's day, because there'd been a fashion for them, making the place look like a baronial hall, that sort of thing. She laid the helmet on my pillow and crossed the gauntlets on the counterpane, with a red rose tucked between the fingers of each one, and one of her handkerchiefs beside them as a lady's favour, with 'To My True Knight' written on it in red ink. The ink had bled into the cotton in places, but you could see what it said. Georgie'd been reading about the holy grail and I think she was rather taken with the idea. There was a book called *The Well at the World's End*, which we were both very keen on, about a prince who goes off to find a magic well. That was a medieval sort of thing, I don't suppose people read it much nowadays, but it was very popular when I was young. Georgie sent me a copy when I was in France during the war. I remember sitting and re-reading it in a filthy little dug-out, water up to the knees, and I don't think I've ever enjoyed a book so much in my life.

Georgie had a game, I suppose it was really a sort of series of tests, the same as the way the knights in the stories were tested. No dragons or anything, it was more to do with finding things: a handkerchief or a hairbrush, objects that belonged to her. She used to hide them somewhere in the house and make up a list of clues, and then I'd have to go and find them. I had to come back before the hall clock struck a certain time and if Father saw me, that meant I'd been wounded, but I might still go on searching, I remember that. If Father spoke to me, that meant I'd been killed, so I'd failed the test. Georgie never came with me, but sometimes she would appear beside me out of nowhere and tell me I was looking in the wrong place. She had this extraordinary trick of moving silently – I never once heard her coming.

I kept the lady's favour handkerchief as a sort of talisman. I suppose at some point I must have decided it was childish to carry it about with me and put it away in a case, but just before I went over to France I was hunting for something and I came across it again, so I took it with me. A lot of chaps did things like that, I remember once there was a great fuss in my company when one of the men, a Catholic, lost a holy medal. Turned the place upside down until it was found, all the men helped, there wasn't one there who didn't treat it seriously. I gave Georgina's special handkerchief to Roland ... Oh God, the whitewash on the wall, don't think don't don't don't *wash me in the water that you wash your dirty daughter* oh, bloody hell ... They found it on his body.

These things don't seem to trouble Georgie as they do me. She'll talk about the present or the future, but never about the past. It's as if her memory is a slate and she rubs out people's names. That was what she did with Freddie. For two people so far apart, Georgie and Father were hand in hand where Freddie was concerned; they both behaved as if he had never existed. The summer he died, when I wasn't allowed home from school, the senior master took me aside and said he was sorry, or something of that sort, and it was never referred to again. For weeks I waited for news from home, someone to tell me something, anything, about what had happened, but no one did and I began to wonder if I hadn't simply imagined the whole thing. I think I was half expecting Freddie to be there when I came home for the Christmas holiday, but of course he wasn't, and everyone behaved as if nothing had happened, except that Father was at Dennys and even I could see that he was different. It tormented me for days. I couldn't think of anything except Freddie. Georgie never volunteered anything about it and I didn't know how to bring up the subject. I remember once we were sitting on the floor playing a game and I asked her, 'Where did they put Freddie?'

'Put him?'

'Bury him, then. Where did they bury him?'

'In the village churchyard.'

'Can we go and see?'

'He'll come for you, if you go there.'

I didn't understand what she meant by 'he'll come for you', but it frightened me and I never asked again. I suppose I'd just wanted to see where he was, that was all. Then I asked her if she'd cried about Freddie and she said she had. I don't think I believed her, but I didn't want to argue with her because I thought she might get angry and banish me from her room. I think she told me she'd cried because she thought that's what I'd expect from a girl. During the war, I used to think how lucky girls were, being able to cry. I mentioned that to Roland once – I'm not sure why, I suppose I must have hoped he'd agree. I remember it because it was such a tremendously difficult thing to put into words, and hard to speak the words because it wasn't the kind of thing one usually said. We were in part of a trench that we'd just cleared of the Boche, waiting for the barrage to lift. I forget why Roland was there, I think his lot must have come unstuck, because there were several men in a very bad way and only Roland and one of the signallers not wounded. It was a dreadful mess: our wounded, dead Germans all over the place, knocked-out guns and the rain pouring down on the lot of us. But for once in my life I felt I'd done something right – it was practically the only occasion in all the time I was out there that I felt I'd managed to do what I was told to do and not made a bloody hash of it, because we'd captured this trench.

When we'd done what we could for the wounded men, Roland and I sat down to wait it out. We had a rather odd conversation, and I explained the business about weeping. I don't know what I expected Roland to say; in fact, I can't imagine what else he could have said except what he did say: 'People will think you're a pansy if you talk like that.' Because you couldn't do anything to upset morale, distress the men. If one of them got the wind up it would spread like wildfire and then you had a problem on your hands. And if you were an officer, of course, as we were, one was supposed to set an example. After that, I remember giving Roland Georgina's handkerchief which said 'To My True Knight'. We shook hands over it and then there was the most terrible racket and Roland's signaller came crashing down on top of us. He'd tried to leave the trench for some reason and taken a bullet in the throat.

I didn't know why I wanted to give Roland the favour and I'm still not sure. People do queer things in those circumstances and besides, I never thought I'd be here now to try and explain it to myself. In my mind, it wasn't a question of 'if I die', but '*when* I die'. That was what made it so hard afterwards, one couldn't see why one should be alive, when there were so many others ... When I gave the favour to Roland, he said 'Thanks, old man' and looked a bit puzzled. He didn't know why I'd done it any more than I did. But you see, he died because I gave it to him. I know that. If I'd kept it, as I was supposed to, as Georgina wanted me to, I would have died, but I wanted Roland to have something – I wanted to give him something, an important thing, because it was a way of saying ... well, saying that you loved someone, I suppose.

I wonder what Roland would say if he could hear me now. He'd probably tell me I'd turned into a pansy.

ADA

The first time I saw Mr James, now that was funny. We had a man at Dennys called Thomas; he used to come up from the village and do a bit round the garden. Mr Lomax wouldn't have anyone else near the place, but for some reason he never minded this man Thomas. There came a time . . . the King – King Edward – was still alive, I do remember that, so I would have been what? Twenty-eight? Twenty-nine? And Miss Georgina about seventeen. And she was beautiful, no doubt about it. If she'd been going out in society, I'm sure she could have had an earl or a lord or anyone she fancied for a husband. She was so lovely she could have had the pick of them. About this time, Mr Lomax told me he'd pay the bills and I was to give all the housekeeping matters into his hands, the money side of course, not the rest. I didn't understand it. I'd been managing well enough, but he'd decided in his mind that folk were swindling him at home as well as in the business. I think that *was* true about the business – well, judging from what Master Edmund has told me there was money being stolen from him behind his back. As I say, only a few came to see him, and I think some of them did go off and cheat him once they realised how matters stood. But it made him start to see thieves everywhere, even me. I used to bite my tongue. Least said, soonest mended, and besides, *I* knew I'd done nothing wrong. He'd never have wanted to do my little accounts if things had been as they should, but a man's got to be master in his own house and if doing a few bills gave him the feeling of it, where was the hurt? Except that he got it into his head there was too much food being ordered, so there was nothing for it, we had to cut back. He didn't tell me any of this, mind you. He went and told Thomas and said for Thomas to tell me, which didn't please me.

Well, one day Thomas came to me and said, 'Mr Lomax says you're to keep rabbits.'

I didn't think I'd heard right at first. Rabbits! You could have knocked me down with a feather. I said to Thomas, 'Where I am going to get rabbits? I don't know anything about them.'

'Oh, don't worry about that, leave it to me.'

Well, the next time he came, he'd got his hammer and nails with him, and he set to in the yard, making these cages. I said, 'I thought we were keeping rabbits, not mice!' Because they were tiny, far too small. I could tell he thought I must be a bit touched, but he knocked two together so they made one, and he put in small windows to give the poor creatures a bit of light. I asked Thomas, 'How many rabbits are you going to bring here?' because he was making enough cages for a zoo. He said, only the buck and the doe, and the rest would follow – which they did before you could say Jack Robinson. Thomas stacked up the cages on the veranda, at the side. I had a look to make sure you couldn't see them from the front – the place looked bad enough from falling slates and want of paint without turning it into a farmyard as well.

I used to love going to see those bunnies. I'd stroke their lovely soft fur and talk to them. Well, I'd no one else and it was better than talking to myself. Miss Georgina never went near them. She evidently wasn't interested – or maybe she just had more sense. You don't want to be pals with something that's going to end up on your plate, do you? Because, every so often, Thomas would kill one and I'd have to cook it, which I hated.

Well, this went on for quite a few months. One day that summer I was in the hall when I saw this rabbit hopping about. It was the big one, the male. I saw afterwards that it had chewed through the wood of the cage, which I wouldn't have thought possible, but it had. That rabbit knew when it was well off, it was jumping up and down and dancing about all over the place, and it wasn't going to let me anywhere near. I was nearly in tears because I couldn't catch the wretched thing and I knew if it burrowed into all the rubbish on the stairs I'd never see it again. So I dashed forward and grabbed. I was practically on top of it, it was kicking and struggling, and I was flat out on the ground: 'Oh no, you don't!' when suddenly I saw, out of the corner of my eyes, a man's legs. Just inside the front door, trouser legs and shiny shoes. As soon as I saw those shoes I knew they couldn't belong to Mr Lomax. It must be a strange gentleman and he'd seen everything! I wanted the floor to swallow me up, but I'd got a tight hold of old Hoppity Houdini, and I wasn't letting go again, not for anyone. So I scrambled up on to my knees – oh, it was ridiculous, there I was, kneeling on the floor, holding this enormous rabbit. I couldn't even straighten my hair because I needed both my hands to hold this animal, and I was huffing and blowing so much I couldn't get my words out straight.

'Beg pardon, Sir, can I help you?' The gentleman was standing half in the shadow so I couldn't see his face properly, but I could tell he was trying not to laugh.

He said, 'Hadn't you better go and put that rabbit back in its box?'

And that was when I met Mr James. You could see he was a business gentleman, an important one, right away. He had good clothes – good tailor – and a look to him that made you think, there's plenty of money there. But he wasn't a young man, even then. Well, I say he wasn't young, he was past his middle thirties and certainly he was old beside Miss Georgina. Quite a big man, you might have said he was portly, and compared to somebody like William you couldn't have called him handsome, although he had a good head of hair. But he was a kind man and he was certainly tickled pink by that rabbit. That was what made me think he was different from the other businessmen who came to Dennys, because it seemed to me they only came to see what they could get out of Mr Lomax. But Mr James wasn't like that, I knew it as soon as I set eyes on him.

Well, my head was spinning, but all the time I was planning how to manage it so that he didn't see one inch of the house more than necessary. I was kicking myself for not checking the front door – Mr Lomax sometimes went off for walks and didn't shut it, so of course anyone could come in. It turned out Mr James had come in a car and the reason I never heard it was that he'd told his chauffeur to stop at the gates, which was a bit sly. And he never sent a telegram or even a letter to warn us, he just arrived. I overheard him say something afterwards about 'just passing', but I never believed it. He had it in mind to do some business with Mr Lomax, where Mr Lomax still had the control of it, and I think he'd heard some rumours and he wanted to see for himself.

I was ashamed of the house, but I had something up my sleeve: one room that I called the 'business room'. Anyone who came, they went straight in there and never saw anything else if I could help it. Because I wasn't having them going away and talking about us all going queer, not those swindlers, saying how the place wasn't kept up and then all flocking back to rob poor old Mr Lomax because of it. This little room, I'd managed to keep it decent by locking it up and I'd hidden all the keys away where neither Mr Lomax nor Miss Georgina could get at them. Otherwise they'd have been in there like a pair of magpies and there wouldn't have been a stick of furniture left to bless it.

I said, 'Won't you come and sit down, Sir, until I fetch Mr Lomax?' I had my hands full of this rabbit, it was struggling and kicking its great big feet, and when I opened the door to my special room it jumped out of my arms and disappeared under the table.

Mr James said, 'Quick, before it escapes!' and whisked me inside the room and shut the door behind us.

I said, 'Oh, I must catch it.'

'No,' he said. 'This is my fault for being so rude as to come uninvited. I'd like to see Mr Lomax, so if you would announce me, I shall catch the rabbit.' And he pulled out a card and gave it to me for Mr Lomax. I thought, that's a good start, I don't think, but I couldn't argue, so off I went. Mr Lomax was asleep on the sofa in his study, but he woke up and said he'd come along. I knew he'd take his time, so I thought: I'll have to fetch the rabbit out of there because I was terrified it would mess on the floor and then what would I do? So I rushed to the kitchen and made a pot of tea as quick as I could and when I opened up the door with my tray, there was the gentleman sitting there and next to him, stroking the rabbit, cool as you like – Miss Georgina!

Well, as Ellen used to say, 'Close your mouth, Ada, there's a bus coming.' Because it was always a great worry of mine, Miss Georgina showing herself in front of strangers, because she had such queer ideas about what was decent. And of course, all who came to the house, she knew. She must have been watching our little pantomime over the banisters and we never saw her. Usually, she'd go and hide until they were gone, but not this time. As to what she was wearing, well! I don't know where she'd found it, but I suppose it must have been her mother's. It was a ball gown. It was ten years out of date at the very least, not that I know much about fashion, but it was the most beautiful thing. Mr James and I were both staring at her, she was exquisite. Her eyes were huge and she'd got her beautiful black hair done up in these combs with jewels on them – and the effect was . . . well, it was quite fantastic. Never mind that it was four o'clock in the afternoon and she was sitting there with her shoulders bare in front of a perfect stranger, and there was a black-and-white rabbit the size of a cat in her arms, and – what I'd been so afraid of – it had done its business on the floor. Miss Georgina was sitting there just as if gentlemen came for tea every afternoon. I couldn't take my eyes off her and, as I say, I wasn't the only one.

She said, 'Tea, how nice. Ada, this is Mr Gresham. He has come to see my father. Why don't you take Bunny away, and then you can bring the tea things on to the veranda.' Bunny! As if it was a pet! The veranda! I was so flabbergasted I didn't say anything, not 'yes, Miss Georgina' or anything like that. I just took the rabbit and left. The thought of the veranda sent me panicking all over again. The garden chairs were filthy, falling to pieces, but Miss Georgina took Mr James – not that I knew him as Mr James then, of course – straight out there and he sat down on one of these revolting things. Thank goodness it was warm enough that the cushions had dried out, that was all I could think, they'd been out there all winter – well, I couldn't do everything and it must have slipped my mind. And of course the table had to be in full view of the blasted rabbit hutches! I took a sniff, discreetly I hope, but the smell wasn't *too* noticeable, thank Heaven. Miss Georgina was carrying on as if she was in Buckingham Palace and, as I came to know later, Mr James was far too much of a gentleman to pass any remarks. Besides, at that time he couldn't notice nothing in the world but her.

He was a man of the world, but he'd obviously never seen anything like Miss Georgina before. That's one thing you can say about her, she's more like herself than anyone else is, if you see what I mean. But she was perfectly ladylike. She hardly said anything, she was doing it all right, listening to what he said, agreeing, asking questions so that he could talk more, very polite, pouring the tea, offering the bread and butter, just as if she'd been doing it all her life. I stopped behind her chair, because I thought he might think it was queer if I left them alone, and I must say I felt ever so proud of her. A duchess couldn't have done better than she did, I'm sure of that. Then Mr Lomax appeared, smelly old scarf over his face as usual. He looked at the pair of us and grunted. If it had been in English, it would have meant 'Get out'. I thought, well, that's put the kibosh on it, now there'll be trouble, but Miss Georgina didn't bat an eyelid. She said, 'This is my father, Mr Gresham. Please excuse me,' and she went back into the house.

Mr Lomax practically threw the teapot at me: 'Bring some more tea for our guest. This is stone cold!' I didn't like that too well, it made me look lazy, but off I went. When I came back with it, Mr Lomax had his lips right up to Mr James's ear, telling him some tale about this man or that man who had cheated him. Sitting so close, as he was, the alcohol fumes coming off him must have brought tears to Mr James's eyes, but he never flinched. Mr Lomax kept saying, 'I can trust you.' He must have said it fifty times if he said it once. But my eyes flew open when I heard that. I thought, this must be someone very special for him to say that. And all the time Mr James sat nodding his head, not interrupting once. Mind you, I don't suppose he could have got a word in if he'd wanted to, Mr Lomax was talking nineteen to the dozen. I poured the tea and went off round the veranda so I could go down the steps and back to the kitchen. Just before I turned the corner I looked back and I suddenly saw, not Mr Lomax, but the old fellows in the pub at home – I say 'home' but Dennys was my home – what I mean is, the tenement where I lived when I was a girl. That was what he reminded me of. The kind of man who used to hang around by the door half drunk, great fish-eyes swivelling round for someone they can tell their troubles to, and they end up in a fight more often than not. It's the ugliest thing in the world, a drunken man. I could understand why Ellen said she couldn't bear it. But after that afternoon I was never again so frightened of Mr Lomax as I had been.

Mr Lomax talked for a good two hours, then Mr James stood up to leave. Miss Georgina came down the stairs as he was going. I could see Mr Lomax didn't much care for it, but Mr James's eyes were out on stalks. Miss Georgina holds out her hand to him. 'I do hope you will come and visit us again, Mr Gresham,' she says. 'My father does so enjoy having a man to talk to about business. I'm afraid I don't understand it at all.' Mr Lomax was glaring at her with eyes so blazing that I was amazed she didn't burst into flames on the spot, but he managed to keep a civil tongue in his head, at least in front of Mr James.

When I opened the front door for Mr James, he asked me, 'What is your name?'

Well, I turned scarlet, what with the rabbit and the veranda and everything. 'Ada, Sir.'

'Well, Ada, mind you take care of those rabbits.' And he laughed.

'Yes, Sir. Be careful of the drive, Sir.' Because you could come a cropper as easy as winking, there were so many potholes.

'Goodbye, Ada.'

'Goodbye, Sir.' I watched him on his way and felt as if I'd suddenly got a friend. It's hard to explain, really, just that it was like he was going to help us; he was on our side somehow. It wouldn't be right to say he was like an angel, but you could say he was our fairy godmother if you want to be sentimental. Except Cinderella wasn't had up for murdering her fairy godmother, at least not in the story I know. Miss Georgina went back upstairs after Mr James had gone and Mr Lomax shouted out 'Jezebel' after her, but she didn't take any notice.

Do you know, Mr James never forgot those rabbits. For years afterwards, if he saw me checking for dust or looking in a cupboard, he'd say 'found any rabbits, Ada?' or 'rabbit pie tonight, Ada?' As I watched him go down the drive at Dennys, I thought, if gambling wasn't wicked, I'd lay my last penny that he'll be back, I was that sure. And I was right.

It turned out that Mr James wanted to buy into the business – that is, what was left of it. Mr Lomax took to him, insisted he must come down again to discuss such and such a matter and go into it all – which of course he did, and more times than he need, I'm sure of that. You didn't have to strain your eyes to see the reason for it. But Miss Georgina was always very well behaved, I'll say that for her, even if her clothes were rather queer – Miss Louisa sent things from time to time, otherwise she wouldn't have had a stitch but what had been her mother's. I'll say another thing about Mr James, too: I'm sure he paid Mr Lomax more than he needed to when he bought his interest in the business, because of Miss Georgina. So then, of course, Mr James owned the biggest part and the one that's got most calls the tune, doesn't he? I don't suppose Mr Lomax's partners liked it, but I know for a fact that Mr James soon put in his own men, who'd do as he wanted. 'Everything he touched turned to gold', that's what people said about Mr James.

But it does amaze me, how two people can look at the same thing and see it totally different. What Mr James saw that first afternoon made him fall in love, where most would have taken one look and had us all ready for the barmy shop. But Mr James had a romantic streak in him where Miss Georgina was concerned and the way he looked at her, you knew he thought she was perfect just how she was, funny old clothes, ramshackle house, the lot, although don't ask me where the romance is in smelling of rabbits. As I said, I thought my prayers were answered. I'd started going to church again at that time and I said a lot of prayers. In fact it was Thomas who got me at it. He did a lot in the church, getting up little plays for the Sunday school, that sort of thing. Of course, all we at Dennys used to go to church in the old days, every Sunday, you had to. Then I used to go with Mrs Mattie, she never missed, but after she left I tried to avoid the village if I could, because people would say things. If they'd said it to my face, I could have given them a straight answer, but no one ever did. They knew about Mr Lomax's drinking and I'm sure one or two thought worse – that the two of us must be having improper relations. Not a word of it true, of course. Thomas said to me, 'You come along to church. Never mind those old gossips, I'll soon tell them what's what,' because he would never let anyone say a word against Mr Lomax. And not one of them ever raised so much as a murmur, because Thomas was that well thought of in the village. It was ever such a nice walk down the lane to the church and I used to love going, especially singing the hymns. I could feel it giving me that little extra bit of strength I needed for the next week.

I used to go afterwards and have a tidy-up round Master Freddie's grave. I'd sort of forgotten it was there, to be honest, and when I saw it, I thought: He must be so lonely all by himself, poor little mite, because his mother was buried up in

London. So then I'd take a few flowers from the garden and put them on, and sit with him for a bit before I went home. Neither Mr Lomax nor Miss Georgina ever went near the place, I know that for a fact. I suppose Master Edmund might have done when he was having his holidays, but if he did he never left no flowers or I'd have seen them. I remember once I was there by the grave, and a woman from the village came along and asked why the sister wasn't buried next to her brother? She'd heard that Miss Georgina was dead! That's what I mean about rumours.

Thomas was a nice man in the main, except that he was a little bit funny in the way he took against people. Miss Georgina, for one. He came into the kitchen once and told me he'd caught her wandering about the garden in her night-gown – which I must say was just the sort of thing she would do, without any thought to who saw her. He was terribly upset about it. Because actually, she did have this sort of way – a certain manner, of moving, looking at you. You knew it wasn't done for you, she just wanted to see what you . . . well, what effect she had really, I suppose. Trying herself out, if you like. I used to think, poor girl, because she was so beautiful, if she'd led a normal life she'd have had strings of admirers. She was all contrasts – her skin was pearly white, her hair and eyelashes as black as black and her eyes were the darkest blue I've ever seen. Of course, I never told Miss Georgina how beautiful she was. It wouldn't have been right and, anyway, she didn't need encouragement.

Thomas started paying court to me. Only in a small way, but he did. 'Miss Ada' he called me, but it was serious, not like the way William had said it. To tell the truth, I found it hard talking to Thomas. With William it was always a joke and a laugh as he went past in the corridor, we never had much time, but I never had any difficulty in knowing what to say, the words just came out. But this Thomas, I never knew what to say to him because he was so solemn. If I ever saw him laugh I don't recall it. Actually, it took me quite a long time to realise that Thomas *was* courting me, because of the way he went about it. I told you he took a dislike to people, well, he'd talk about women in the village, he'd say this one was wicked, that one was wanton, the other one was no better than she ought to be and then he'd finish it up: 'But you aren't like that. You're a good woman, Miss Ada, a respectable woman.' And again, when one of the village girls got into trouble, he'd say, 'She wasn't modest, she didn't mind herself, but of course you're not like that, Miss Ada, not at all.' I thought, well, you're always telling me what I'm not, so what am I? But I never said that, because he was quite a good deal older than me, so it wouldn't have been respectful. That's why I say he wasn't like William: I wouldn't have thought twice about saying it to William. I tried to persuade myself, well, you can't have a marriage where they can just say any old thing to each other, it wouldn't be right – but it was really to convince myself I wanted something when I didn't. Because I knew in my heart that I could never feel the same way for him that I did for William, but I liked talking to him because it was company, and if he'd asked me, I would have said yes. And before you say that's wicked because it wasn't love, remember, people thought different in those days – you had to. Thomas had a cottage and a little bit of land so it would have been a good thing for me, because I had nothing. But that question never arose, fortunately – I say 'fortunately' now, although I was upset about it at the time. Of course, Thomas would never have wanted to marry me if he'd thought I wasn't pure, but he never knew about that. What stopped him was Miss Georgina. She put him off coming to the house by flitting about in her night-gown in the middle of the afternoon and spying on him, that sort of thing. From the day Miss Georgina met Mr James it all changed and there wasn't any more of that, but it was too late for Thomas. He said he wouldn't come while she was there and he gave notice to Mr Lomax. Never a word to me. I suppose I hoped he might come back to see me one day, but he didn't. I think, because he was so against Miss Georgina, in his mind I was bad because I lived in the same house with her. And he was the sort that once his mind's made up, he won't change for anyone.

So then I was disappointed, because I thought: I'm on the shelf now, I'll never have another chance. I was a bit upset, but I wouldn't say I was angry with Miss Georgina, exactly, not then. I was too worn out with trying to keep the place going to think much about it, really. Because I was saving, scrimping – when I hear people saying they've had it rough with all the rationing, well, that was nothing to what I had to do in those days. Mr Lomax wouldn't pay any of the bills, he wouldn't give me a penny for food, and every time I asked he flew into a rage and said that the tradespeople were cheating him or I was pocketing the money, so I always came away empty-handed.

I did what I'd seen my mother do, went without so they could have theirs. I remember at home, my father always had the most on his plate. He'd say to her, 'Aren't you having some?'

'Oh, I've had mine, don't you worry.' All we children knew she hadn't, but she'd give us a look so we wouldn't say anything. It made me sad to think of that, because I used to think: I'd gladly go without if it was my husband, my children. I'd sit in the kitchen at Dennys, thinking about it, and that kitchen was no place to get yourself miserable, I can tell you. It was nasty, rotten vegetables everywhere. Thomas had grown some carrots and what-have-you – we got a whole lot of stuff that all came ready together and he had to pick it before he left. I was trying so hard to make these things last that I kept them far too long, and they were all burst and gone soft – oh, it was disgusting – but with Thomas gone I couldn't bring myself to kill a single one of those poor bunnies. That was his job, he'd always done that. I suppose it was a bit daft, but looking back I think I must have been affected in the head through not having enough to eat, the way I was hoarding those rotten vegetables and thinking I could cook them. I mean, I could see the marks of it on myself. I was thin and scrawny, and I had a great thing come up on my arm, an abscess. I used to make poultices with flour and water and put those on, but it never made any difference. In the end I couldn't raise my arm; I had to go into the village to the doctor. I thought, I'm going rotten inside like the vegetables. The day before I went, well, I think some of the badness from the abscess must have gone to my head because I went out to the rabbits. It was a beautiful, sunny day and I had this idea that I was going to let them all out on to the lawn. I don't know how I thought I was going to get them back; I just felt sorry for them, cooped up like that with all that lovely grass outside. Well, I undid the first hutch and the rabbit was just hopping off over the lawn, and then bang! it shot up in the air. Mr Lomax was stood on the veranda with his big gun: 'Don't let it go, you stupid girl. Get after it!' He'd hit the poor thing, but it wasn't killed, it was still kicking, trying to get away. I had to give it a bang on the head with a piece of wood in the end, to kill it, and that was horrible, doing that. I remember I sat there on the veranda holding this dead thing on my lap, with blood all over its head and all down my apron, and I was crying my eyes out.

If I'd been Mr James, that's what I'd have been asking myself, was there any madness in the family? Because he was no fool, otherwise how would he have made all the money he did? But he was that much in love with Miss Georgina, he couldn't see anything else. I doubt if all the king's horses and all the king's men would have parted him from her, never mind Mr Lomax three sheets to the wind. Still, when Mr James came, I took care that he didn't see any but the best furniture, even if the dining-room chairs didn't look much when they were out on the veranda. I'd half killed myself trying to wash Miss Georgina's things and get them nice, but if you got up close you could still see all these brown marks where the damp had got them. As for Mr Lomax, he still had that filthy old string of cloth round his neck – he'd never let me come near enough to get it away from him – and the state his clothes were in, anyone would have thought he was a tramp.

But then Master Edmund met Mr James and you could see they hit it off right away. Mr James used to send his chauffeur off to the pub in the village, then he would drive the car himself and take Master Edmund and Miss Georgina on rides all around the country. I'd always know when they'd been through the village because someone would come up to me after church: 'Oh, we saw the car last week.' Because it was unusual in those days, to see a car.

Well, things being as they were, Mr James asked Miss Georgina to marry him. I remember when Master Edmund came home from university, she'd written to him to tell him about it and he came dashing through the front door and up the stairs and whirled her round and round, and she put her arms round his neck and they rocked backwards and forwards, laughing and laughing. I heard Miss Georgina say to Master Edmund, 'It's all fixed. You can come and live with us in London. Jimmy says so.'

Then they stopped laughing and he said, 'Will you mind being married, Georgie?'

'Why should it make any difference?'

'You'll be Mrs James Gresham.'

That set her off laughing again.

'Mrs James Gresham, how ridiculous!'

'We'll still be first friends, won't we, Georgie?'

'Of course we will. I'd like to see Mr James Gresham try and change that!' Well, I thought, that's a funny way to speak about your intended, but I was tickled pink to see them both so happy.

Mr James had saved Mr Lomax's bacon by buying when he did, I know that for a fact, and now he was marrying Miss Georgina and she was going to be rich – any father would have been overjoyed, but Mr Lomax never said 'Congratulations' or anything, just went on the same as before. He did like Mr James, though. Mr James used to visit him even after the wedding, every few months he'd drive down from London to see him. But Miss Georgina never went with him – in fact, she never went back to Dennys at all except for her father's funeral.

Well, when Miss Georgina got engaged, that was the beginning of the fun. Mr Lomax had said she could marry, so then she had to have trips to London for her clothes and trousseau, and she brought back all sorts of wonderful things. She used to go with Mr James's mother, who was French so of course she dressed beautifully. Mr James had to pay for it all himself, which wasn't the right way, but he didn't seem to mind. Miss Georgina's wedding dress was loveliest thing I've ever seen. It was the latest style, with the narrow skirt and all in lace so fine you'd have thought fairies had made it. Oh, Miss Georgina loved that, picking out all the clothes and the big hats they wore then with the feathers. It was like watching a child let loose in a sweet-shop and I'm sure no mannequin could have worn those clothes better than she did.

I was very worried about the state of the house because of having the wedding there, but Master Edmund told me I was to get some of the women from the village and some workmen, and before long the place was almost back to its old self. Oh, it was lovely to have it all bustling again, and get the windows mended and the tiles back on the roof, and the cobwebs down and everything scrubbed and polished. Master Edmund was everywhere at once, he even helped the men to move the furniture. I don't think I've ever seen him so excited. He went up to the village and managed to persuade Thomas to come and rescue the garden, which was just as well because it looked like the wilderness.

He walked straight into the kitchen, Thomas did: 'Good-day, Miss Ada.' You could have knocked me down with a feather! Never a hint of what had passed, so I thought: Well, two can play at that game and I kept my distance. I was a bit worried, to tell the truth, because if I'm honest, I had been to Thomas's cottage – only the once, mind you – but I did go there, just to say hello, and knocked on the door, only he wasn't at home so I came away. But one of the farmers' wives had seen me coming out of his gate and it crossed my mind more than once that my visit might have got back to him. But least said, soonest mended, that's what they say, and besides, I didn't have to worry no more because Mr James had asked me would I go and be housekeeper for them in London when they were married? He'd told me that Mr Lomax was already suited, that Master Edmund had asked Thomas to come and look after him, and Thomas had said he would give up his cottage to live at Dennys. I thought it was a rum thing to do, but Mr James told me that that was what Mr Lomax wanted and anyway, it wasn't none of my business. I felt as if I was being set free and I was thrilled. I used to imagine it, how it was going to be when Miss Georgina was married. Mr James was such a good man and he'd have given her the moon if she'd asked for it. I was sure they'd have lots of children, all beautiful. I couldn't wait to see those children. I had a picture in my mind, like a real painting with a fancy gold frame in that style they had in the old days, of Miss Georgina with four lovely children. She'd be sitting in the middle with two big boys standing beside her and two little girls in front with white dresses and pink sashes. I felt those children were just waiting to come to us and if I shut my eyes I could almost see them holding out their little hands. I wanted them as much as if they were my own. I'd even thought about what names to give them. Because it was the best I could get, you see, I knew that.

I wish Mrs Mattie could have seen that house the way it looked on the morning of Miss Georgina's wedding, she'd have been so proud of it. Mr James had some of his servants come down from London and they were all rushing about, so I took the chance to have a walk through the house on my own. I went down the nursery corridor. I wasn't thinking to stop by Miss Georgina's room, particularly, only I wondered if a familiar face among so many strangers would help her if she was nervous. Anyway, the door to her room was open and there she was, all alone, sitting in front of the dresser and looking into the mirror. She had a book on her lap with a red cover and she was scrubbing at it with a scrap of silk to get some red for her cheeks. All brides are lovely, or that's what they say, but Miss Georgina would have taken your breath away. At that moment, when she saw me in the mirror, she looked more beautiful than I'd ever seen her.

She said: 'I'm glad you came, Ada.' She said it as if she was expecting me, although she hadn't called me. Then she said, 'dear Ada,' and held out her hand to me. I'd thought she might be a bit frightened or nervous, but her hand was still as a stone and she looked straight into my eyes and didn't even blink. It felt as if I was in a dream, or being hypnotised or something, and I could swear I was on tiptoe going across that carpet towards her. She took my hand in both of hers: 'Do you want to come and live with me in London, Ada?'

'Oh, yes, it's all arranged, Miss Georgina, I'm to come.'

'Do you promise you'll never leave me, Ada?' I just shook my head, I couldn't trust myself to speak. 'I must have your solemn promise.'

It sounds daft, but I think I would have done anything she asked me at that moment, so I said, 'I promise.'

'Good. Wish me luck, Ada.'

'Good luck, Miss Georgina.'

Then off she went to be married.

As for me, I had one last thing I wanted to do before I left. What I'd promised myself to do was, I was waiting on the veranda for Mr James's chauffeur to bring the car, and I'd put my hat and coat on the rail so they'd keep nice and clean, then I went round the corner to the rabbit hutches and undid the latch on every single one. Ever so slowly, the rabbits came out, and I was worried sick in case Mr Lomax should look out of the window and see what I'd done. They huddled up on the veranda, they were all trembling, noses sniff-sniff-sniffing. Then suddenly one of them gave a jump and they all went lollopy-lollop down the steps and across the lawn to the woods.

GEORGINA

Jimmy wasn't much of a one for bed, which was a shame because I rather enjoyed it once I got the knack of it. At first I couldn't imagine what Jimmy was doing. I thought he must be trying to suffocate me. It would have been easier if he'd explained, but of course he couldn't. I've always thought it strange that people can do something so intimate to each other but never be able to talk about it. Teddy used to maintain that gentlemen found it difficult with ladies, because they never had any to practise on, only tarts, but I shouldn't think Jimmy had had much practice even with tarts. Teddy did, though. Do you know, he told me once that I was the only proper lady he'd ever had – I was the only one he hadn't paid. But I wouldn't have minded a present from 'Uncle' – a nice fur coat, perhaps, a bracelet, why not? Jimmy wasn't suspicious, but of course I should never have got anything past my maid Jones or Ada. Women have such nasty minds, servants especially. Ada's frightful and she's got no business to be, we've always looked after her, she's never had to worry about a thing, and she repays us by disapproving. It was she who told Jimmy about Teddy, I'm sure of that.

I asked Teddy once if he was at our wedding and he said he was. I don't remember him, but he could have been because he was in business with Jimmy in those days. All the people at our wedding were Jimmy's, because I didn't have any except Edmund and Louisa. I hated it, all those people touching me and kissing me. I felt coated with their breath. I wanted to run away and jump into a bath and scrub it all off, but Jimmy kept steering me through this ghastly crowd of baying faces with his hand clamped on my elbow. I felt as if I was covered in bruises from all those people pawing at me. And Dennys looked so extraordinary, with so much food, I'd never seen so much food ... Edmund told me that, after everyone had gone, Father collected up all the leftovers for him and the gardener to eat. It was Edmund who gave me away – Father took himself off to the gardener's house and stayed there until it was over. Jimmy went there to say goodbye to him before we left.

It was so much easier to go about when one had the right clothes. People still looked, but because one was well turned out, not because one was some sort of freak, and I found I rather liked that. We went to the Isle of Wight. I realised on the honeymoon that Jimmy and I didn't have much in common. Really, my brother Edmund was the only man I knew apart from Jimmy and we never had any shortage of things to say to each other. We used to lie on the bed and talk and talk until we fell asleep in our clothes, and Ada would tiptoe in and cover us with blankets, but I had no experience of talking to any other man. Jimmy's conversation was like a prize-winning composition. He would tell me things about politics and the economy – it was like a lecture, a series of facts, and then he would ask me what I thought of it. It was ridiculous – how could I have an opinion? Until I was married I'd never read a newspaper in my life. My father took one, but he wouldn't have let me touch it even if I'd wanted to. Jimmy wanted to educate me, which was tiresome. He wanted me to think about all these weighty matters and form opinions, but I wasn't really interested. Why should I be? It all seemed so little do to with me that I couldn't even *guess* at what I was meant to say. The things I actually *thought* – the things I would have said aloud if I'd been with Edmund – about the landscape and the houses and the people, those didn't seem to be the things that Jimmy wanted to talk about. I was sure most husbands and wives didn't talk in *subjects* the way Jimmy did, but I didn't know any other people, so really I had no idea how they went about it. I'd never been anywhere in my life, never done anything, and there we were, stuck in this stuffy hotel with these stuffy people on this stuffy little island, and I didn't know what to do. I remembered Edmund's advice about copying other people, but they were all so dull that I thought: if I have to behave like that I'll bore myself to death. And then I thought, why *should* I do what other people do? It's tedious and, besides, I'm not like other people, so why pretend that I am? If I'd known such a word existed, I would have said, 'Oh, bugger it!' That's how I felt.

But a honeymoon is supposed to be the time when you get to know someone. I didn't feel I knew Jimmy any better afterwards than on the day we met. I remember one day, I was alone in the hotel room, waiting for him to come back from somewhere. There was a beautiful Oriental rug there, and I decided I'd do what Cleopatra did and roll myself up in it. I'd read that she'd done this so that her guards could smuggle her into the Imperial Palace and unroll her in front of Caesar. Well, I thought that would be quite amusing, so I got some soot from the grate and painted my eyes to look like the Egyptian people one sees in pictures, then I took off all my clothes and lay down on one end of the rug and wrapped myself up in it. Well, Jimmy came back and I said 'Hello-o!' He looked right round the room before he saw me on the floor with my head sticking out of this roll of carpet.

'What are you doing on the floor, Georgina? Have you had an accident?'

I said, 'I'm Cleopatra, can't you tell?'

'Cleopatra?'

'A present for Caesar. You're supposed to unroll the carpet, Jimmy.'

'Unroll it?' He was staring at me as if I was mad. 'Supposing somebody comes in?' As if anybody would just saunter into one's hotel room without knocking.

Well, I thought, I might as well unroll myself, that'll surprise him. So I did. I lay on the floor, completely naked, and blew an imaginary trumpet, 'Ta-daah!'

'For God's sake, put some clothes on.'

I was thoroughly fed up with him so I said, 'If you don't stop being so stuffy, I'll walk right out on to the balcony like this.' It was mid-afternoon and I'd closed the curtains, but I ran across the room and yanked them open before Jimmy could stop me. 'There! That'll give them all something to talk about.' I honestly thought Jimmy was going to have apoplexy. He grabbed the curtains and pulled them shut so hard that the pole came down. One of the curtains landed on top of him like a cloth over a birdcage. He was staggering around bumping into things, but I couldn't help him because I was lying on the bed, crying with laughter. He was making enough noise to wake the dead, so it wasn't long before the manager came banging on the door. Jimmy ripped the curtain off his head, scooped me up from the bed and practically *threw* me into the bathroom, with my clothes after me. When I looked in the glass I saw that the soot had smudged and I looked more like a chimney-sweep than the queen of Egypt – no wonder Jimmy couldn't recognise me. Of course, I absolutely screamed with laughter. Poor Jimmy was trying to explain to the manager about the curtain and my howling away in the bathroom can't have helped at all.

He was livid about the whole escapade. 'I don't know what's the matter with you, Georgina. You're behaving as if you're drunk.'

I said, 'Perhaps I should try it. At least it might be more entertaining.'

He looked so hurt I almost wanted to hit him. He said, 'Perhaps you'll be kind enough not to talk about this in future.' But he brought it up again when we were at dinner. 'You won't mention it to Edmund, will you?'

'Mention what?'

'This afternoon.'

'You said I wasn't to. Anyway, why on earth would Edmund want to hear about it?'

Jimmy said, 'Oh, I don't suppose he would.' I thought that was rather odd of him, because Edmund and I have always had an unspoken rule that we didn't discuss Jimmy, just as we don't talk about Father. Jimmy wasn't to know that, I suppose. Poor Jimmy. I never did try any fun with him after that. He didn't understand it. At the beginning, I thought perhaps he'd had to work too hard for what he'd got to treat anything lightly . . . but I came to realise that he didn't possess a sense of humour. When Edmund and I would come out with our games and catch-phrases and all the rest of it, he'd watch our lips as if we were speaking a foreign language and he wanted to understand what the words meant. I used to call it his 'yellow dog expression'. That was because of a big dog Edmund and I saw on the Heath once. It had been let off the leash and was having a whale of a time digging a hole. Its master kept telling it to stop, and up came its head out of the hole looking so confused – all its instincts were telling it to go after the rabbit and its training was telling it to obey the man. Jimmy would get exactly the same look on his face when the two of us got going. I used to say, 'Who let the dog in?'

Then he'd smile and look as if I'd caught him out: 'Oh, dear, was I doing it again?'

I remember vividly the day we came back from our

honeymoon and I saw Hope House for the first time. The sun was setting and we were in the car, with Herbert driving us up the road and round the corner, and there it was, this monstrous building. Jimmy turned to me and said, 'I built it for you.'

'Oh, thank you.'

I must have sounded like a lady mayoress who's just been handed a bouquet of wilted violets, because he said, 'Don't you like it?'

'Well, it's terribly grand.' Of course, the awful thing was that I *didn't* like it and I always had this dreadful feeling of being burdened because it was such a magnificent gesture, rather like the Taj Mahal except that one wasn't dead. One should have been terribly grateful, but I was actually jolly glad when we had to leave. Ada wasn't. She thought it was a great come-down, moving here, I was left in no doubt about that. She's never been the same towards me since. I'm sure she holds me responsible and of course she's quite right because I *am* responsible, although perhaps not quite in the way she thinks. Of course, I've never actually *denied* killing Jimmy, except in court, but it's a question of loyalty. It went without saying that servants were loyal when I was a girl, but not any more. If you want loyalty nowadays, buy yourself a spaniel, that's my advice.

The war started soon after that. The Great War. That was my war, really, mine and Edmund's. Those were my men, marching away, my brother, my cousin, then Herbert the chauffeur, the gardeners and every single man I knew except my husband – Jimmy was too old. I didn't meet Teddy properly until after the war. I didn't have anyone in this last one – well, Edmund tootled off to Harrods and bought a military sabre from the cutlery department, but the Local Defence lot wouldn't have him, which was beastly of them, although they did let him do a spot of fire-watching to make up for it.

Edmund's letters from France never told me anything. They were rather peculiar – all 'keep smiling' and 'mustn't grumble' – more like a character in a play than a real person. Sometimes it wasn't even a letter that you got, but a thing like a luggage label, with sentences printed on it: 'I am quite well', 'I have been admitted into hospital' and other things like that. The soldier crossed out the sentences that he didn't want and signed his name at the bottom. They used to call them 'whizz-bangs'. At first I was jealous of Edmund being in France. I thought it was like the knights who won their spurs in the marvellous adventures we'd read together when we were young. I used to write to him saying how much I envied him for the fun he must be having. I loved sending him parcels, all the clever things you could buy . . . once I sent him a special officers' tea-set with two bone china cups in a tiny leather box and, another time, a miniature folding bookshelf. But of course it turned out to be no fun at all, just slaughter. When Edmund came home on leave he still kept smiling, just like his letters said, but his eyes looked dreadfully sad. I don't mean self-pity, but that the war made a terrible impression on him and he couldn't seem to stop thinking about it. We went to see Louisa and her bandage-folders, we dined and went to the shows, I even took him to see all the potatoes that Jimmy had grown in the garden, but I couldn't manage to raise him out of this sadness. I could see he was making the most terrific effort to be jolly, that was the frightful thing, but he just couldn't seem to come out of it. He wouldn't really talk about anything and he would stare at odd things, a point on the table-cloth beside his plate or the label on the decanter. I knew that he wasn't seeing them or listening to what I was saying, but often I had the feeling that he might be about to cry and I knew I had to prevent that from happening. So I was like a side-show, really, until the moment had passed. I don't know why this happened, but it did, fairly often. You see, I'd invariably known what the things were that Edmund was afraid of, like the pony and having to have his dinner downstairs with Father. I'd always understood it before, but not this time. None of us did who weren't in France, because it was so dreadful that no one who'd actually been there wanted you to know. Even though they were so near to us, it was as if we weren't real to them. Only the trenches were real.

Edmund never spoke to me about Roland's death. He wrote to me: 'I expect you have heard about poor Roland by now. Well, the best always go soonest,' and ended with a joke: 'There isn't a man here (or a horse) who doesn't wish for peace.' It was the one thing he wrote to me from France that actually meant anything. When Edmund was over there I missed him even more than when he was away at school or university, but I missed him most when he was right beside me at home. The war took him away from me and my battle was to bring him back. Because Edmund and I belong together. Before I was married, Edmund said to me, 'I couldn't have managed without you, you know.'

I said, 'Well, I couldn't have managed without you, either.'

Then he asked, 'What would have happened if we'd been two different people?'

'We'd have found each other.'

That's why we're going to die together.

I dreamed about Edmund so often when he was in France. I always woke up very frightened because I thought that if I'd dreamed of him it meant he'd been killed. I dreamed about the *Luisitania*, too, when we heard that it had been hit and so many people drowned, not soldiers but whole families. I dreamed about the drowned children, that there were rows of coffins beside the sea with their lids thrown off and for some reason I was walking around looking for Edmund, hoping to find him in one of the coffins. The dead children were wearing the clothes in which they'd drowned, the sea breeze was drying them, blowing their hair across their faces so it was hard to see who they were, but when I moved closer, they were all my brother Freddie. All of them, in different positions, different clothes, sometimes two in one coffin with their arms round each other, but always Freddie.

If Edmund had been killed in France I would have committed suicide. Every time I woke up from one of those dreams and thought he was dead, it was as if my life had crashed into a brick wall. I didn't make any plans – no gun or pills or anything like that – but I would have found the means to do it. Of course, if I *had* died, Jimmy might still be alive today. He'd be eighty-one. An old man. And given the numbers that died in Flanders, that always seems much more likely than the other. I wonder what the odds were against it happening? If Teddy were here I'm sure he could have told me.

ADA

Hope House was Mr James's pride and joy. He said to me once, 'I always had a dream of building a big house for the woman I loved.' I thought it was the most romantic thing I'd ever heard. Mr James told me that he could see the house as clear as anything in his head, every single room, he told me that was how the great architects had visions of palaces and churches; even if it was as big as St Paul's Cathedral they would know every detail, how it had to be done. Well, of course, Mr James wasn't an architect himself so he had to get a man to come and draw the plans, but he stood right by that man and never let a thing go by unless he saw it was done right. As soon as he made his first big money he bought the land and had the building begun, at that time he never had enough money to finish, but he went along step by step – it took him twelve years all told, but he did it.

Hope House was much grander than Dennys. It looked like those places they show you in the magazines, when you get photographs of where the big film stars live in America, that's what it looked like. When I first went there, I was so shook up by going in Mr James's car that by the time I arrived I didn't care if it was the monkey house at the zoo, just so long as I could have a sit-down and a cup of tea, but I loved Hope House from the first moment I set eyes on it. It was all set on different levels because of being built on the side of a hill, and it was made of brick, with big stone windows and wooden doors like you'd have on a castle with iron studs and bars all up and down. But the funny thing was, it didn't really look like a castle, it had a roof like a normal house with tiles and spiral brick chimneys. Mr James told me he'd had them copied from the ones at Hampton Court, from the time of King Henry VIII, and that some of the other things were from medieval castles. So it wasn't just in one style, but all different kinds – Mr James said he wanted the best of every type of old building. You could see it from the road – that's how I first saw it – but it was built well back and the lawn in the front was like a small hill in itself, with the house sitting on top of it. When you looked out of the front windows you could see for miles, because it was at Hampstead and the Heath was stretched out in front. Inside, it was all big rooms with tall ceilings and wood panelling. Mr James had it carved specially in patterns from the olden days and he'd had big stone fireplaces built, with the chimney pieces going right up to the ceiling. And there were stone carvings and coats of arms all over, because Mr James was very keen on those sorts of things. He'd had stone creatures made, too, lions and griffins, and they sat at the bottom of the main staircases – to be honest, I thought they were a bit silly; they always reminded me of big daft dogs sitting up to beg.

Hope House had a beautiful garden, too. That was got to from the drawing-room, through big double doors with leaded glass. It was all terraces, you went out to a flat part paved with stones and a pool with a fountain, full of goldfish as big as your hand. There were stone steps up the middle of the garden with these terraces on either side, with the lawns sloping down to thick holly hedges at the bottom of each one. At the top there was a lovely bower, with a sunken garden behind, and further up a summer-house, and a stone circle with poles round and great ropes strung between like a giant's skipping ropes, and roses twining round them.

I was all by myself for the first couple of days I was there, but I didn't mind, I had a lovely time getting a good look at everything. A lot of people who've been in service will tell you it was a terrible life and in some ways they'd be right, although there's less respect nowadays and people seem to think they've a right to complain about every little thing. But one thing I'll never regret: that I had the chance to live in a beautiful house with lovely things in it, because that was the only way someone like me could learn about the better things in life. Even if we couldn't have them ourselves, we could appreciate them as well as anybody and I'm grateful for that.

Mr James told me he'd promised himself never to marry until his house was finished. He wanted it all to be perfect, you see. We both did, Mr James and me, we wanted it perfect. But when Mr James told me about his house, I got a little thought come buzzing round me like a fly that wouldn't leave me alone. What it was was this: you can dream up as many houses as there's fish in the sea and build them, but you can't design a human being. Perhaps Mr James had an idea of a wife and Miss Georgina seemed to suit, I don't know, but you can't design a wife, although I'm sure a lot of men would wish it. They'd probably design one with no tongue in her mouth, or with just the one big lip so the mouth couldn't open to scold them. Well, there I was, thinking it's a new start, a new life, for Miss Georgina and for me, how good it's going to be, but all the time I knew that Mr James didn't really know what she was like. Because I'd watched the way Miss Georgina showed herself to him, how she hid her will from him. I suppose I thought she would change, being married and away from her father, although she didn't have a notion of how a lady should behave and it worried me that if she decided she didn't want to learn she wouldn't, because I've never met anyone with so strong a will as Miss Georgina. But it didn't go wrong for want of wishing, I'll tell you that. And one thing I was sure of was that she'd change when the children came.

I never gave old Mr Lomax a thought, I was so wrapped up in my work at Hope House. Because Mr James had chosen me when he could have had anyone, and I was determined not to let him down. I was going to have it all running like clockwork and more than once I had occasion to bless Mrs Mattie for all she'd taught me. I'd quite a few girls under me and that took a bit of getting used to, giving orders, because I never had that before. Mr James never had a butler; the only male servants apart from the gardeners were his valet and the chauffeur, Mr Herbert. Looking back, I'd say that it was a happy time, in the main, because Miss Georgina seemed to take to being married quite well when you consider what had gone before. She and Mr James came back happy and smiling enough from the honeymoon, and she was soon settled in and going on like the Queen of Sheba, never so happy as when she had three or four to attend to her every need. She'd had a lady's maid engaged for her, Elspeth Jones, and she never let the poor girl alone for a moment.

I don't know what Mr James thought about it all, but he was that much in love with Miss Georgina, he never seemed to mind *what* she did. It was only where the house and garden were concerned: he wanted her to love them as much as he did, but unless it was clothes, she wasn't really interested. I remember they were having breakfast one morning and there she was, sitting at the dining-room table, beautifully dressed as usual, and Mr James had his coffee cup in his hand, standing at the window looking out at the garden. I was in there and I heard him say to her, 'How about planting some lilies under the terraces? Would you like that?' And he turned round for her answer. You could see it was important to him what she thought. But all she said was, 'Whatever you like, James,' as if it was boring her even to think about it.

He said, 'If you don't like lilies, we can plant something else.'

'For heaven's sake, James, it's all the same to me. I can't tell an oak tree from a daisy.'

'I could show you – there's a book.'

'Oh, no, don't bother about it. I'm sure it'll look beautiful, whatever you do.'

I saw his thumb that was on the saucer come down tight like a clamp, and he turned round to look at the garden again and didn't say any more. She never even noticed he was angry, or if she did she gave no sign. But that was typical – with the house, Mr James liked to choose everything himself, down to the smallest detail; he would ask her what she thought of such-and-such a pattern or material or something and she'd always say, 'Oh, do what you like, don't ask me,' or 'I don't know, why don't you ask Edmund?' Mr James never said one word of reproach, or if he did, it wasn't in my hearing. If Master Edmund was there, or Miss Louisa, when she paid a visit, I'd see them talk to Mr James about his plans and look at his drawings, but you could see him looking round for Miss Georgina, hoping she'd join in – after all it was her home, not just some hotel she was staying in. I never understood why she couldn't just *pretend* to be interested, it would have made all the difference to him. But she's never been much of a one for considering other people's feelings.

There was a picture painted of Miss Georgina and Miss Louisa. Mr James paid for it to be done. I can't recall the name of the artist, but I do remember someone remarking it was an old-fashioned style – I think that was because you could see what it was supposed to be! Mr James was very particular to the artist that it must be done in a certain way: three-quarters of the face showing, side by side and both looking in the same direction, neither of them wearing a scrap of jewellery and loose hair all tumbled behind, because that was before the new short hair came in. The picture used to hang in the library at Hope House. I suppose it must have been taken down when we left, but I don't know what happened to it. Perhaps it ended up here, but I'll never see it again, it'll be buried under heaps of stuff by now. It's a lovely picture, though, with the one dark and the other one fair. Mr James was thrilled with it.

I always hoped that Master Edmund and Miss Louisa might get married. I know they had blood they shared from being cousins, but if ever two people could have been happy together I'm sure it was the two of them. Master Edmund would always turn up when the artist was working so that he could see Miss Louisa, and I remember thinking that he must ask her very soon. When the Great War came, all the boys were asking their sweethearts to wed before they went to fight and there wasn't one of us at Hope House that didn't think Master Edmund would propose to Miss Louisa, but he never did.

I think Miss Louisa would have liked to go as a nurse, but her father wouldn't have it, so she went to the Hospital Supply Depot instead – they'd got one set up in the Finchley Road, so she came to live at Hope House and went up there every day to help make up bandages and pyjamas for the wounded soldiers. Quite a few of the big places near us were requisitioned for hospitals and convalescent homes, and a lot of the things they made went to those. That was when I first came to know Miss Louisa, really. Every afternoon when she'd come back from her work, and instead of going into the drawing-room to have tea with Miss Georgina, she used to come and knock on the door of my little sitting-room instead. It had a big desk so I could do my lists and accounts, but I kept it nice and cheerful with flowers and a couple of comfy chairs, and it had a lovely view out over the Heath. I remember the first time Miss Louisa came in, I was surprised.

'Is there something the matter, Miss?'

But she said, 'Do you mind if I sit down?' Mind? I was pleased as punch! She was so natural about the way she spoke and she used to get so excited. 'We've got a new target this week, Ada,' and then she'd tell me how many dressings they'd made and who'd done the most. She thought it was a great lark trying to beat all the others. Miss Louisa had her bandages, but the only thing I remember Miss Georgina doing was that she learned to drive a car. That was a shocker, seeing ladies driving cars, even vans, some of them. Driving along ever so pleased with themselves: 'Releasing a man for the Front,' they said – and half of them still keeping on the chauffeur as well. But I used to love those chats I had with Miss Louisa. I don't know that I ever said very much, it was more listening, really, that I did, but it was always a pleasure. I used to rush through my afternoon's work so that I'd be sitting ready in my housekeeper's room at half past four when Miss Louisa came in, to look as if I was making a list or something, but I was just holding the pen, really. I always made up the tray myself for her tea, and I used to tell the girl, 'You bring that in at five-and-twenty to, not one minute later.' I used to look forward to that all day, tea with Miss Louisa. And she still steps down to see me, every time she comes here. She remembers my birthday, too. I had a present last time she came, a lovely brooch. It's shaped like a thistle, with a purple stone and the leaves done in silver all round. It comes from Scotland, that's where she bought it. I've not worn it yet, not had the chance. I'm saving it for a special occasion.

Miss Louisa always asked after my family, how they were going along, but I didn't tell her much – well, I told her about Mother and my brother Charlie, who'd gone to France, and my sister Winifred, but I didn't want to say too much or it would upset her. Besides, I had my pride, I wasn't going to tell Miss Louisa all our business. Because my family did have a bad time – a lot of the poorer ones did. My brother Charlie was still living with my mother in 1914, he brought home quite a good wage and he used to give most of it over to her for the housekeeping, so she was well provided for. But his firm put a lot of pressure on the men to enlist: 'Enlist or leave!' that was what it came down to, so Charlie didn't have much choice. Besides, he wanted to do his bit, so he joined Kitchener's army and went off for the training. I've still got the letters he wrote to me from the camp, the funniest things they got up to! They were sleeping in a field, Charlie said, 'like sheep' except they had some tents and boards underneath to lie on, only the ground was wet and water used to come up through the boards and soak into their blankets. And then they had to walk two miles every morning for a cup of tea and a bite of breakfast! When Charlie was sent to France I was worried, but I didn't know what was happening, just that they all had to go and fight for king and country. The king, the government, whoever it was, if that's what they told you, that's what you did, it was your country and it was right.

Charlie was killed on the Somme, and I still cry when I think of him. I pray we'll meet again, 'up higher' as the soldiers used to say. All I could think, when I heard, was how could they kill my little brother? Because that was how I thought of him, even when he was a grown-up man wearing a soldier's uniform. I was only five when he was born, but I used to mind him for my mother. I used to carry him everywhere and he was nearly as big as I was. He was the next one after me because my mother had two that died before Charlie came along. After he died I started having these dreadful thoughts, if I saw a young man in his uniform, I had this terrible sadness inside: oh, he's going to die, they're all going to die. A lot of them did, of course. I used to like to see the soldiers before, some of them did their training on the Heath and I used to watch them from my window, but after Charlie was killed, I never wanted to look at them again.

There was another thing I used to think about – William. I couldn't help myself. And in a funny way it made me feel better. I didn't even know if he was in the war or not, I thought he must be, but I didn't know for certain. I used to wonder what it would be like to be his wife, waiting for him at home. I'd tell myself to leave the subject alone till I was blue in the face, but I never listened. So I'd say to myself, you want the world and a handle to carry it, you do. It's all nonsense what you think, he'll have married some girl. Because he could have had any girl he fancied, there wasn't one who'd turn him down with his looks. And of course there was all that going on in France. The boys used to sing 'Mademoiselle from Armentieres, Hasn't been kissed in forty years' – I don't think! Forty seconds, more likely. But I thought, with William, there was bound to be one, an English girl I mean, that didn't let him get away like I did. And then I'd wonder how it could have turned out different, perhaps if I hadn't given myself to him, but then I didn't give myself to him, not in the usual way of it. You always think you could have done things different, better, that's human nature. But it isn't true. All you could have done is what you did do, same as the poor boys that were fighting in the war. Oh, I don't say I went against the war like some of them, but it was a terrible business.

But who wants to know about my life? People don't want to hear about me, or only because of Miss Georgina. When you read books it's always Lord This and Lady That, or it's about Americans, like in the films. That's who people want to know about, not me. Same with Charlie. All the ones that write stories about the war, they're the leaders, educated people who can explain everything properly. Charlie used to collect cigarette cards: 'VC Heroes of the Boer War'. The men on those cards, they were all Lord This and Sir That. A brave working man doesn't count for so much – they don't even give him so much of a medal, he only gets a little one. But that doesn't mean he isn't just as brave. Charlie was brave. I know in my heart he fought as hard as any of them.

That was my family, but we weren't the only ones that lost. Miss Louisa's brother was killed the next year and we had two gardeners at Hope House who never came back, and there was a young lad that used to help them. He must have lied about his age or they'd never have taken him. Mr Herbert the chauffeur came back, though. He always was a quiet man and I never did find out where he'd been or what he'd done in the war. You learned not to ask. It was always the ones who hadn't done it that wanted to talk, but that's the same with everything, isn't it?

We got Master Edmund back, only he wasn't the same as the one we sent. He wasn't wounded badly in his body – that was something I never got used to, all those half or three-quarter men, one arm or one leg missing and some poor souls with no legs left at all. There was a lot of big houses they'd turned into convalescent homes near us and you'd see them all the time. But Master Edmund was more wounded in his mind. I don't think it was the shell-shock, because there was one nearby my sister Winnie's who had shell-shock and he used to beat the air with a stick, his arm flailing up and down all the time and not able to stop it. Master Edmund didn't do anything like that, it was just that he wasn't like himself any more. I suppose you'd call it nervous trouble, I don't know, but we – I mean the servants – noticed it right away. Because he'd always been so friendly and then, when he came back, nothing. Wouldn't stop and talk, wouldn't look you in the face, barely looked at you at all, come to that. The maids would tell me, 'I said, "Good-morning, Sir" and Mr Lomax just looked straight through me as if I wasn't there.' Honestly, if I heard that once, I heard it a thousand times. I started to wonder about it myself, because before, Master Edmund had always popped his head round the door of my room to have a word: 'How are you this morning' or 'What's for dinner' or something of that sort, then suddenly he wouldn't give me the time of day. Mr Herbert knew I was worried and he said to me, 'He'll come round, don't you fret. One minute he's going over the top and the next minute it's tea in the garden. He just needs time to make the adjustment, that's all.' Well, I should have thought that anyone would be glad to have tea in the garden after spending the best part of three years on a muddy old battlefield, but if Mr Herbert didn't know what he was talking about, then who did?

The one who surprised me, though, was Miss Georgina. If I hadn't seen it with my own eyes I'd never have believed that she had the patience to nurse Master Edmund like she did. Florence Nightingale couldn't have done a better job. Master Edmund used to have trouble sleeping and she'd sit up with him all night if she had to, she'd never let anyone else take a turn. They asked the doctor for something to help him, but it can't have worked because he often used to get up and walk around at night; the maids used to find glasses and cigarettes round the house where he'd been, and her with him, she was always with him. I didn't always sleep so well myself and several times I've woken up in the middle of the night and come down to the kitchen, and then I've heard them in the drawing-room, talking. Once I found them dancing together. It was three o'clock in the morning, they'd no music or anything, they were just waltzing across the floor. Not speaking, very solemn, both in their night-clothes, dancing a waltz.

I had to smile when I saw that, but I took care they never knew I was there as they might have thought I was spying on them. Because they became very close at that time, like two children with a secret, that won't let anyone else have a share of it. I can look back and see the three of them, Master Edmund, Miss Georgina and Mr James, just as if they were a picture hanging on my wall: after dinner, Master Edmund and Mr James sitting in the drawing-room in tall-backed armchairs side by side, Master Edmund smoking one of his cigarettes and Mr James with his cigar. Miss Georgina's behind them, leaning over the backs of the chairs, wearing the black-and-silver evening dress made by Madame Alix Grès with the long sweep behind. She's got one arm on the back of each chair, telling them some story, and they're listening and laughing, because it's a funny one. But the queer thing is, *I* know she's only talking to Master Edmund. Of course she's talking to Mr James too, but only because he's in the room. If he was to get up and walk out, she'd carry on, whereas if Master Edmund went out she'd keep mum until he came back. Because that was where her attention was, the whole time. On Master Edmund.

I was happy enough to see her looking after him, because I used to think it shows she's got some proper feelings in her, to look after her brother so well when he's poorly. Miss Louisa said to me, 'I must say, I think Georgie's doing a first-class job looking after Edmund.' Poor Miss Louisa, she'd have been glad enough to do the same for Master Roland, if only she'd been given the chance. So, as I say, I thought it was a good thing for Miss Georgina, a proper thing for a lady to do.

Even though she was thirty by then, I'd never given up hope that she and Mr James would be blessed with little ones. But

I thought Miss Georgina might have done with being a bit more affectionate towards Mr James, because they were shutting him out, really, the two of them. Well, I say the two of them, but it wasn't Master Edmund's fault. In fact, if Master Edmund had been in his right mind. I'm sure it wouldn't have happened. Because they had this special language, he and she. I think they must have been using it in private for years, but then they started doing it in front of Mr James and that was the first time I heard it. I thought it must be some foreign language, although I couldn't think what, because Master Edmund speaks French, but Miss Georgina doesn't, so how come it was all jabber, jabber, jabber, all of a sudden? Then I started to pick up the odd word and I realised it was just English being spoken funny, words backwards and jumbled up, etteragic when they meant cigarette, that sort of thing. Then they had words they used to mean other than what they do mean. And it wasn't like a normal language, where a word means the same thing every time you say it, because they'd take a fancy to a certain word and just keep using it, and it could mean anything, just like you might have a Joker in a game of cards. They were always funny-sounding words. Spelunk, that was one of their favourites for a long time, and then there was decorticate, and bandersnatch, and flolollopy. I used to nip into the library and look them up in the dictionary, but I think some of them were invented because I couldn't find them. It was people's names as well that they used, they'd start off with the name properly, then they'd mix up all the letters so it didn't sound anything like. Pandit Nehru was one they had a few years ago, when you got a lot about India in the papers, and Reg Dixon that plays the organ in the cinema. And Stafford Cripps. He was good for hours of amusement, was Stafford Cripps. I thought they might show a bit more respect with him being in the government, but it didn't make any difference. It was Miss Georgina mostly, doing all this. They both love playing word games, of course, but with her it's one of the ways she has of having something that she knows and others don't, to be that bit superior. Her very own special language, that only he and she understand – and him not always because I've heard him say 'What's that when it's in English?' more than once. But I don't hear much of it any more, not down here.

By the summer months of 1919, late summer, when Master Edmund got a bit more his old self, it used to remind me of the old days at Dennys, the two of them sitting in Master Edmund's room, playing games and cards. If you went past the door you'd hear gales of laughter. I can picture that, too, the two of them in his room in the evening, with the smoke floating around them in the lamplight, sitting on the bed, heads together with hair the exact same shade of black-blue. They'd look up at the same moment and you've never seen two pairs of eyes so alike. They've always loved games and puzzles, and there was a lot of new ones after the war. Every fad that came along, they had to do it: mah-jong, the crossword puzzle, the Monopoly game, that one where it's meant to give you a better memory, all of them. That's not to say Mr James didn't have his own crazes – he did. He used to build radio sets. He used to sit at the end of the long table in the drawing-room for hours fiddling wires around and Mr Herbert used to help him. Mr Herbert was just as mad about taking things apart and putting them together as Mr James was, even though he was the chauffeur. 'Like two big schoolboys,' Miss Georgina used to say, and it was. It was funny to see Mr James sitting there with the radio's bits and pieces strewn all down that big table – the drawing-room was done out to look like a room inside a castle and it was big enough for one, except that the ceiling was the normal height and I've never heard of a castle with french windows. I always thought a radio looked all wrong in there, especially the great monster Mr James had, which nothing ever came out of but crackles as far as I could tell. But the radio was only one of Mr James's machines, he always had the latest things because of his business and a lot of them ended up at Hope House.

I remember he got hold of an electric cooker which drove every cook we had nearly off her head. And there was a great big refrigerator, one of the very first ones, that came from America. What a monster! The first time I saw it, I didn't know what it was. I'd never seen one before, none of us had. The kitchen maids were scared of the noises it made so they used to put all the food in the pantry same as always. I believe Mr James made quite a lot of money out of refrigerators, but I've never seen the need myself. The trouble was, Mr James was always coming into the kitchen to see how his machines were doing. I think he almost wanted us to tell him that they were causing trouble, he and Mr Herbert would have had their jackets off and the parts all over the kitchen floor in a minute if we had. But of course we always said, 'Oh yes, it's very good, very useful.' If Mr James had lived in different circumstances, I'm sure he'd have been one of those men that's always in a shed at the bottom of the garden with their sleeves rolled up and mourning borders round the nails from tinkering with a lot of old iron.

But of course, Miss Georgina couldn't share those interests. They weren't lady's things and she wasn't the type to put herself out for anyone – unless it was for Master Edmund. She got into the way of doing little things for him when he was ill and she still looks after him to this day. Miss Georgina takes the trouble to dress for dinner even now, just like in the old days. She's only got the one set of jewellery, but the lovely clothes Mr James bought her, she still wears them – they may not be the latest fashion, but you'd be hard pressed to find that quality nowadays, I can tell you, and I've never in my life seen a back so straight as hers. Every night at half past seven she comes down those stairs like a duchess – with the kitchen mincer tucked underneath her arm! You'd think it was a beautiful evening bag the way she holds it, instead of an ugly old lump of metal. I've told her I'll give it a polish, but she won't let me so much as touch it.

Then down comes Master Edmund in his evening clothes – over twenty-five years old, some of those suits he's got, and he still wears them. Of course they're hanging off him now, poor Master Edmund. He's so thin you'd think a breath of wind would knock him over and that's her doing, of course, having the worry of her. Anyway, he and she drink their sherry. Then at a quarter to eight she bangs on the floor with the broom handle, and I've got all their dinner put ready on the dumb waiter and up it goes. Master Edmund had the dumb waiter put in a few years ago. I was against it at first, I mean it doesn't matter what anything looks like down here, but it's a pity to spoil Miss Georgina's sitting-room with that great wooden monster. They always had proper dinner in the dining-room before the war, but now that's so filled up with stuff you can't get into it. But Master Edmund wouldn't hear a word against his precious dumb waiter and I'm ever so glad of it now; my legs couldn't stand to go up and down with those heavy dishes six times a day. I used to get up to the sitting-room and put up the little card table for them to eat off, but I can't even do that now, not every day. Master Edmund was ever so good about it, he said not to worry, they can do it themselves with the cloth and all the silver and that, just show him where it is. Well, you can imagine how I felt about that! But with my legs being the way they are, I didn't have any choice. So they set up the table by themselves and then Miss Georgina takes all Master

Edmund's food and runs it through the mincer till it's nothing but little strips. For his teeth, you see. I've told her, I can do it down here, but I'm not let to touch the blasted thing and I've no idea where she washes it. In their bathroom, I suppose. Very nice, I don't think! But she does it because she loves him, so I'm not complaining.

EDMUND

I don't understand women. I'd say I was like most chaps in that respect and in any case, one was never encouraged to look too deeply into these things, it only leads to morbidity. But I have always been fond of Louisa. Ever since I can remember, she's been my – well, my pin-up girl, if you like to use these modern terms. When we were children, if I knew she was coming to see us, she and her brother, I'd look forward to it more than anything else. I'd wake up on that day and think: Louisa's coming today, and I'd feel happy and excited. Special, you might say. Something special was going to happen. I don't know why – why does any man prefer one girl to another? Not even the scientists know that and they seem to know everything else nowadays. Louisa had this wonderful soft hair and she was always smiling. You couldn't say that she was elegant or beautiful like Georgie, but she had a kind face and her hair was nice and wispy. She's still quite lovely now, only much older, of course – we all are. Everyone wants to talk to Louisa because she listens to what they say and she never laughs at anyone or says clever things to make them look foolish. Both men and women enjoy talking to her, I've noticed that. People don't seem to like talking to Georgie much, I think she frightens them. She treats Louisa terribly, says dreadful things about her. Never to her face, of course. Louisa's always been so kind to her, but sometimes I think Georgie's got some demon inside her that can't be silenced.

It's no use wishing now, but one can't help thinking if I had proposed to Louisa before I went to France and she had accepted me, everything would have been quite different. Louisa would have met Davy Kellway afterwards, of course, but she would have been my wife by then, so she wouldn't have fallen in love with him, or I suppose she wouldn't. And even if she had taken a shine to him, nothing would have come of it because she would have been married to me.

But I didn't have the confidence, certainly I never had the confidence of a chap like Davy, or Roland, or even Jimmy, come to that. Roland had confidence shining out of him. If he'd proposed to a girl it would simply never have occurred to him that she might turn him down. Wouldn't have occurred to her either, I shouldn't think. But I didn't know if Louisa would . . . I didn't know if she cared enough to marry me. I used to tell myself that it was all for the best. Suppose we'd been married and I'd lost a limb in the war, or been blinded, or had half my face shot away, what sort of a husband would I have been then? That was what I told myself, but it wasn't the true reason. I didn't ask her because I was afraid she'd say no. It's as simple as that. It was bad enough at the time, when one didn't know how she felt, but then to be given the knowledge, to have lived and to have *known* all these years that one could have simply asked . . . that's worst of all.

I went to see my father before I left for France. It was the first time I'd seen him for quite a few years, to be honest, and the prospect of going back to Dennys without Georgie was dreadful. For months, years, I'd told myself I had to go, but I put it off and put it off, and of course the longer I put it off, the harder it became. I wrote letters from time to time, but that was all. I knew the man Thomas was there – he was to let me know if there was anything wrong – but of course when the time came to go to France I simply couldn't go on making excuses. I asked Georgie if she'd care to come with me, but she refused. 'Why should I? I don't wish to see him and he doesn't wish to see me, and that's the end of it.'

'But you haven't seen him since you were married.'

'That was the plan, remember? You ought to, you were the one who suggested it.'

When I pointed out that it was almost five years since she'd left Dennys she was almost shrewish. 'You only want me to come because you're afraid of him. I can't do everything for you, Edmund. For heaven's sake, stop expecting me to nursemaid you.'

Before I left, I went up to her room to see if I could patch things up a bit. She wouldn't let me in. I said, 'I've come to say goodbye.'

'Oh, Edmund, don't fuss.'

'Shall I give Father your best wishes?' I knew even as I said it that I'd never dare to.

'You can give him the Archbishop of Canterbury's best wishes for all I care.'

I said, 'Please let me say goodbye to you,' because I didn't want there to be any bad feeling between us, but she said, 'Please, darling, I simply can't bear it if you fuss. Just *go*.'

But the incredible thing was that my father was pleased to see me! He was almost sentimental. It was the most extraordinary thing. I sat on the train telling myself that he'd never fought in a war, that I was going to do something he had never done, trying to make myself less afraid of him. I was wearing my uniform, I suppose because I thought that dressing like a soldier would make me behave more like one. When I wasn't wearing it, the idea of myself as a soldier – an officer, no less, giving orders to other chaps, leading them over the top and all that rot – seemed like some awful joke.

My father was shorter than I remembered, more frail – more like a human being, really. I'd taken the evening train because I was going to have dinner and then return to London the next morning, and we sat either side of the fire in his study until it was time for dinner. I was waiting for him to shout at me – that's what I was prepared for – but he didn't. He asked about the regiment, how I thought the war was going, that sort of thing. And Father's man, Thomas, produced the most wonderful dinner. I was staggered. I mean, the food was never up to much in Ada's day, although she did her best, God bless her. I remarked on how nice it all was and my father said, 'Thomas cooks it.' Come to think of it, that's quite good, 'Thomas cooks it,' because of the travel agency, you know. I must tell that to Georgie, she'd like that. Anyway, then he said, 'It's one of our hens. Thomas keeps them at the back.' I said 'Oh?' or something like that and he said, 'Still got the rabbits on the veranda. Had to be rabbit or chicken, but I told Thomas you'd want the chicken.' It really was quite bizarre. I kept trying to imagine the two of them having a conversation about whether I'd prefer rabbit or chicken. I wouldn't have thought my father would have known the difference between them. He certainly couldn't have done anything in a kitchen, he'd have broken every dish he touched. Mind you, I don't suppose I'd be an awful lot better myself; it's a complete mystery to me, how it all gets on to the plate like that.

Father said, 'Does James still employ that dreadful woman?'

'Ada? Yes, she's still with us.'

'Can't think why, woman's half-witted. But Jimmy always was one for taking in stray dogs. Compassion, that's the measure of the man. That stupid woman let all the rabbits out. Only found out the next day. Never caught a single one.'

I said, 'I don't remember that. Why on earth would she want to do a thing like that?'

'Scatter-brained.' He cleared his throat as if he was going to say something important. 'Hare-brained, you might say.' And he laughed! I wanted to ask him if he liked making puns because I enjoy it myself and it would be nice to think that one had something in common with one's father, even if it was only that, but he started telling me how Thomas had dug up one of the lawns for vegetables and things, like a sort of allotment. He seemed to know all about it, how it was planted and all the rest of it. I told him about Jimmy's vegetable garden that he'd started because of the war and I thought: Georgie will never believe me if I tell her about this, because there we were, having an ordinary sort of chin-wag, not about anything very important, but to me it was a miracle. But of course I never did tell her, because . . . well, because it would have been like boasting and it wouldn't have been fair, somehow. But I began to wonder if perhaps I could come up to see Father again. I could tell him about the war and he might be pleased, he might start to be proud of me . . . but the man Thomas put the kibosh on that. I'd noticed during dinner that he was making his presence felt, hovering about behind Father and glaring at me, but Father didn't seem to mind, so I thought it must be his usual manner.

Later, when I asked Thomas where I was to sleep, he said, 'The top of the house is all shut up now. You'll have to take the housekeeper's room. You'll manage for the one night, I'm sure.'

I couldn't think what he was talking about. 'I'm sorry, I don't think—'

'You'll recognise it soon enough. Come on, follow me.' We went traipsing round to the kitchen corridor and several times I nearly ran into him because it was absolutely pitch dark. It felt suffocating, as if we were walking through a tunnel.

'Can't you light the gas, Thomas?'

'No gas here. Waste of money.'

'I'm sure there used to be—'

'Never had gas in this part of the house.' He turned round and stood in front of me in the dark. I couldn't see him, but I could feel his breath. 'Why should you worry, Mr Lomax? You'll be gone in the morning.'

'Yes, but surely it would be easier—'

'Well, we've managed without you and your advice for years, haven't we? I'm sure we can manage for a few more.'

It turned out he was taking me to Ada's old room beside the kitchen. I must say, it smelled jolly peculiar. I don't think anyone could have slept in it since she left. Thomas had put clean sheets on the bed, but the mattress was quite damp and he must have known about it. The armchair wasn't too bad, so I spent the night in that. When I woke up in the morning it was still pitch dark. I couldn't work it out at first, but then I saw that the windows were completely smothered by creeper, just like the corridor. It was even finding its way inside the frames and reaching along the walls of the room. Thomas didn't reappear in the morning. He left a cup of tea and a bowl of shaving water outside the door, both stone cold.

They had some ancient horse and cart to take me to the station – all the decent animals were long gone – and I was just about to climb aboard when my father suddenly appeared on the veranda with a shawl round his shoulders, slashing at the creepers with his stick like a native clearing a path through the jungle. He leaned over the balcony and said, 'Let me give you a spot of advice before you go. I don't know about this war, but if you come through, you be careful. Don't get caught up in all that women's business, marriage. Stay out of it. No need for it, you're better off without.' God knows what I said in reply, I can't remember. Then he asked me to thank Jimmy for him.

I thought, this must be something to do with Georgie, at last he's going to say something about Georgie, so I asked: 'What am I to thank him for?'

'The money he sends me.'

'I could send you money.'

'No, Edmund, I don't want your money. I never gave you very much of anything, did I? You go now. Good luck in France.'

'The money he sends me.' I felt dreadful when I heard that. I had a job because of Jimmy and a roof over my head, everything I had in the world was because of Jimmy and now he was sending money to support my father. It had never occurred to me that my father might need money. Of course, I knew that the allowance I received at university came from my mother's money, but I had just assumed he was financially sound . . . because I didn't want to think about him, I suppose. Yet he hadn't said those words to me with reproach, rather the opposite, as if he didn't deserve anything from me. It suddenly came to me – it was the same as Georgie. The acceptance, I mean. As if it was some sort of punishment . . . as if they were punishing each other. And although they each behaved as if the other didn't exist, they were closer in understanding, somehow, than I could ever be . . .

When I got back to Hope House I asked Georgie if she'd known about the money and she said she had. 'Jimmy has done it ever since we got married. He asked me about it and I said it was a good idea.' I didn't know what to say – she never, ever mentioned our father, yet she was quite matter of fact about it, as if it was all quite ordinary. I was confused, frustrated by it, but most of all there was this strong feeling that I was simply stuck, that events must take their course. I suppose that was partly because of the war, one had to go and do one's bit and just – well, just leave everything else alone, really. Georgie said to me: 'Jimmy can afford it. Besides, he *wants* to send it. For heaven's sake, Edmund, it doesn't matter. Why ever should it matter?' And then she smiled and turned the subject to something else. I felt as if I was in the middle of a game of blind man's buff and it was always my turn to wear the blindfold. I could never catch Georgie and, nowadays, I've stopped trying.

People are very quick with the word 'hell': the weather is hell, the crowds are hell, the traffic is hell. You hear all the time that something is hell. But when you've walked across a battlefield in Flanders – well, I believe that is the nearest to hell that anyone can come in this world. Passchendaele is the one that really stands out in my memory, but it is almost impossible to describe what it was like. It rained most of the time, and I remember walking along beside saturated horses and watching the water pouring off their manes, with harnesses so slippery that the drivers could barely hold the reins to guide them. When the rain stopped, for as far as you could see there was mud. Just mud itself is nothing, nobody minds a bit of mud. But this wasn't just a bit. There wasn't a decent house, not a bush, not a tree that you could see, just shell crater after shell crater, all of them filled up with muddy water deep enough to drown in and nothing safe and flat to walk on but the lines of boards laid down in between. Some of those craters were so close together they had only a narrow, slippery rim of mud between them and you'd fall straight in if you tried to get across. The water in most of those holes was so tainted by gas that it would burn your skin if you touched it. In some places, you'd see four or five craters that had joined up together to make one big lake – and if you fell in one of those you didn't have a hope of getting out unless your pal could help, and then not always because the chances were he'd end up in there with you. In some of them you could see blood on the surface of the water, so you knew what must be underneath. There were bubbles, too, great bubbles that burst when the bodies in there released their gases. No one could fetch them away for burial, you see. They had enough to do taking care of the wounded – the dead had to fend for themselves. You walked along those endless lines of boards and you'd see dead men everywhere you looked. The ones that were just lumps in the mud weren't so bad, because you couldn't see the faces or hands. Unless you trod on one – that was pretty grim. If there was a gap in the boards, well, it had to be filled somehow, and there was a certain texture that you could tell immediately wasn't mud, your boot came down on something soft, not sticky like the mud but something that made a sort of waving, yielding movement beneath your foot, and you knew you must be treading on a dead man's stomach.

It is extraordinarily difficult to speak about this, even after so many years. That was the reason I never told Georgie. Because nobody can explain something so evil – because that's what it was to me, an evil place. But it wasn't just the mud and the death that made it like a nightmare. It was that it heightened so terribly the sensation that one didn't know what was going on. It was absolute confusion, a voice permanently bawling in one's ear, giving orders with no apparent rhyme or reason. You just struggled through and did your bit and never looked beyond your nose. It was just getting the gun from this place to that and if you'd tried to think of anything else you'd have gone raving mad. Judging by what I've read since, that was quite a common experience. You didn't know about the higher strategy and all the rest of it, you just got on with it. The hardest thing was never showing you were afraid. Sometimes I was more frightened of showing fear than I was of the war itself.

Of course, there were some chaps who'd worked it out. Roland was one of that sort – they make the best soldiers.

Enjoy it, too. He joined up very early on, a public schools battalion. It was one of the pals battalions, but by 1917 when he and I met, nearly all the pals were dead and you wouldn't have recognised the battalion because most of the men hadn't been near a public school in their lives. Not that it made any difference to the Boche, of course, he'd kill you just the same. In any case, by the time Roland and I bumped in to each other he wasn't with that battalion any more, they'd loaned him out to another lot because of his experience. He was always calm, you see, never got the wind up. One of the best – he'd been decorated with the Military Cross for gallantry during the Battle of Loos and I suppose you wouldn't be too wide of the mark if you said that Roland was a hero to me.

I found out later that I must have been only a quarter of a mile away from Roland when he died. We'd had a terrible day – rain pouring down and the guns hopelessly stuck in the mud. Every time we fired it grew worse and the guns had to be got out before we could go again. We were supposed to be providing the barrage for the infantry attack. There were six guns in all, going off at intervals, but by midday we'd lost four of them and at least half of the men as well, with plenty of others wounded. The place looked like a casualty clearing station. If they could walk, we told them to try and get to the dressing station. As for the others, well, we didn't see a single stretcher party all day and there was nothing we could do for them.

There was an old German pillbox nearby, so we settled down there for the night. I say 'settled down' – but it was just a square concrete hut with a hole for the door. The rain was coming down nineteen to the dozen and the floor was a great puddle of dirty water. Not that it made any difference, because every man there was already soaked to the skin. In any case, there were ten or twelve of us and there wasn't enough room for everyone to fit in at once, so we had to take it in turns. We'd got no rations, so we sucked our hard biscuits – it was either that or dunk them in the puddle, otherwise it was impossible to swallow the things. We were the lucky ones. We'd moved all those men who were seriously wounded, but it was impossible to get them through the pillbox door and in any case there were seven or eight of them. They were just laid on boards with the rain pounding down on them. We covered them with groundsheets to keep it off, but all the time the mud was sucking them down – they were literally drowning as they lay there. We tried everything we knew, we even propped them up with our weapons, but they just kept on sinking down into the mud. I calculated afterwards that I must have been awake for over sixty hours by the time we arrived at that pillbox, but I barely slept. I won't forget that night as long as I live, sucking those bloody biscuits and listening to the men dying outside, the choking sounds they made as the mud ran into their mouths and nostrils. There was one man who'd had both his legs shattered by a shell. He didn't groan or cry out, he just kept repeating 'Oh dear, oh dear' to himself, very quietly. I don't know if he was in a state of delirium or what, but it seemed so odd that he should be making this sound – more like a vicar who's fallen off his bicycle than a mortally wounded soldier. It was said with just the same tone as Ada when she's going upstairs and her knees are hurting her: 'Oh dear, oh dear'. Whenever I hear her I think of that soldier. He must have been about my age – my age then that is, not now. I dozed off a bit towards morning and when I woke up the sound had stopped. He'd died while I was asleep.

I was wounded a couple of nights after that, a Blighty one in the chest, so that was the end of the war for me. I was in hospital when I heard about Roland. He'd bled to death from a stomach wound, waiting for a stretcher party – it wasn't their fault, the mud was as impossible for them as it was for everyone else and it took twice as many men to carry a stretcher in those conditions. In any case, they would only take those they reckoned to save, that was what the doctors told them to do. It wasn't official, of course, but it made more sense than wasting hours on a man who might go west as soon as he got to the hospital. Roland was too far gone – the chap who told me was his sergeant, he'd been with him when he died. The sergeant seemed a good sort and I wanted to say 'I'm glad someone was with him', but it was too much the sort of thing a wife or mother would say and I wasn't a civilian who didn't know what it was like. I'd seen enough men in that state to know there wasn't any noble deathbed scene. I remembered I'd given Roland Georgie's favour and I had a terrible sense of the injustice of it, the *wrongness*. Because my life is nothing, it's worse than nothing – if I'd died, then I'd be gone and forgotten, and out of this miserable existence.

When I was wounded, a man called O'Hare took me back to the dressing station. I don't remember much about it except that it was a very dark night and the two of us were stumbling from shell hole to shell hole like drunkards. I was surprised by the sight of my own blood, that it was coming out of me, I suppose, and not someone else. O'Hare was pretty well holding me up and he kept on talking to me, but I couldn't really hear what he was saying or make any sense of it. At one point he started to sing, very quietly, I suppose to keep his own spirits up as much as mine – *At seventeen, he falls in love quite madly.* My mind must have been affected, because I suddenly saw Freddie coming towards me. I was afraid for him, he looked so small and I thought he'd get hit, but he didn't, he seemed quite happy, playing in the shell craters as if they were puddles in a park. I tried to join in with O'Hare's singing, because I had an idea that Freddie might hear it and come towards us, but my voice wouldn't work. I remember the words: . . . *flirting sadly / With two or three or more / When he thinks that he is past love / It is then he meets his last love / And he loves her as he's never loved before.* Poor Freddie. If he'd grown up to be a soldier he wouldn't have stood a chance. You could see his hair from miles away.

ADA

Miss Louisa and Lord Kellway were married in 1920 and it was in all the newspapers. I was disappointed, because I really did think that she and Master Edmund . . . but I suppose it was all to do with the war. I'm sure Master Edmund was upset about it, although of course he didn't show it. He went back to his work once he was better. He was very conscientious about it, but it wasn't in his blood the way it was in Mr James's. Mr James was away most of the time, always travelling around, and occasionally Master Edmund went with him, but normally he went to the office in town – unless *Madam* stopped him, that is. That was a great thing with her if Mr James was away. Mr Herbert would bring the car round in the morning and it would be stood on the steps for half an hour sometimes while she and Master Edmund argued. Miss Georgina would use the whole bag of tricks, feeling sorry for herself, saying Master Edmund and Mr James didn't want her or they wouldn't leave her by herself, everything. After six months, I'd heard it so often I knew it as well as my prayers. Master Edmund would say, 'Georgie, I've got work to do.'

'But what about me? What am I going to do?'

'Georgie, I have to go. Jimmy's not here.'

'Jimmy's never here and I haven't any idea where he's gone. He could be in Australia for all I know. I can't think why the two of you don't just throw me out and then you can run around with your stupid business as much as you like.'

'I'll only be gone six hours.'

'What am I supposed to do in the meantime? I don't just cease to exist when you leave the house, Edmund, although I can see it would be jolly convenient for you if I did.'

'I know that, Georgie, but there are things I have to do.'

They'd go on and on like that, and sometimes it used to get nasty, because Miss Georgina's got quite a temper when she wants. Once she said, 'I can't think why Jimmy doesn't pay you to look after me. I'm sure you'd be much better at it than whatever you do in your horrid office.'

Master Edmund said, 'Like a eunuch guarding a harem, you mean?' Well, she'd got her mouth open, all ready to spit out something catty, but then she saw me and shut it, which was a blessing. The truth was, Miss Georgina wouldn't do any of the things that ladies are supposed to do, going to tea and charities and that sort of thing, so of course she was bound to be bored with nobody to pay attention to her.

That was where Mr Booth came in. He had some money in Mr James's business. He was a jolly gentleman, always joking and playing the clown to make people laugh. 'Teddy's coming, he'll buck you up' – that was what Mr James used to say to Miss Georgina. I was amazed she took to Mr Booth the way she did, because he wasn't young or handsome – if anything, I'd have said he was older than Mr James and he had a big red face. But he was always smiling, that's what drew people to him. He was mad for racing cars, he used to go everywhere to the races, even to France, and sometimes he took Miss Georgina with him. Cars and parties, that was what he liked. The first time I remember him coming to Hope House he lugged a great box of champagne into my kitchen: 'I've brought my own refreshments!' He'd carried it all the way up from the car himself, wouldn't let his chauffeur so much as touch it. 'The bubbles keep me happy,' that's what he told me. He thought that there wasn't a problem in the world that couldn't be solved with a glass of champagne. His chauffeur told Mr Herbert once that he even kept some spare bottles in the car 'in case there was an accident'.

I suppose he was what you'd call a character, really. At first I never thought a thing of him going about with Miss Georgina the way he did – after all, it was Mr James himself who'd suggested it. But then some things started to happen that made me change my mind. The first one was this: Mr Booth and Miss Georgina had been to see a show and then I think they must have been out dancing, because they came back ever so late, laughing and singing, making a dreadful racket. It sounded like bedlam and I couldn't think what the noise was, so down I went and found the two of them cavorting about in the hall. I was just standing at the top of the staircase, about to go down to them, when Master Edmund nearly knocked me for six rushing straight past me. He was fully dressed and as angry as I've ever seen him. 'What the hell do you think you're doing?' That's exactly what he said and he never swears, not unless it's an emergency. Then he looks at Miss Georgina and says, 'What have you done to your face?'

She gave herself a little preen and said: 'Oh! Don't you like it?'

He said: 'No, I don't like it. You look like a prostitute. Go and wash it off.'

Because she was wearing this dark make-up, you see, smeared round her eyes. Master Edmund wasn't the only one staring, either, because in 1924 women didn't wear paint on their eyes – well, they did on the films, but I'd never seen a real person wearing it. It looked as if Miss Georgina's eyes had been blacked, what we used to call 'an Irish beauty' when I was young. Oh, she looked like a demon then, she'd been drinking Mr Booth's champagne and her face was flushed, with those great big eyes glittering, and Master Edmund looked quite as mad as she did. 'It's my house, Edmund. I do *live* here. I am so sorry if we woke you up. Let me make it up to you, darling. Give him some champagne, Teddy.'

'I don't want his bloody champagne!'

I'd got my head in my hands – I was like an ostrich, hoping she wouldn't see me, but by then I wasn't ten feet away from her, and of course she did. 'Bring some glasses, Ada. My dear brother is going to have a drink.'

Master Edmund shouted 'No!' so loud I nearly fell down the stairs.

Then Miss Georgina said to me, 'I do hope you heard that, Ada. Apparently Edmund isn't thirsty after all,' and she smiled down at her feet as if she had a secret joke.

Well, Master Edmund could see she was mocking him and I thought Miss Georgina was going to get a real black eye, because he just exploded at her, 'Listen to me, you little slut,' like that, and put up his arm to hit her, but Mr Booth got between them and grabbed hold of him.

'Steady the Buffs,' he said to Master Edmund. 'No harm done. Let's go upstairs and sit down, shall we?'

Master Edmund said, 'I don't want to sit down,' but before he could get any further, Miss Georgina leaned past Mr Booth and took hold of Master Edmund's arm.

'You listen to me, Edmund. I'm going away next weekend. I'm going with Teddy. So what have you got to say about that?' They were both shaking like leaves and before Master Edmund turned away from her, just in that little moment when they stared at each other, I could have sworn they looked frightened. Not angry, or triumphant, or what you'd expect; they both looked terrified.

Well, I didn't know what that was all about, but if you'd seen the second thing I'm going to tell you, you wouldn't have needed no tea-leaves to see what the future held. Mr Booth didn't seem one bit put off by Miss Georgina and Master Edmund quarrelling, he always arrived with a great fanfare to take Miss Georgina out somewhere. Some weeks we'd see him every single day and I don't suppose there was anyone in the house who didn't think there was something going on. Except Mr James, that is, but he wasn't there most of the time. Well, we may have been servants, but we weren't born yesterday. Anyway, one afternoon Miss Georgina and Mr Booth went for a walk in the garden, and one of the gardeners came rushing down and told me that Miss Georgina had been stung by a bee and I was to send something up immediately. Well, the man told me they were in the summer-house, which was near the top of the garden, so I went straight up there with some blue to rub the place. When I got there the first thing I saw was Miss Georgina sitting with her leg propped up on Mr Booth's lap and her skirt hiked right up past the knee.

Well, I didn't know where to put myself and the gardener must have been as put out as I was, because he took himself off pretty sharply. Miss Georgina was sitting there with all her leg showing and she was practically sitting on Mr Booth's lap. I showed her the blue and she said, 'Oh, Teddy can do it.' I started to say, 'Well, I don't think that would be right, Miss Georgina,' but she just looked at Mr Booth and repeated, 'You can rub my leg, can't you, Teddy?' At least he had the grace to look embarrassed. Well, I handed it over and then I thought: I don't care, I'm not staying and watching this carry-on, so off I went. But I saw Mr Booth put his hand on her leg and I didn't like that at all. I couldn't put that out of my mind for days, him touching her like that. It was horrible.

But the next thing that happened was worse. Two o'clock one morning, Miss Georgina's maid, Miss Jones, came and woke me up. She was in a terrible state. 'Miss Pepper, come quick! Mrs Gresham's dying!' So we rushed down and there was Miss Georgina lying on the bathroom floor with all blood coming out. As soon as I saw her I knew she must have been going to have a baby. I didn't know if it was like a wound or what it was, but I'd heard of women bleeding to death from trying to rid themselves of a baby. Well, I didn't know if she'd done anything like that, but I didn't want everyone woken up and knowing about it, so I said to Miss Jones, 'We'll have to manage this by ourselves.' All I knew was, we must stop the blood. I'd no idea how to do it, but I sent her off for more towels and sat Miss Georgina up, so she was resting against the side of the bath, and then I got out the aspirin and gave her some of those with a drop of brandy.

Well, then poor Miss Jones rushed back and came a cropper on the wet floor: 'Oh, my wrist, it's gone!' I was worried she'd woken Master Edmund, because he had the room just across, and I was so flustered I nearly gave her a slap. But I stopped myself. I just told her to keep quiet and go and put new sheets on Miss Georgina's bed, because that was all messed up from the blood.

I was frightened because Miss Georgina was still bleeding and I didn't know what to do. When I bent down to ask her how she was feeling, she whispered: 'Don't leave me, Ada.'

I said, 'Will you let me fetch the doctor?'

'No, don't go.'

I said, 'Have you done something bad to yourself?' because I thought the doctor would be able to tell if she'd done something like that and perhaps that was why she didn't want to see him.

She said, 'I haven't done anything.' She looked so weak and frail that I thought: Supposing she dies?

I said, 'Will you give me your promise that you haven't done something?'

'I told you, I haven't.'

'So can I fetch the doctor now?'

I thought she was going to say no again, but she said, 'Yes, but don't leave me on my own.'

Well, we had to wait while Miss Jones sorted the bed out and I began to feel as if I was going to keel over myself, so I sat down beside Miss Georgina on the bathroom floor. It was a beautiful bathroom she had, Mr James had it done out in green marble from Connemara. We sat there side by side on the floor; there was towels and mess everywhere and Miss Georgina looked dreadful. She asked me, would I talk to her. Well, I'd been along to the big Empire Exhibition, so I told her about that, about seeing Queen Mary's dolls' house. She said, 'That's nice,' but in a bit of a mumble, and then she was quiet for a bit and I noticed her head had slipped off to one side and she made a sort of snoring sound, and I thought: She's going to die. Then I didn't really know what to do, so I pulled her up against me to get a proper look at her. She had her eyes closed, and I remember looking at her eyelids. They were purple, with tiny veins, so delicate, and her face was stark white, and she seemed to me to be hardly breathing at all.

Now, as to what I felt . . . I was sorry for her, but – well, I'd be a liar if I didn't tell you that it was sort of a relief that I felt, not gladness, but just somehow that a door that had been closed to me – well, it was coming open just a little crack. It sounds queer to say it, because that was my job, my life, and what else did I have to do? I didn't have nowhere else to go, but I could sort of imagine this other life, not even what it was, but a sort of . . . a sort of freedom, perhaps, or power, I don't know. I know it was a wicked thing to think, but I couldn't help it, it just came rushing into my mind. I said, 'Miss Georgina, do you know what happened to Master Freddie?' I was holding up her chin so her face was pulled against mine, almost close enough for a kiss. I said, 'There's no one here but me, so you tell me what happened.'

She said, 'Freddie,' or I think that's what she said, it was only a whisper.

I said, 'Go on, you tell me, I won't let on,' and I gave her chin a little shake. She started mumbling again. 'Louder, speak louder, I can't hear you,' and then I gave her a slap on the chin, just a tap to wake her up.

Then I heard her say what sounded like 'my fault'.

'What do you mean, it was your fault?'

'Not my fault.'

'What are you talking about? What wasn't your fault?'

She said again, 'Freddie,' and that was all, because then I heard Miss Jones coming back, so I put my hand over Miss Georgina's mouth before she said anything else.

The two of us got Miss Georgina into bed and I saw there was a big mark on her chin where I'd held on to her. I didn't want Miss Jones to see it so I said to her, 'Go and tell Mr Herbert to fetch the doctor for Miss Georgina, but don't you say nothing more.'

When she'd gone, Miss Georgina's eyes came open again. She stared at me for a moment as if she didn't know who I was, then she said, 'Don't go, Ada, don't leave me.'

'I'll be here, Miss Georgina, don't you worry.' I sat down by the bed. I didn't look at her or anything. Didn't want to. I'd wanted there to be a baby for so long, I should have been sad about it, but something told me it wasn't Mr James's child. The whole thing felt dirty and wrong and I didn't want anything to do with it. I said, 'Did you know you were going to have a baby?'

'Of course not.' I didn't believe her, but I didn't say so.

I said, 'I suppose there's no point in my asking if we should send a telegram to Mr James?' Because he was away at the time, I think it was Scotland where he was, but I'm not sure.

Miss Georgina said, 'Don't tell Jimmy.'

'He'll have to know some time, Miss Georgina.'

'Yes, but not now. I couldn't bear it now.' Well, I thought, it's a shame you never thought of that before, isn't it? But I never said.

Miss Georgina put out her hand to me. I didn't want her to touch me so I moved my chair away from the bed a little. 'Please, Ada.'

'Please what?'

'Don't go.'

'I've said, haven't I? I'll stay.' As soon as I said that, my little feeling I had about freedom all flew away and that was it, back to normal.

Well, the doctor came and gave Miss Georgina something to make her go off to sleep. When he asked about the bruise on her face, I told him she'd fallen down. He took a look at Miss Jones's wrist as well and told her to go down to the hospital in the morning to have it seen to. By the time he'd gone it was up like a football and the poor girl was as white as chalk, so I sent her off to bed with a mug of cocoa and then I had a terrible to-do with all the sheets and towels, trying to get them bundled away and everything tidy before any of the maids came down. It turned out that the wrist was broken. I said to her, 'If anyone asks you how you did that, you say you slipped. You don't have to say anything else.' I sent her back to her mother for the rest of the week; I didn't want the house turned upside down with everyone asking daft questions.

No one had told Mr Booth, of course, and the next day, along he came. Miss Georgina was too poorly to see anyone so I packed him off again, but he sent round a van full of flowers, a whole florist's shop by the looks of it, and I put them all in vases in her room, but after a few days she told me to get rid of them. Soon Mr Booth was coming round every day, regular as clockwork, with his bottles. 'Champagne! That's what we need!' From the way he went on, you'd never have known that Miss Georgina was ill at all. He'd go up to her room and play the gramophone all afternoon, but I noticed that he always left before Master Edmund came back from work.

If Miss Georgina remembered our conversation about Master Freddie, which I doubt, she never spoke of it. I was glad she didn't, really, because I think she was just confused in her mind and didn't know what she was saying. I certainly couldn't make any sense out of it. Anyway, what's past is past, isn't it? There's nothing any of us can do about it now.

The doctor had told Miss Georgina that she had to stay in bed for a time, I forget how long, but it was quite a few weeks before she was really up and about again. Certainly she seemed just the same in her manner, but suddenly a lot of people started coming to the house, which they never had before, and there were a lot of noisy parties. I think many of the people who came weren't particularly good sort of people. I thought at first they must be Mr Booth's friends, motor-racing people, but they weren't, they were just people they'd met and Miss Georgina had invited them. I had the impression that quite a few of them didn't really know Miss Georgina and Mr Booth at all, let alone Mr James, because all this used to happen when he was away. It was like running two separate households, really. As if Mr Booth was master of the house when Mr James wasn't there, with Miss Georgina egging him on, of course. They were always having parties and never with any sort of notice. They'd go out in the evening and bring people back, whoever they could find. They'd have the gramophone with the music blaring out till all hours, and all the windows and doors open at the back with everyone dancing and a lot of silly stuff, pushing people into the pond and that sort of thing.

One of the guests fell out of an upstairs window. What he was doing up there I have no idea and I don't want to. But it was one of the windows over where the scullery was, and one of the big sinks was by the window so if you were standing in front of it, you were facing a little bit of the garden at the back. Two of the girls were washing glasses when they heard a woman screaming and suddenly this man fell right down past the window in front of them and went *wap!* on the grass. On his feet, would you believe it? He'd drunk so much that he was like a rag doll, which was just as well because if he'd been sober I should think he'd have broken his neck. And his hat came down with him. I remember that because he picked it up off the ground and raised it to the girls, and of course they screamed their silly heads off when they saw that. Well, Mr Herbert and I went out to him and he kept raising his hat to us and saying he didn't want to put us out. He seemed to think Mr Herbert was a policeman, because he kept saying, 'Don't trouble yourself, officer, I can manage.' In the end Mr Herbert helped him to his car and he drove away. I did wonder if he got safe home, because we never saw him again. The girl who'd been up there with him came flying down the stairs half naked, screaming her head off. She must have seen him fall, but I don't think she had the faintest idea what was going on. When she heard his car going off, she went running down the road after him, no hat or shoes or anything. We never saw her again, either.

A lot of that sort of behaviour went on, and Mr Booth and his champagne were usually to be found in the middle of it. Needless to say, Lord Kellway and Miss Louisa never came to any of these parties and Master Edmund usually stayed away as well. I didn't like it and neither did Mr Herbert. He never said much, but it upset him – it upset all of us because it wasn't respectful to Mr James. Not only that, but all the maids would be grumbling because of the extra work they were put to, not to mention having to stay up half the night. Because most of those that called themselves guests were people who didn't know any better; they gave themselves airs as if they were dukes and duchesses, and treated us like dirt. One summer we got through three different cooks and of course it was a terrible upheaval each time. The last one, Mrs Seddon, she stayed. I don't know what I'd have done if she hadn't. She did plain food, that's what Mr James liked, a good solid roast meal. She was a good sort, very patient – well, she had to be, to put up with all the carry-on as long as she did.

Sometimes they used to play tennis. Mr James had had two nets put up on the sunken lawn at the top of the garden and of course the maids couldn't bring the trays up the centre steps in the middle of the terraces where everyone could see, so they had to go the other way round, which was a slippery, muddy slope behind a load of trees with branches sticking out in all directions. You had to duck and dodge round them, and that wasn't easy if it was almost dark and you had a tray full of drinks. I was always having girls come to me crying because they'd fallen over and messed up their uniforms or sprained their ankles.

I don't think Miss Georgina played tennis herself and I can't imagine Mr Booth was much of a one for running about. She was the umpire, keeping the score. You always knew who was going to win, not because they were good players, but because she always favoured the best-looking people, especially if they were men, so if a handsome man was playing, he'd win even if he didn't hit one ball straight. 'Oh, darling, you can win today, you're awfully good. You're the winner. Bunny's the winner, everyone!' Or Boysie, or Binkie, or some other silly pet name they went in for. But everyone seemed to take it in good part and, besides, there must have been more drinking than tennis that took place, judging by the amount that had to be carted up there. Some of them played with a tennis bat in one hand and a glass in the other, and there was always broken glass for the gardeners to pick up afterwards.

We all knew that Mr James wouldn't like it if he found out, but who was going to tell him? I knew Master Edmund didn't like it either and I couldn't think why he didn't say something to Mr James, but he must have had his reasons. You always know where the power lies in a house: we knew it was with Miss Georgina, not Mr James, and a lot of the servants were petrified of her. The worst party that Miss Georgina and Mr Booth had ended up with her standing on the long table at the end of the drawing-room. She'd got a golf club and she was swinging at golf balls, trying to hit them into the fireplace at the other end of the room. I think she must have had quite a few drinks, because these balls weren't going anywhere near the fireplace, they were flying off in all directions, crashing against the panelling, the furniture, even one of Mr James's Morlands, but it only hit the frame, thank Heaven, because it was one of his favourites. And then of course the others were all queuing up to do the same and hitting these hard balls and Miss Georgina was laughing and encouraging them. I'd seen from the hall that this was going on and I was worried about the damage . . . but what could I do? I couldn't go in there and stop them. I was so upset I went round to the back of the house outside the french windows where you could see into the drawing-room. There was a little paved part outside the windows and thick bushes on each side, and I came creeping round there so that no one could see me. It had been raining and there was a nip in the air, so they'd got the doors shut.

Well, I could see all this going on inside from where I was standing, when suddenly I realised there was a man there, sitting down on the step with his back to the windows. He wasn't doing anything, just sitting there in the dark. Well, I thought: He must be the worse for drink, I'd better get him out of that wet before he catches his death, so I went over to speak to him and it was Mr Booth. He said, 'Hello, Miss Pepper, won't you have some champagne?' and then I saw he had a bottle and two glasses beside him.

I thought: Oh, well, that's the last straw, trying to bring me into their caper. I wanted him to know I still had my pride in spite of everything, so I said, 'Excuse me, Mr Booth, there are things I must attend to.'

He said, 'Won't you stay for a moment, Miss Pepper?'

There was something about him, his voice – he had his cigar and his champagne all right, but he didn't look his usual jolly self at all. Mr Booth took a lot of drink, but I must say that I never saw him the worse for it, only that night, and even then he wasn't what you'd call drunk, just a little bit unsteady when he got to his feet. I said to him, 'You must excuse me,' because of course I had no good reason to be there, but he said again 'please stay'. We were standing side by side looking in through the window. I felt so sad, watching Miss Georgina spoiling those beautiful things with nothing I could do to stop any of it. I felt it as if they were my own, after all I was the housekeeper – not that she gave me any respect, but just treated me as if I was nothing – but the worst of it was, how could she do that to Mr James? I thought she really had gone mad and it upset me so much I just wanted to go upstairs and hide my head, but I had the girls to think of – I couldn't leave them downstairs on their own with all that going on. I was standing there thinking this, and then I heard Mr Booth say, 'I am sorry about this.'

It gave me such a shock to hear that, I forgot myself and said, 'What do you mean, sorry?'

He said, 'I can't stop her.' It was on the tip of my tongue to say, 'Well, why did you start her, then?' because I thought, well, all these parties, it's six of one and half a dozen of the other, when he said, 'I can't help her.' It sounded as if he was talking to himself, not to me, so I didn't say anything. I thought, she doesn't need help, she needs someone to give her a good slap, but of course I didn't say it.

Then Mr Booth said, 'I don't know what to do.'

He was in his shirt-sleeves and I noticed he'd put his jacket over one of the bushes, so I said, 'Well, let me take this inside for you and dry it out. The lining'll be all damp.'

He looked at me as if he hadn't heard me and said it again: 'I don't know what to do.'

It was hearing him say that decided me, to be honest. Because nobody knew what to do, not Mr Booth, nor Mr Edmund, nor anyone else, and Mr James, he didn't know what was happening. Well, I thought it was high time that Mr James put his foot down. After all, he should be master in his own house, not some other man. Then Mr Booth said, 'Please, won't you have a drink with me, Miss Pepper?'

Well, of course, I said, 'No, thank you.'

But he wasn't having any of it; he almost forced the glass into my hand. 'Please, Miss Pepper, you're the only decent person in the whole house.' So I did, I had a glass of champagne with him. After all, why shouldn't I? It may be the rich man in his castle, the poor man at his gate, but we're all the same before God, aren't we? Mr Booth said, 'I'll drink to you, Miss Pepper' and raised his glass. And I stood there and thought: Yes, I'll drink to me as well – here's to you, Ada. I thought: Miss Georgina may treat you like nothing, but you're not nothing and you won't be nothing, not any more. So I raised my glass and gave it a little clink against Mr Booth's, and then I had a drink.

I suppose Miss Georgina thought the fairies would put everything back in its place overnight, all those marks on the wall where the golf balls had hit, but we had to have men in to repair some of them and that cost money. I couldn't just magic it out of my housekeeping and I don't know what she thought I was going to tell Mr James. Not what I *did* tell him, that's for certain. He came back a few days later and the next thing is, he wants to see me in the drawing-room. So I went in and he was standing by the Morland picture, the one that was his favourite, just touching the frame with his fingers. He didn't look angry, just very calm. I couldn't tell what was in his mind at all. 'Will you tell me what happened, Ada?'

I thought, in for a penny, in for a pound, and I said, 'It was only a game, Sir, but a dangerous one if you don't mind my saying. Miss Georgina had a party, Sir, while you were away.'

Mr James said, 'Not the first.'

'No, Sir, not the first.'

'One of many?'

'Yes, Sir, one of many.'

'Since her illness?'

'Yes, Sir.'

Once I'd started, it was as easy as saying the catechism. Then he asked me: 'Was Mr Booth the – occasion – of her illness?'

That was what he said. I remember every word of that conversation. Although I was saying Sir this and Sir that, I didn't feel like a servant, I didn't feel anything. It took me a moment to understand what he meant about the occasion of her illness, then I answered: 'I think so, Sir.'

'Thank you, Ada, you may go.'

'Thank you, Sir.' Then I left the room. And I'll tell you something: that party was the last time Mr Booth ever set foot in Hope House and very glad we servants were to see the back of him, I can tell you.

Well, I say that, but it was queer about Mr Booth. Because you might say he was a bad man, but I don't think he was, not altogether. I watched his face when he was looking through the window at Miss Georgina and I thought: He does love her, or else he wouldn't look so sad as he did. Mind you, I'm not saying it was right, what they did, because it wasn't. It was very, very wrong. Mr Booth did the right thing at the trial, of course, but then he would because he was a gentleman, not like all those others who came smashing up Mr James's lovely house. I can't say I'd ever really taken to him, what with all that waving champagne bottles and dashing about the place, but when I saw him watching Miss Georgina that night, I just felt sorry for him. I remember he said, 'It's not me she wants.' Just to himself, like that. I didn't know what he was talking about, because it sounded like a lot of nonsense, Miss Georgina wanting things, when she had that beautiful house and more clothes than she knew what to do with, and a good husband like Mr James. And as I say, I looked at Mr Booth standing there in the darkness and I couldn't make it out really, what I thought.

GEORGINA

It was Ada who told Jimmy about Teddy. He was bound to find out sooner or later. I thought I would mind about it terribly, but when it happened I didn't care very much. I suppose the funniest thing was that Teddy was not a romantic man and he certainly wasn't a passionate lover. I suppose it isn't necessary to be very passionate with tarts and Teddy had had lots of those. But one would really have to say that his chief characteristic was reluctance. And what was charming was the way he overcame it – well, how could he help himself? But I was very fond of Teddy and I certainly had more fun in bed with him than I ever had with Jimmy. I often sit here and think of Teddy. It makes me happy to think of him. Thinking about Jimmy just makes me feel blue.

Although Teddy told me he was at our wedding, the first time I actually remember speaking to him was at a house party. It was several years after the Great War ended, but things weren't completely back to normal, well, not unless you'd made money from the war, which Jimmy certainly had, and Teddy as well, of course. Anyway, I was finding the whole thing very dull and wondering how I could escape when Teddy came up to me and said, 'If you sit there any longer, you'll be covered in cobwebs. Come on, I'll take you out for a drive.' And he whisked me off to the stables and showed me the most wonderful silver car. I remember he said, 'I've got six cars, but this is my favourite.' Good heavens, I thought, six! I was very impressed because Jimmy only had one in those days, and it was black and looked like a tin box. Teddy's cars were always his pride and joy. He said, 'Hang on to your hat,' and absolutely raced me round the countryside. It never occurred to him that I might want to look at the scenery, all he cared about was showing me how fast his car could go. At one point we met a flock of sheep coming the other way, but he didn't let up for one moment. The shepherd leaped into the hedge and the sheep shot off in all directions.

I thought it was the funniest thing I'd ever seen. I said, 'This is much more fun than all that chat.'

'Well, there's a time for everything, but you looked in urgent need of a bit of excitement.'

I said, 'Oh, I was,' and I leaned over and gave him a kiss.

I'll never forget what he said then: 'Good lord, I don't think that's a very good idea, do you?' But he was smiling when he said it. You see, Teddy was decent, he was – to use an old-fashioned word – honourable. He liked Jimmy and hated the idea of cuckolding him. People are so stupid, they always assume that it's the man who makes the overtures. I knew that Teddy wanted me, but I also knew that he would never have done a thing about it. So what could I do? If you were to put it crudely, which is what most people seem to do these days, you would say that I offered myself to him on a plate.

It was one evening in the summer and Teddy had come to Hope House to see Jimmy about some business. It must have been very important, because normally Jimmy did all that sort of thing at the office. There were some other men there as well and Teddy wandered out of the meeting early, so I offered to show him the garden. It wasn't planned or anything, because I hadn't known he would be there, it was just a lucky chance. There was a large wooded area at the top of our garden near the summer-house and I thought the gardeners wouldn't be there so late, so that was where I took him. I knew I had to be direct, you see, if I was going to seduce him. I hadn't done anything quite like it before, but I'd hit on an idea which would be a novelty to him and I thought it would work. We were walking along, just exchanging the normal pleasantries – always so peaceful at this time of day and so on – when I thought, well, it's now or never, so I said, 'Oh look up there,' and pointed, so that he would think it was some special sort of squirrel or bird or something, and while he was trying to see what was up there I ran off and hid behind a tree. I took off all my clothes except my shoes and stockings and when he came to look for me I stepped right out in front of him . . . unfortunately it wasn't a terribly warm evening and I must have looked rather mauve.

He was so kind; the first thing he said was, 'You're quite lovely, but you're going to catch pneumonia.' And then he put his arms round me and gave me a kiss and said, 'I can't imagine why you should want me, I'm far too old and fat.'

'Oh, but I do want you, very much.'

Teddy said, 'Well, at least I can keep you warm.'

Poor Teddy. But Jimmy was always somewhere else, or when he was at home, he was taken up with a ridiculous obsession about model communities. He was forever talking about Robert Owen, which was rather mad because Jimmy wasn't a socialist – how could he be with all that money? It's just a lot of fancy names for interfering in people's lives, in my opinion. I used to ask Jimmy, 'How do you know that these people want to live in your houses? They're probably happier than we are where they are now.' Jimmy could never answer that. Because that was the point of it, you see. Jimmy always had to have some vision, some idea he could try to turn into reality. I'd been a dismal failure, so he'd replaced me with a row of cottages with indoor lavatories. I never blamed Jimmy for that, but it was the most monumental bore. Poor Edmund had to take the brunt of it – he's always had more patience than I have and I really felt I would explode if I had to listen to any more Utopian nonsense. Jimmy had the most enormous pile of plans and sketches of model cottages and factories and schools and everything, he'd done most of it himself and he was forever talking about how he was going to send it to George Bernard Shaw. I don't know what became of that, because I don't think he ever wrote to Mr Shaw. But he had great plans for this village: they were all to wash the clothes together in one big laundry and make food together in one kitchen, and have all the children in one nursery, and hold educational classes for the men after their work was finished and all sorts of things. I said to him once, 'Jimmy, supposing these people don't like each other, what then? You're making everything communal except sexual intercourse.'

'Don't be disgusting.'

Jimmy hated anything like that, especially if I said it, but I didn't care, I was so fed up with the whole thing. It was always that, or the garden, or making radios with the chauffeur, or *something*. That was the thing about Teddy: he understood how to enjoy himself; Jimmy never did.

That was the great difference between them. Jimmy lived for his work and, whatever he was doing, he had to understand it down to the last detail. Like those wretched machines he was always buying for the servants and then bothering over them in the kitchen. It was almost an obsession with him, to understand how a machine worked. Teddy didn't want details. If he saw a good thing he'd put his money into it and the money would do the work while he amused himself. He never talked about business things to me, of course, because I wouldn't have understood, but I know he did well out of them. He liked music and dancing and car racing – he loved that. He used to take me to Brooklands sometimes. I'd love to go there just once more, but they've closed it down. They used to keep the cars in stables as if they were horses and there was a place they always called the paddock, full of cars waiting to race. Teddy used to get *so* excited . . .

Even if Ada hadn't told him, Jimmy must have known that he couldn't be the child's father because we no longer had sexual relations. I know Ada thought I'd done something to cause the miscarriage – women have such nasty minds, particularly lower-class women – but nothing so vile would have occurred to Teddy. Or Jimmy, for that matter. And I didn't try to abort the baby. I wouldn't have known how. I've always thought it aborted itself because I didn't deserve to have a child, not that I wanted one. The whole business sounds revoltingly medieval and I can't imagine why anybody does it.

My relationship with Teddy – the physical relationship, I mean – only lasted until the miscarriage. He thought he'd hurt me, you see, that it was his fault, and that frightened him terribly. 'We needn't, need we? Not again?'

I said, 'No, we don't have to.'

'But we can still have a lot of fun together, can't we?'

He thought that was what I wanted, you see, what I needed to stop me feeling blue about the baby. Because even though I hadn't wanted it, losing it like that did leave me feeling rather peculiar. And Teddy tried to make fun – *I* tried, too, to be gay and not to care about anything, I tried very hard, but there was a change between us and we couldn't seem to get back to our old ways. We'd go off and dance and do things, but it wasn't the same. It was as if Teddy was frightened to be alone with me. He'd always collected people, wherever he went, with his champagne and cigars, he wanted people to enjoy themselves. He'd invite complete strangers to Hope House. Women I'd never seen before in my life were always draping themselves over me and saying, 'Darling, it was so sweet of you to invite me.' One couldn't very well say, 'I didn't.' The men were the kind who pay absurd compliments. There was one fellow who told me that he was my slave. He said, 'You can order me to do whatever you like and I'll do it. You have only to say the word.' Well, this got very tedious because he was constantly following me around, waiting for these orders, and I could never think of anything for him to do except bring me cocktails. He must have got awfully bored because he started throwing himself at my feet and trying to kiss my shoes, and it all got rather sordid and embarrassing. Teddy had to ask his chauffeur to frog-march him out of the house in the end. I can't remember what his name was, if I ever knew it. I didn't know any of their names and I don't suppose half of them knew mine. But it was as if Teddy and I were wearing a sign saying 'Don't leave us alone'.

I suppose . . . the sorts of things we did, that was the time as much as anything. Everyone was a bit mad then. Driving around London in the middle of the night having treasure hunts, that sort of thing. Nothing seemed to matter very much . . . I didn't especially *want* to do the things I was doing – certainly I didn't like the people, I thought they were a great lot of phonies, all talking at the tops of their voices about nothing at all – but one had to do something. I remember one party at Hope House, walking through a great throng of these people in the garden, all strangers, all drunk and I was drunk too, they swung themselves round at me with their teeth showing like horses on a merry-go-round that come towards you and past you, towards you and past you, round and round again and again, and never stop for you to climb on board . . .

But I needed them to be there. Teddy and I would go to one of the night-clubs and bring them back, hordes of them, roaring up the drive shrieking and sounding their horns, the girls running up and down the paths in short dresses, tipsy and laughing. They just wanted to enjoy themselves, they didn't care how. I wanted not to be alone and there they were.

I suppose I had hoped that Teddy would look after me, somehow, but he couldn't. I wanted him to protect me from Jimmy and from myself. The emptiness I felt inside, knowing I'd failed with Jimmy, that I couldn't talk to him or anyone . . . but how could Teddy protect me from that? He couldn't, of course he couldn't, and everything was wrong and I didn't know what to do. I'd even driven Edmund away. One could hardly blame him – what was it the soldier said, in that famous cartoon? 'If you know of a better 'ole, go to it.'

But people will always believe what they see and Ada's no different from the rest, whatever she may think. She thought I'd been pregnant with Teddy's child and that was what she told Jimmy. When Jimmy asked me, I agreed that Teddy was the child's father and of course that was what Teddy thought, too. It was better that way. And, as things turned out, I couldn't have chosen a sweeter, kinder person.

EDMUND

Once you were wounded they handed you round like a parcel, in and out of trains and hospital wards with doctors and nurses and all the rest of it, but I didn't mind. I didn't much care what happened to me, to tell the truth. I couldn't think of one single, solitary reason why I should still be alive, when Roland and thousands of other men were dead. What had I done that I should be allowed to live? It didn't make any sort of sense to me then and it doesn't now. Being a parcel was bearable because one didn't have to do or say anything, but when one had to come back among the people one knew, the effort one had to make just to be like one's self, the old, peacetime self, was quite remarkable.

I know this business took men in different ways. I knew that Roland would have just shrugged it off, that's the thing, and I tried to live up to that. Remembering Roland would help me to get along, but I felt – I say 'I felt' as if it's in the past, but it's part of that old whitewash on the wall, the old lie that one is a decent human being, because it's the same old wall underneath the paint and I still experience this overwhelming feeling of guilt that I should be alive and Roland dead. Even with Ada, I knew her brother had been killed and I imagined that she must look at me and think, Why did *he* deserve to come back and not my brother? I couldn't bear to look at her. But one lived in a normal house and the servants expected you to tell them you wanted things, to give orders – and I felt as if I had been struck dumb. It was like the dinners with my father when I was a child: the churning in the gut, the cork in the throat, the not being able to swallow . . . It's strange to think of it now, but for quite a time I couldn't bear to see Louisa at all. It became so bad that I even asked Georgie to tell her she shouldn't visit. And when Georgie told me that Louisa was marrying Davy I almost felt glad of it because I knew I didn't deserve her. Nowadays, her visits are the one thing I look forward to. I mark time between them and when she's here I try to hide my pleasure from Georgie, although I suppose she must see it.

It took quite a time for the wound in my chest to heal, because the bullet had left rather a mess, but when it had begun to clear up a bit, the doctor suggested exercise. At first I went for walks outside, but then I became afraid of what I would see. It was the faces, men's faces. I kept thinking I could see Roland. A man might be the same height, have the same colour hair or just the uniform and, if the light was poor, or he was some distance away . . . a few times I even called out and once a man turned and said, 'Your pal's dead, isn't he?'

I said, 'Yes.' He told me he'd done the same himself.

I gave up on walks and plodded round the garden instead, but I still couldn't get rid of the feeling in my stomach, as if my guts were twisting themselves into knots. Georgie said, 'It's a good job you're not a horse.' Because they'd shoot a horse with twisted guts, you see, they'd have to. If I'd had any sense I might have shot myself.

Perhaps it was all that which led me to do . . . to what happened, I don't know. You see, I had to spend a lot of time in bed because of the wound and I used to get very bored, so Georgie would come to my room and play cards. Georgie always cheats at cards and my being ill made no difference at all – she'd cheat a child of six if she thought she could get away with it. I can tell by her eyes when she's doing it, but the bridge players never noticed, except for one man, and I think Georgie knew he'd got his eye on her because he was hardly ever invited. But Georgie never asks anyone for bridge nowadays – not that there's many to come, they've all moved away or died. No one visits now except Louisa.

None of this is what I was trying to say . . . but how does one speak of what Georgie and I did? What is one supposed to *say*? Talking about it makes it seem so unpleasant, sordid, and it wasn't that. You think of these slums where they all pile into the same bed and the girl has a child and they don't know if it's the brother's, or the father's, or whose it is. Everyone's heard of that sort of thing, but it was nothing like that. At the time I didn't think – well, what we were doing didn't involve anyone else. Although it did, of course, in the end. Like throwing a stone into a still pond and watching the ripples spread out. But it didn't seem so dreadful, in fact at first it was marvellously innocent, like being children again, and I felt so safe . . . I don't suppose that makes much sense, but it's true. One can't explain without making excuses, though, and there are no excuses for what we did.

Who began it, started it? I suppose one has to say it was one or the other, but really it wasn't either of us. It wasn't as if – well, of course there had been a few girls in France, but that was here today, gone tomorrow, you never thought about it afterwards and I don't suppose they did, either. It must have happened first in the evening, because I remember that I was in bed and Georgie came into the room wearing a lovely pair of silk pyjamas. 'Make some room,' she said. 'I'm cold,' and she got into bed next to me. We'd often done that as children, at least when we were on our own, so there was nothing particularly strange about it. We were alone in the house – well, the servants were there, of course, but what I mean is that Jimmy wasn't. Georgie got into bed beside me and we got on with our game of cards. Then I noticed her trying to get a look at my hand and she saw me watching her, so she said, 'Oh, you've been cheating,' because Georgie always puts the blame on the other fellow when she's been caught out at cards.

Well, normally I didn't say anything when she cheated, but this time I said, 'You can stop that, because I know you've been cheating,' and then we had a little tussle over the cards, because she wanted to get hold of mine and I wouldn't let her. Or that's how it started out: 'Let go, those are mine.'

'No, you let go, you oaf,' and she started giggling like a schoolgirl.

At first it felt the same as when we were children, the absence of any of what I suppose you'd call physical feeling, but then there came a moment where Georgie was lying across my lap, holding me round the waist; I had my cards hidden behind my back and she was trying to snatch them. She was making little lunges to try and reach the cards: 'I'm-going-to-make-you-give-them-to-me-Edmund,' like that. I looked down at the top of her head and then there was the sensation of how warm her body was, and suddenly I found myself – I found that I was – aroused – by her – by what she was doing – and I suppose she must have discovered it too, because she stopped moving and straightened up. Her arm stayed round my waist, but she became quite still. She could have turned her head and looked at me quite easily where she was, but she didn't, her face was turned away from me, and I have an idea her eyes were shut. She said 'Edmund'. Not a question, not an accusation, more like a sigh: 'Edmund.' So then I shut my eyes as well and I felt her touch my cheek. I didn't want her to take her hand off my face. In fact, I think I may have moved it back when she tried to take it away. She said, 'I love you, Edmund. Don't worry, no one will ever know.' I can't remember what I said in answer. Perhaps I didn't say anything. I don't know.

When I watched her take the pyjamas off, because she had no coyness or false modesty or anything of that sort, I realised that I had never seen a woman entirely naked before. Statues and pictures, yes, but not a real woman. With the girls in France, there was always a chemise, or some sort of garment, and it had never occurred to me that anyone *would* take all their clothes off. I could tell by the way Georgie was looking at me that she didn't unclothe herself like that for Jimmy and I suppose I felt a sort of pride about that. She was kneeling up on the bed, with her knees slightly apart and, although the bedclothes bunched up around her legs, I could see that the hair between them was curled like mine and of course it was the same colour, black. It looked so dark against her skin, which was pale and smooth, and lovely to touch, and it fitted so well. That may sound strange, but the girls in France – perhaps it was because of the difficult times with the war and shortage of food and so forth – sometimes they seemed to have too much skin for what was inside, and it was often quite dark and coarse, even rough. But Georgie's skin was soft and it fitted her like a perfect kid glove.

I wanted to tell her she was beautiful, but I couldn't, I couldn't talk or even swallow, because she was staring at me. Nobody had ever looked at me like that. I wanted to look at her body but I could only look at her eyes. I couldn't stop looking at them. It was like a contest to see who would look away first. Georgie moved her face nearer and nearer to mine and leaned over so that our noses where touching, like she used to when we were children. 'How many eyes?' she said. 'How many eyes have I got?'

When we were done, I thought she might be angry and blame me, but she didn't, she lay back and smiled, and said, 'You liked that, didn't you? We should have done that a long time ago.' Well, of course I did enjoy it, partly because of the sexual side, the fact that one was able to function in a normal way as much as anything else, but also because while it was happening I wasn't thinking of anything else. I can't make clever explanations, never could, but while I was there with her the faces outside, the men's faces and Roland, the fear, the reproach – the whole bloody lot – it wasn't there any more.

Georgie came back to my room the next evening and the next, and it became a pattern: she came into the bed, and sometimes we only played cards and talked, but at other times we – we did the physical thing with each other. Then, when I could get up and about, I had the habit of going to my room for a rest in the afternoon, and she would come and join me. I was quite deliberate with myself that I would not think about it at any other time, because I wanted to keep it quite separate, as if it had no connection with the rest of my life or Georgina's. It was only when Georgie went to Teddy Booth that I fully realised what a dreadful thing I'd done, to have debauched my own sister, or why would she have gone to another man? Because I know damn well that she was the seducer, not Teddy. He brought her home one night from a party and Georgie told me straight out that she was going away with him for the weekend. I suddenly saw how depraved she'd become, as if she simply didn't care what anyone thought, she was standing there announcing this in front of the servants with this hideous black-and-white paint smeared all over her face like a common street-walker. We almost came to blows – heaven knows what Ada must have thought, because she witnessed the whole thing. Well, she took Georgie upstairs and put her to bed, and when the coast was clear I tiptoed across the landing and knocked on the bedroom door. 'Georgie, I have to talk to you.' Dead silence. I tried the handle but the door was locked. 'Georgie, you can't let Booth take you away like that. What about Jimmy?'

Then I heard her voice on the other side of the door, very low: 'Jimmy doesn't care about me any more. Don't you know that?'

'Then what about me?' She didn't answer immediately and I thought she'd gone away. 'Georgie, don't be so bloody childish. What about me?'

Then she said, 'I'm sorry, Edmund.'

'Well, if you're sorry, what are you doing it for? Just tell Booth it's off, that's all.'

'I'm sorry, Edmund, I can't.'

'Why not? Why can't you? Booth won't mind. You don't think he cares about you, do you?'

'No, I suppose he doesn't.'

'Then why are you doing this?'

'I told you, I have to. Good night, Edmund.' That was the proof of it, you see, she couldn't help herself. Once she'd had one man who wasn't her husband, of course she would want another – after all, what decent woman would throw herself at a man the way she set herself at Teddy? I felt as if I'd taken the stopper out of a bottle and it could never be put back, because you can't have innocence back when it's gone for ever. It was all part of the bloody great mess I'd made of everything . . . it disgusted me, all of it, the way she behaved with Teddy . . . how brazen she'd become. As if she could just . . . just make up her own rules and everyone else could go hang.

GEORGINA

I have never told Edmund that it was his child. I thought that it must be like a Cyclops or some sort of monster and the doctor might be able to tell, that he might say it was the child of degenerates – although Edmund and I are not degenerates and what we did wasn't degenerate. But to talk about that sort of thing makes it seem coarse and sordid, which it wasn't. It was perfect.

And it was the most wonderful fun keeping the secret. First there was a great to-do because we had all the furniture in Edmund's bedroom moved. Edmund was funny about sleeping with his back or even his side to the window, he wanted to face it head on so the bed had to be turned round, and then there was a wardrobe with a mirrored door opposite the bed and he would wake up in the night and think there was someone in the room, so it had to go. It was just like when we were young and used to do things together. I would bring flowers from the garden and arrange them in his room and he would teach me to smoke. He just did it to amuse himself, really, because I never got the knack of it at all. We used to open all the windows wide so that Ada wouldn't smell it, but she always did, and she used to tut and sigh and flap the curtains like anything. I have never smoked in public in my life, I might add. I've never got used to the sight of women smoking all over the place. I couldn't bear that, during the last war, seeing all those girls walking about in trousers with cigarettes hanging out of their mouths. All those horrible square shoulders and sensible shoes and nasty, greasy rolls of hair, as if they were pretending to be men. It was such a relief when the dresses came back and proper evening clothes, and everyone started looking like themselves again.

Anyway, Ada made a dreadful fuss about the smoke and Edmund worried awfully about upsetting her, so in the end I said, 'I know how to solve the problem, it's our house and we simply shan't let her in, then she won't know.' So that was it, we said we wouldn't have her or any of the servants in the room, we made them leave trays outside the door and then I'd dash out and pick up Edmund's dinner when no one was looking.

It sounds strange to say this now, but the whole business of the baby was a very great shock to me. Not only the pain, but I had never been entirely sure about how babies actually happened – of course, I was married so I knew one didn't get a baby by shaking hands, but I certainly didn't understand how they were born. I suppose people like Ada must have known about these things, but *we* didn't. I mean, I doubt if Louisa knew any more than I did and she had a real baby. I suppose Jimmy wasn't able to make one – he can't have been able to because I certainly didn't know what to do to stop one coming and with Teddy, well, there already was a baby, that was rather the point. Of course, Teddy never asked about any of that, but then men don't need to worry, do they? Still, I suppose women are not required to die in wars. Or at least they never used to be, but I suppose the air raids changed all that. Not that I minded air raids, I thought they were rather exciting. I thought it might have been a good death for us, a direct hit. If Edmund was there and it was quick, I shouldn't have cared a bit.

There's a poem by A. E. Housman that Edmund read to me, that says something about the name dying before the man.

That's what's happened to me, you know. When I die, if anybody notices, they'll say, 'Oh, her, wasn't she the one who did her husband in all those years ago and got away with it?' The older ones, that is. The younger ones won't even know my name.

EDMUND

My father died in June 1927, a year before Jimmy. I can't pretend I didn't feel relief. But it shows character if you don't make a fuss, or that's what they say, so there was absolutely no difficulty there, for once. It was as if I'd somehow beaten the old man by outliving him, in spite of the bloody war. That seems a dreadful thing to enter one's mind, but it was what I thought.

Jimmy didn't go to the funeral. He said he couldn't get away from the business. He simply told us he wouldn't be able to go and we didn't argue. But I was rather sorry about it, because Father had liked Jimmy more than he'd liked Georgie or me.

Father was buried in the village churchyard. Some of the local people, the older ones, were there, but not many. Because my father wasn't a man who was liked, he wasn't the sort of chap who'd pass the time of day or anything like that – in fact, there'd been trouble in the village because he'd started wandering about in the evenings, behaving rather oddly – there were a few children who'd complained that he'd thrown stones at them and once he pushed a young girl into a ditch, and there was another occasion when he'd found a young woman walking home in the dusk and started abusing her because she was out by herself. A local man told me that after that incident the village policeman, Constable Whatmough, had spoken to Thomas and told him to keep an eye on my father, in case he did anything else – and Thomas had answered that the girl deserved it. My chap said that Thomas said women and children shouldn't go rambling all over the place in the dark or they'd get what was coming to them. Quite extraordinary, when you think that the poor girl was only walking down the lane.

I was in the churchyard, having a look at the headstones after the funeral, and I came across a small grave with a plain stone that said *Frederick Fairbanks Lomax 1894–1899*. It was the first time I'd seen Freddie's grave. That was all it said, the name and dates. There were no flowers, but it looked tidy. When I told Ada that my father had died, we'd fallen to talking about the old times at Dennys and I'd asked her about Freddie's funeral. She told me: 'Your father wanted Master Freddie in the earth and covered up as fast as he could. It was all hurried off, Master Edmund, hurried off and no one was to talk about it.' When I asked her why, she said, 'It was too much for him, poor man, after your mother. I don't think he ever forgave her for dying and leaving him like that, and then Master Freddie on top . . . it was too much.'

I said, 'What do you think it was, an accident – Freddie, I mean?'

'I don't know, Master Edmund. I never did understand it and I don't suppose I ever shall.' Well, I was still in the dark about the whys and wherefores, but it was a relief to hear Ada mention Freddie's name, even if she did it with pursed lips. Because most of the time he seemed to be an invisible object that one had to skirt around in the conversation and one never quite knew what shape it was, if you see what I mean. Only that one had to avoid touching it at all costs. As a child, I was afraid that if I thought about Freddie for too long, I'd sort of become contaminated and other people would know it, and then they wouldn't speak to me. I started to try and explain all this to Ada, but I can't have made a very good job of it because she said, 'Don't upset yourself, Master Edmund. Master

Freddie's at peace now and it won't do no good to disturb him.' Well, that wasn't what I meant at all, but it was obviously hopeless trying to explain, so I took myself off.

There was no mystery about my father's death, but the manner of it was rather odd. No one had seen him for a week, and then a man from the village knocked on the door at Dennys and there was no response, so in the end Constable Whatmough was fetched, and he broke into the house and found my father and Thomas lying at the foot of the stairs, both quite dead. The doctor thought that they must have slipped and fallen down the stairs together, one trying to save the other, perhaps. Thomas had his neck broken – he died immediately – but my father's leg and hip were badly smashed up and the doctor said he could have gone on for quite a few days. He couldn't have pulled himself along for any distance to get help, because he was in a very frail state, quite apart from the broken bones, so he must have had a fairly grim time of it. The doctor told me this in private. I didn't mention it to Georgie.

Thomas was buried in the village churchyard too – next to my father, as it turned out. I don't think I'd have fancied lying next to Thomas for all eternity, but a man can't choose unless he's reserved a place in advance. It was the natural place for Thomas, of course, because he'd been born in the village and lived there all his life, but I was rather surprised that my father hadn't elected to be buried with my mother in London.

There was a pub in the village called The Hand and Flower, and Georgie and I stayed in a couple of rooms there. Constable Whatmough gave me the keys to Dennys after the funeral. That was an awful thing, because we knew that the house must belong to me under the terms of the will, but when I asked

Georgie what to do, she said, 'Throw the keys into the village pond.'

'I wish I could.'

'Well, I don't see why you can't. Anyway, I don't care what you do, just so long as I never have to set eyes on it again.'

I knew that was her attitude, which was why I was flabbergasted when she agreed to come to the funeral in the first place. Jimmy told her she ought to go, and she said, 'Well, I will.' She'd seemed terribly offhand about coming along, but we drove the whole way down in silence and I could tell she was nervous as hell. The two of us stood on the porch at Dennys trying to get our courage up. The whole veranda was completely tied up with ivy and Virginia creeper, which was probably what was holding it together. There was a pile of smashed-up tiles in the drive that had fallen off the roof and most of the windows seemed to be boarded up. The wooden steps to the front door were completely rotten, and I think they must have had an accident getting the coffins out of the house, because two of them had completely caved in and there were bits of wood and moss everywhere. When Georgie saw the holes, she said, 'Well, I suppose we should be grateful he left by the front door.' All the time, she held on to my hand, wouldn't let it go.

We managed to get the front door of the house open and immediately there was this vile smell which sort of assaulted you. I honestly think it was worse than the trenches, because the foul air was trapped with no breeze to blow it away. The hall floor had been decorated with a pattern of coloured tiles, but you couldn't see it because it was crusted with muck and straw, packed down hard as if the place was some sort of farmyard, and the few remaining sticks of furniture were battered almost to pieces. There were various rooms off the hall and I noticed flies buzzing around outside two of the doors, where the smell was particularly strong. I went as close as I could stomach and the upper panels of the doors had been hacked out, so I had a look inside. It was the most pitiful sight. They'd been keeping animals in these rooms, rabbits in one and poultry in another, and they must have been passing hay and food for them through the holes in the doors. The poor creatures had all starved to death and there were corpses everywhere, covered in droppings and alive with flies. The instant I saw that I knew I had to get out before I vomited, but when I turned to look for Georgie she'd disappeared.

I truly don't think I could have stayed inside that house one moment longer. It wasn't just the stench, but the atmosphere was *so* – well, I suppose it was knowing that my father had died there and thinking of him lying in that filth, in terrible pain . . . I couldn't rid my mind of the picture of him beside Thomas, waiting for death to come while those desperate animals were clawing at the doors in search of food.

I nearly broke my neck on the front porch on the way out, looking for Georgie. For several months before my father died I'd hardly seen her at all – I couldn't bear the strangers racketing round the house and never any peace, so I cleared out. I was going to put up at my club, but Louisa found out and invited me to stay there, with her and Davy and the baby, because Caroline was just a tot in those days. I stayed with them for three or four months in the end. I kept offering to move out – it wasn't fair to them to stay so long – but they wouldn't hear of it. Louisa was always so kind. When I told her how much I hated the way Georgie was behaving, she said, 'She's unhappy about losing the baby. You shouldn't be angry with her, Edmund.' It had never occurred to me that Georgie might have actually wanted a baby until Louisa said that. I tried to imagine Georgie with a baby, but I couldn't make it fit at all, somehow. But all women want babies, or I suppose they must, or they wouldn't keep on having them.

Louisa certainly seemed to want her baby. She was a marvellous mother. I used to go up to the nursery with her to see Caroline sometimes, and Louisa would always take her in her arms and kiss her. I'd say, 'She's a lucky baby to have a mother like you,' and Louisa would laugh at me, but I meant it.

Seeing Louisa every day should have made me the happiest man alive and some of the time it did, as long as I could forget the rest of it. It sounds childish, but sometimes when the car brought me back from the office, I used to pretend that Louisa was my wife, not Davy's, and that Caroline was my daughter. I didn't tell her about that, but we did talk about a lot of other things – well, I suppose I talked, mostly, but Louisa was always quite happy to listen. We talked about the summers at Dennys and about Roland . . . I used to wonder if she liked to hear me talk because it reminded her of him. I wouldn't have minded if that was the case, because being with her made me feel nearer to Roland, too. But when she looked at me, straight into my face, in that quiet, serene way of hers, I felt like the lowest being on the earth. Because how can you forget that you've betrayed the person you love most in the world when they look you in the eye? Even if they don't know what you've done, *you* know it and you know that you can't undo it.

I went round to the back of the house to look for Georgie. I couldn't find her anywhere. The flower beds were choked with weeds and the yard was in a filthy state, but the hedge was still there, massively overgrown, with the little hut behind it that used to be the servants' toilet. Georgie and I were fascinated by it as young children because we were never allowed to go near it. You couldn't see the entrance to the hut any more, or even its shape, it was just a great mound of creeper – something rather smelly with a greenish-white blossom – which had grown so much that it was smothering all the trees within range and there were waist-high stinging nettles everywhere.

I found Georgie standing in the shadow of the hut in the middle of a clump of nettles. She had her handkerchief pressed against her face and she looked as if she'd been crying. She said, 'This was where Freddie died.'

'I didn't know that.'

'It's true. They all went into the house and waited until he was dead, then they fetched the policeman.' She ran straight towards me and grabbed hold of my arms. 'They let him die, Edmund!'

'Georgie, you don't know what you're saying.'

'Yes I do. I do know! He wasn't dead when I saw him. He was breathing. But *they* left him out here – Mrs Mattie and Nurse and all of them. It was them, their fault! They ran away and waited for him to die.'

She was sobbing. I'd told myself – promised myself – that I would not touch her, but when she ran towards me I had to, I had to hold her in my arms until she stopped weeping. That was all I did, I didn't kiss her or do anything, I just put my arms round her. I don't remember ever being told that Freddie's body was found outside the hut and I suppose I might have expected to feel something of an emotional sort, standing on the place where he was found. But I couldn't imagine it at all and there was nothing there except Georgie and a lot of nettles.

Georgie said, 'I want to go back to the car.'

'Come on, then.' I had a hip flask with me and a bottle from The Hand and Flower. Brandy. Father's favourite. Georgie waited while I broke one of the kitchen windows and hopped over the sill to get a couple of glasses.

Georgie grabbed them and said, 'Let's get drunk.' She made

a toast: 'Here's to keeping up family traditions.' Then we sat in the car and got drunk. There's no other way to describe it, because that's what we did, quite deliberately. I think Georgie started to feel the effects before I did, because she was giggling and singing to herself. Then she suddenly said, 'Edmund, I've simply got to take off my stockings.' She'd torn them running through the nettles and her legs were quite badly stung. I didn't want to watch her take her stockings off, so I said I'd go and fetch a dock leaf, but by that time I wasn't very steady and for some reason, well, mainly it was because I didn't want to go back to the car, I ended up with a dock leaf and a lot of grass and flowers as well. I remember reaching right into the middle of a bush for some big white roses – in fact, I scratched my wrist rather badly, although I hardly noticed it at the time. I heard Georgie singing 'O, O, Antonio, he's gone away, Left me alone-io, all on my own-io' at the top of her voice, and then she started shouting 'Edmund, come back! Where are you? Don't leave me all on my own-io! You don't have one scrap of love for me, Edmund, not one ounce . . .' I stood in the bushes for a few minutes where she couldn't see me, but she only shouted louder. Then I heard the sound of breaking glass, so I thought I'd better go and see what she was up to.

I found her swigging brandy from the flask, sitting with her bare legs stuck out in front of her. The sun was going down and they looked like ivory in the fading light. She was laughing. 'Sorry, Edmund, I dropped the glasses.' I didn't want to look at her. It wasn't her legs that were disturbing to me, somehow, but her feet. I suppose because a car was the wrong place for bare feet, they looked very undressed, next to the brake and the steering wheel, and the effect was rather unsettling. I pitched all the roses and other stuff into her lap and sat down sideways on the driver's seat with my back to her, and I lit a cigarette. She said, 'Won't you take some of these flowers, Edmund? I only want the dock.'

I didn't turn round, I only said, 'Throw them out of the window, then.' We just sat there in silence after that, me with my back to her, passing the bottle back and forth. I turned round after a while and I saw she'd wound the flowers into a sort of garland and put it on her head. It made me smile and I think perhaps I leaned over to touch it: 'Flora.'

She said, 'If Jimmy were here, we wouldn't be doing this.' As if we were two children making mischief. Then she said, 'I'm not frightened. I thought I would be, but I'm not.' I didn't know what she meant, I thought she must mean frightened of the dark, because the light was completely gone.

I said, 'You're never frightened.'

She laughed. 'No, I'm not, am I?'

When the bottle was empty, she grabbed it and jumped out of the car. She ran towards the house on her bare feet, dancing, leaping in the air, scything the bottle from side to side and whirling in circles. She was wearing a black dress and all I could see in the dark were flashes of her white face and legs. Her eyes were like slits, black slits. Then she stopped dancing and hurled the bottle at the house as hard as she could. It was too dark to see where it landed, but I heard a window shatter. 'I hope it rots. I hope it burns down.' Then she ran back and hurled herself into the passenger seat. 'Start the car. Now! Start it now!' I was fumbling so much in the dark that I almost broke my thumb on the starting handle. Georgie had the garland she'd made in her lap and she was ripping it to pieces. 'Take me away,' she kept saying. 'Take me away.'

We made it out of the main gates, but I hadn't driven more than a hundred yards down the road when she grabbed my arm and nearly landed us in a ditch. 'Edmund, stop. I can't bear it. Stop the car. Stop it now!' She was white, shaking, weeping – I'd never seen her like that and it frightened me. By the time I'd got control of the wheel again and pulled up, her face was buried in my waistcoat and she was sobbing like a child. The thought of returning to Dennys made my heart sink, but I said, 'Do you want to go back?' because I thought that must be it.

She said, 'We're never going back. Edmund, I don't care what happens. We are never going back.' I stroked her head. I could see that there were still some bits of flowers and leaves on her clothes and hair, so I started picking them off and I don't know if she misunderstood what I was doing, or if it was her, or me, or what it was, but after a while she kissed me . . . you must remember the circumstances, and that we'd both had a great deal to drink. When Georgie kissed me, I had Louisa's face in my mind. I wished she were Louisa with all my heart.

It was pitch dark, so there was no chance of anyone seeing us – we couldn't even see each other. We sat for a long time in the dark, holding hands. Georgie said, 'Will you come back to Hope House now, for good?'

'Yes.'

'There's no need to be afraid. It's just us now, isn't it? I love you, Edmund.'

And then I said the stupidest thing I could have said. If I hadn't been half cut, if I'd thought before I'd spoken, the words would never have left my mouth. Because I couldn't see her, I felt less . . . well, I suppose it was as if she couldn't hear me. But I said it. 'I love you, too.'

ADA

The spring after Mr Lomax's death, I met William again. I did! I was walking down the street in Finchley – it was my afternoon off and I wasn't going anywhere much, just minding my own business – when I suddenly heard this voice: 'Good afternoon.' And there he was.

'William Ferguson!'

'Ada Pepper!'

I said, 'How do you know it's still Pepper?' I went to put my hands behind my back, but William beat me to it – I wasn't wearing any gloves, as luck would have it.

He said, 'Isn't it?' So of course, I had to say it was.

I can remember every single word of the conversation we had. The minute I looked up and saw William's face, I was lost. He was still a very handsome man, with a way about him; I noticed that even quite young girls were giving him looks as he went by. I'd been that angry with him, but all the things I'd meant to say to him about what a so-and-so he was, I never said one of them. They all flew out of my head the moment I set eyes on him. He said, 'You been waiting for me, then?' Typical! Then he said, 'You got a boy?' just like the young ones used to say at the time. I had to laugh. He said, 'You come with me, I'll see you right.' And before I knew it he was taking me off for a cup of tea and a bun. So there I was, walking down the street with my arm in his, and if my feet were touching the pavement, well – I couldn't feel a thing.

It was the dirtiest, most horrible tea-shop I have ever been in, the rudest waitress with nails as black as my shoe, and I have never felt happier in all my life. This girl in a filthy apron came slouching towards us: 'What do you want?'

When we'd given the order, William whispered to me, 'Do you think she's going out the back to dig for the tea-cakes?' and I had a terrible job not to laugh right then with her not three feet away. She crashed down the pot so that the tea slopped out on the cloth and then came the plates, crash! wallop! all spinning about. She'd just gone slap, slap, slap with the margarine on the bread – honestly, my sister Winnie making the tea for her kiddies would have done it more carefully.

Well, I'd poured out our tea and we each had our slice of bread on our plate, when the waitress came back and stood over us again.

'Plain cakes or fancy cakes?'

William looked at me, very serious: 'Oh, I think the occasion calls for fancy cakes, don't you, Miss Pepper?'

I knew I couldn't look at him or I'd be in dead trouble, but I never had time to draw breath because this girl bellows 'Gentleman wants fancy cakes' in a voice you could have heard in Yorkshire. Then she goes stumping off and comes back with a plate. Slam! down it goes on the table. 'Fancy cakes is extra.' Then she goes, 'There's three there. You can have one each. You've got a choice.' Well, those cakes had certainly seen better days; and one of them looked as if she'd trod on it. If I'd been on my own I'd have sent them straight back, but when I looked at the plate, the idea of paying extra for that lot seemed so barmy that it started me off laughing again. I had a quick glance at William, but he wasn't any better than I was. I heard him say 'thank you' to the waitress, but I couldn't trust myself to look at him. I was looking down into my lap, trying to get myself under control, but then of course I had to go and drop my napkin, and we both bent down to pick it up and almost banged heads.

There was a huge black beetle under the table and William said, 'Oh look, there's Lon Chaney. He's waiting for Miss Grace and Charm to come off her shift.' Well, that was the last straw; I nearly burst. I had tears rolling down my cheeks, the lot. William said to me, 'You always were a terrible giggler.' And it was true, I was. Ellen and I were always laughing, but I'd forgotten.

How can I explain what that feels like, the years just falling away like that? I felt that I was seventeen again and, when I looked at William, I could feel my heart swell up inside my chest I was so happy. When he was counting out the money for the bill, he whispered 'Fancy cakes is extra' and of course, that set me off again, and we both had to dash outside and down the street in case anyone in the shop saw us.

I know we walked about for a bit, but I couldn't tell you where we went. We were talking and laughing a mile a minute when a terrible fear got hold of me that William had a wife and family – he'd asked me if I was married, but I hadn't thought to ask him. Because if you'd seen him, you'd never have believed that some girl hadn't managed to net him. I was shaking inside when I asked him, I don't mind admitting it, but I thought: well, I've got to know. So I came straight out with it: 'Are you married?'

I'll never forget the way he looked at me when he said 'No'. Then he said, 'We've got a lot of things to talk about, haven't we, Ada?' I understood his meaning well enough and I must have turned red as a poppy. I'm sure that's very charming if you're a schoolgirl, but when you're going on for fifty it's ridiculous. I looked away for a moment to recover myself – there was a stand with a man selling flowers, so I looked at them. William said, 'Well, we can talk about them next time, can't we?' I still didn't trust myself, I just kept on looking at the silly violets, or roses, or whatever they were. Then William said, 'Will there be a next time, Ada?'

'Oh, yes, I'd like that.'

So we made an arrangement to meet, then I had to catch my bus. William said to me, 'Wait a minute,' and he bought me a bunch of roses from the stall. When he held them out to give them to me, he said, 'Bought and paid for, fair and square,' and I knew he was talking about when he'd given the roses to me and Ellen, and I'd asked how he'd come by them. You could have knocked me down with a feather, because that was how many years ago? I never thought a *man* would remember a thing like that, but he had.

I suppose I might have cried, because no man had ever bought me flowers before, but I'd have been crying tears of joy, not sadness. They were red roses and I was holding on to them tight all the way home on the bus. I was just going up the road towards Hope House when I saw Miss Georgina with Master Edmund, driving out of the big gates. Master Edmund stopped the car to talk to me: 'Such lovely flowers, Ada, a present from an admirer?'

Well, I might have told him if *Madam* hadn't said her piece: 'Don't be mad, Edmund. Ada doesn't have admirers, do you, Ada?' I never said anything, I was too angry. I've told you my face wouldn't win any prizes, but there was no need for that. Well, they went off, and I stood there with my flowers and thought: that's all you know about it.

Because Miss Georgina always thinks she's the one with the secrets, but this was one she didn't know. Like with that funny language she's always speaking with Master Edmund. I was telling William about that – because I did meet him again after that and not just the once, either – and he said, 'What does it sound like?' So I told him how it was words muddled up and back-to-front and all that, and he said, 'Oh, the men at the market do that.' I asked him what he meant, and he said that the butchers and greengrocers and everyone spoke certain words backwards like a sort of code, and that if they were talking fast you couldn't make head or tail of it. I laughed fit to burst when I heard that. There's Miss Georgina thinking she's so special and it's only what they do in the market. When Master Edmund and I made up our own things we used to say, Miss Georgina didn't like that at all. It was in the last war, before Master Edmund bought the wireless for me, and he fixed up their wireless down in my sitting-room. We used to listen to ITMA and all the shows we liked – *she* said it was vulgar, but some of the things they got up to on the wireless, it was enough to make a cat laugh. I used to put my head round the door and say to Master Edmund, 'Can I do you now, Sir?' like Mrs Mop. Miss Georgina would give me such a look.

Well, now William was *my* secret. His hair was a little grey, he was a bit heavier round the middle and there were some lines on his face, but I'd say he'd changed more in his character than in his looks. When William was a young man he was very vain of himself, but that had gone and, best of all, I didn't feel that he was laughing at me, not the way he used to. I thought that he must care about me, at least a little bit. But women look old sooner than men, don't they? I saw my reflection in the bus window on the way home that evening and I thought: whatever does William see in me? I'd got my own teeth – still have, believe it or not – and my hair was still nice, but like I said, I was no beauty queen, even as a girl. No one ever looked round in the street after me, except William. I'll never understand why, but he did.

I arranged to meet William at the station at Hampstead the next time, and we went for a walk on the Heath and had our tea. I said I must pay for the tea, or I wouldn't go. William didn't like that one bit, but he had to let me. We did talk about *those things* – not in the tea-shop, of course, but on the Heath. I said to him, 'I could have had a baby, you know.'

He said, 'No you couldn't. I took care of that.'

I said, 'What are you talking about, you took care of it?' He saw I didn't understand him, so he explained it to me. I thought I should have died with the embarrassment! He meant, where he'd wet my legs. Well, I hadn't known what it was at the time, but hearing him say those words, I couldn't believe my ears. It was shocking to hear William talking about the facts of life as if it was something you could just talk about. I did learn something I hadn't known before, but fancy learning it like that from a man! But whatever anyone says, *I* say it's more shame that there I was nearly fifty years old and still in ignorance about certain matters. But imagine if someone had overheard!

William was quite upset with himself, so I said, 'Well, it was a long time ago, so we won't worry about it now,' because I thought it was time to change the subject.

But he said, 'My God, Ada, I'm so sorry. It must have been hell, thinking you were going to have a baby.' He kept shaking his head. 'It was my fault. It should never have happened.'

Well, that wasn't fair, so I said, 'It takes two.'

He said, 'But you can't tell me you enjoyed it, Ada.' Well, if I'd been scarlet before – *enjoyed* it? Well, I dared not say anything to that, it would have led to goodness knows how much more embarrassing talk. 'I always seem to be making you blush.' That was what William said. 'Pink cheeks suit you.'

Then he put his hands on my shoulders and gave me a kiss. Just a peck on the cheek, that was all he ever did, he never took any liberties with me, except only that one time when we were young. He said, 'I'm glad you never cut your hair. It's like looking into a fire.' Wasn't that nice? It had just started to go grey then, but there was still plenty of the old colour left.

I said, 'Well, better make the most of it while it lasts.'

William said, 'I don't care if it turns green.'

We went out every other week after that. Sometimes we went to the pictures, but what I liked best was if the weather was warm, we'd buy some fruit and eat it in the park. Once when we were there, I asked William, 'Do you remember Master Freddie that was killed?'

'That was a bad business. You couldn't forget a thing like that.'

'Do you remember the girl they took away, the simple one?'

'Jenny? I remember sitting in the yard with you the day they came for her. There was a fair old fuss about it, wasn't there?'

'I never thought she'd done it.'

'What do you mean? 'Course she did it.' I was a bit taken back when William said that.

'Oh,' I said. 'I always thought you didn't reckon it was her, either.'

'Well, if it wasn't her, who else was it? There wasn't anyone else there.'

'Well, I always thought it was a tramp or something. But anyway, there were other people, there was the governess, she was outside with the children.'

'Yes, but why would she want to thump one of them on the head? There's no reason to do a thing like that. You'd have to be mad, or an imbecile. Besides, do you remember Jenny had a turn? Well, I helped carry her into the house and there was blood on her dress and apron.'

'Well, she fell down on the ground, didn't she? She might have rolled in it.'

'Didn't look like rolling to me. More like a splash. I saw it, Ada.'

'But she could have tried to lift Master Freddie up or something.'

'You liked Jenny, didn't you?'

'Yes, that's why I thought it was so unfair, picking on the weakest one because she couldn't stand up for herself.'

'Listen, Ada. When I was in the army, we had one like Jenny. Bert Morris, he was called. Fat chap. If any of the men got a parcel of food from home and didn't keep his eye on it, Bert Morris would pinch the lot and scoff it. There was a row about it every time and Bert would promise not to do it again, but he always did. To his mind, he was hungry and he couldn't see no further than that. Jenny was the same – didn't think what would happen next.'

'But everyone knows what happens if you whack a five-year-old child on the head!'

'It must have been her, Ada. It doesn't make sense otherwise.'

He said it ever so gently and I suppose I felt I'd been a bit stupid, thinking Jenny was innocent. I mean, William had seen this blood on her clothes and what he said was so sensible that I thought: Well, I've been wrong all along. But I've always had this strong feeling that what happened to Jenny wasn't right. It's queer, really, because I'm not a fanciful sort, not like Ellen. But still, I can't help it. Daft, but there it is.

We liked our times in the park so much that I'd got into the habit of taking some sandwiches and buns wrapped up in paper so that we didn't have to bother with a tea-shop. So there we were, sitting on a bench, and William was telling me about his job. He could have gone on and done very well in service, I'm sure of it, but he'd been given a job as a driver when he enlisted and he'd learned about mechanics. Well, he found he liked it, so he got into that trade when the war ended and he was all set up in a garage of his own just near where I met him in Finchley, and he had a man working for him. He told me this and then he said, 'I was such a fool!' I asked him what he meant and he said, 'Oh, I thought I was something all right, I thought I was love's young dream.' My heart felt as if it was trying to climb up and jump out of my mouth. I looked at the sandwich I was eating and I thought: I'm not going to manage any more of this. Don't ask me how I knew what he was going to say, but I did. What he said was, 'Do you reckon we could make a go of it?'

Now, do you remember I told you that Cornford's pickles don't agree with me? Well, that's when I found it out. I wasn't sure what would come out if I opened my mouth, otherwise I would havc said ycs straight away. But William saw me hesitate and he said, 'Why don't you think about it?' And after that, I thought: Well, perhaps that's the proper thing to do, not to give an answer for a week and then say yes. So I nodded that I would. And I felt glad I'd never said yes then and there, because it might have seemed . . . well, forward. Especially after what happened. I'm sure that must sound very funny to someone who's used to being courted by men, and having lots of proposals and all the rest of it, but it was new to me; all I knew was what I'd read in books.

That was the happiest week of my whole life. Thinking about how I would say it to William – not that I was going to say anything fancy, just 'yes' – imagining how it would be when we were married – oh, I was over the hills and far away, that week. I thought: I've worked hard all my life; when I get married, it'll be like a holiday. Because I didn't think of that as work, not looking after William, not in our own house. I'd like to say I didn't let it go to my head, but the truth was, I'd been living for those afternoons with William and I wasn't paying as much attention as I should to other things. But there wasn't only William distracting me, there was my sister Winnie as well. Because at that time things were getting bad for a lot of people. Not people like Miss Georgina and Master Edmund, but working people and their families.

My sister Winnie married again in 1920, after her first husband was killed in the war. Her second was a man called Frank Peel. He'd had a good job as a foreman at a factory where they made boots and shoes, but they'd laid them all off and he couldn't get anything else. He was a big, strong man, but he got so low and bad he'd sit and stare into the grate, and this was all day, every day, mind you. It got on Winnie's nerves to see him brooding and bringing nothing in, but what could she do? Poor Winnie. She was forty when Frank married her and she never expected any children from it, but she got them: twins! Frankie and Peter their names were, but of course they were still at school and she'd got nothing coming in from them but the odd few coppers. Better-off people said the children didn't get enough to eat because the women were bad managers, but it wasn't like that – I'd like to see some of them that said it trying to manage on nothing and then they'd see how they liked it. Winnie'd been quite ill when the twins were born and I don't think she ever got back to her old self, not really. I'm not saying Frank wasn't a good provider when he was earning, but he was a selfish man at the best of times.

If there wasn't enough meat, which was most days, it all had to come on his plate. Nobody begrudged him, but it was the way he did it. He'd sit up at the table with his eyes going all round, and if he thought one of the kiddies were getting more than their share, it was 'I'll have that' and it would be straight off their plate and on to his. His reasoning was, he brought in the money, he must have the best. Fair enough. But then when he couldn't bring in the money, that was terrible to him. Because they've got to feel that they are a man, haven't they? And losing the job takes it away from them. Oh, he used to drive Winnie mad, trailing about after her: 'Let me have a bit of bread, I want a bit of bread.' Like a baby. Well, the day came when there was nothing to eat in the house and Frank knew it as well as the rest of them, but he kept on and on at Winnie, 'Give me some bread,' and in the end she picked up her big knife and went for him. The twins had to pull her off else she'd have killed him. He was out cold as it was. They had to fetch a neighbour and put Frank in a handcart and wheel him the mile to the hospital, which can't have been easy, two boys and an old woman – because Winnie said, 'I'm not coming with you, I don't care if he pegs out' – and Frank must have weighed seventeen stone.

The first I knew of it was a message to say that there had been an accident at Winnie's and someone should be there with her. Mr James couldn't have been kinder, straight away he said to me, 'There's no question about it. You must go there at once and stay with your sister for the night.'

Well, I had no idea what I was going to find, but Winnie's neighbour Mrs Elliot was out waiting for me. 'Oh,' she said. 'It was fearful. The twins came charging in here and I thought the house was on fire because I couldn't get one word of sense out of either of them. So in I go and there's Winnie, stood there as calm as you like, Frank on the lino and blood all over the place.' Well, the hospital put enough stitches into Frank's face and chest to make a trousseau and he had the scars till the day he died, but the queer thing was, he would never admit it was Winnie that did it. I ask you! He told them at the hospital that a man had attacked him, said he was after his money. Of course, the neighbour went and told the whole street it was Winnie, but none of them would ever say it to Frank's face because they knew he'd have half killed them. Besides, she'd given him this one scar that run right down the side of his face from his eyebrow to his mouth and it made him look so fierce that no one dared to cross him.

Anyway, that night I slept at Winnie's. As I say, she was calm enough, so after we'd been down to see Frank at the hospital and I'd tidied the house and got a bit of food in, I came home. All the way on the bus I was thinking: Thank goodness I'm not about to marry one like that.

It was about eleven o'clock when I got back to Hope House and Mrs Seddon was sat up waiting for me in the kitchen. I said, 'Oh, you shouldn't,' because I thought that it was ever so kind to wait up like that.

But she said, 'You must go in and see Mr Lomax at once. I'll be waiting for you here.' I thought I must have done something wrong, or why would Master Edmund be summoning me to see him? Because he always came to me if he wanted anything doing, just the same as when he was a boy.

Well, I went into the drawing-room and there was Master Edmund, standing in front of the fireplace. I'll never forget walking across that room. Master Edmund was looking down at his shoes. When I came close, he turned his back and pretended to move something in the grate, although there was no fire, being summer. He said, 'Please sit down, Ada,' but he never turned round. I remember how he was stood as clear as if I had a photograph; I could see his profile, with his head bent down and the grey in his hair, which was just starting to come at the side. He drew the back of his hand across his mouth, with his black sleeve and white cuff, and the gold ring shining on the little finger. 'I am afraid that Mr Gresham is dead.'

You'd think I must have said *something*, wouldn't you? Asked a question or something? But I never. It was Mrs Seddon who told me the details, not Master Edmund. The only words he said to me was to tell me Mr James was dead. He never turned his face to look at me properly, he just gave a little cough, then he was out of the room. It had a door on either side of the fireplace and he shot through one of them like a cat in a rainstorm. I was just left sitting there on this great big velvet chair, listening to his feet going off down the corridor. Master Edmund had told me to sit down and there wasn't a hard chair, so I had to sit somewhere. Then I thought: Well, I can't sit here all night, so I went off back to the kitchen. Mrs Seddon was waiting for me and we went into my special room beside the kitchen. She'd made up a tray with some tea on it and I think there were some biscuits or cake or something. I sat down at my desk. There was all my account books and whatnot in front of me, and I nearly found myself pulling out my pen as if we were going to go through the orders for the week, because it didn't seem as if it was real, what I'd been told. Mrs Seddon told me as much as she knew, but I couldn't follow it. Anyone who'd overheard me would have thought I was a simpleton because I kept asking the same questions, I couldn't seem to understand it.

I asked her 'Where is he?' I meant, where was Mr James's body, because I thought he'd gone up to Manchester. I didn't understand when Mrs Seddon said he'd been found upstairs and I was even more confused when she said they'd taken him away to do an examination. 'What sort of examination would that be?'

She said, 'Well, I don't really know, the police said it was to find out if he'd taken these pills.'

'What pills?'

'I don't know, but they said he might have taken some pills and that's why he died.'

'Was it poison?'

'Some sort of medicine, I think they said.'

'But he doesn't take any medicine, not that I know of.'

'Well, they said it came from the doctor and Mr James might have had more than he ought.'

I said, 'Well, I don't know what medicine that could be,' because I'd never known Mr James take so much as a tonic. His doctor was Dr Durrant, same as Miss Georgina. He'd paid plenty of visits to Hope House to see her when she was poorly, but I'd never known him be called to Mr James. I said, 'Oh, I can't believe this.' Because I couldn't think straight at all and none of it made sense to me, what Mrs Seddon was saying.

'It was Master Edmund found him. Half past six in the morning. Mr James was in his dressing-room. Mr Edmund went to pay a call of nature and when he came past the door it was open, so he looked inside and there was Mr James, sat bolt upright in his chair, fully dressed with a rose in his buttonhole, stone dead.'

'What was he doing with a buttonhole at half past six?' Mr James used to go out every morning in the summer and cut a bloom for himself, but he always did it after breakfast.

'I don't know, but one of the girls saw a bunch of roses on the side, quite fresh, so somebody must have picked them, but if it was Mr James, nobody saw him do it.'

'How come he was sitting in a chair?'

'Well, Mr Herbert told me it was sort of wedged under the table where he puts his hair brushes.'

'He must have been looking out at the garden.' Because that room had one of the nicest views and the garden was a real picture in summer with all the flowers out. 'Does Miss Georgina know?'

'Oh, yes. But don't worry, Miss Pepper, the doctor gave her something.'

'Well,' I said. 'I suppose we should be grateful for small mercies,' and then I thought: Oh, it didn't sound respectful the way I said that, but it came out before I could stop it. I asked Mrs Seddon when the police would find out about the medicines, but she didn't know that. As I say, I couldn't really take it in what she was saying. All I knew was, when I'd left to go to Winnie's Mr James was as right as rain. I'd seen him myself, talked to him and everything, and he was fine. Now here was Master Edmund saying he was dead and no one knew why. I told Mrs Seddon, 'I'm going to bed.' I'd heard enough and, to be honest, I just wanted to be left on my own. I said, 'Don't worry about the tray, I'll take it in the morning,' and she didn't make a fuss, she let me do it my own way.

But I didn't sleep a wink. I had all this stuff going round and round in my mind all night. I didn't even know *what* I was thinking about half the time, it was things I didn't want to think, all tangled up. And then I was thinking about William – what was I going to tell him? I thought, I must write him a letter, I must tell him, and I was lying there trying to work out what to say, but I'd get one sentence started and never finish it because then I'd see Mr James jammed in his chair, dead, with his eyes wide open and staring at the garden. I didn't know if his eyes *were* open, I suppose I just thought that people always died with their eyes open; I don't know if that's true, but then you put pennies on the eyelids . . . It was all things like that, they kept coming back to me again and again, so I got dressed and went to Mr James's dressing-room. It was locked up, but I had my keys and I went in. The first thing I saw was the roses. Nobody'd thought to put them in water and they were just lying on the side. It seemed a shame to let them die, so I put them in the basin in Miss Georgina's bathroom and I sat there on the side of the bath looking at them. I must have sat there two, three hours, but they never perked up so I took them downstairs and threw them out. I can't tell you what I was thinking – I can, though, some of it, it was about the children.

The ones they never had. I would have loved children. Poor little things. And Mr James. Poor, poor Mr James.

I don't like to think about it, but I was in a bad way after Mr James died. I never got the chance to speak to Miss Georgina or Master Edmund – they shut themselves up in their rooms mostly, especially her. I don't think she came downstairs once in three weeks. We had to bring the food up on a tray and leave it outside on the landing. No one was to go into their rooms – they'd leave the tray outside again when they'd eaten, just like when they were children, just the same. If they wanted anything doing, they'd write a note and push it under the door. Do this, fetch that. Not even signed.

Master Edmund went into the office most days – there was a lot for him to sort out in the business – but when he came back he was straight up the stairs so fast that you could barely see him. It was a sort of a suite of rooms they had, you see, him and Miss Georgina and Mr James, and there were big doors that closed it off from the main staircase and then it had a little private hallway of its own. Anyway, Master Edmund would dash off up there and we wouldn't see him again until next morning, and then only for his coat and hat. I remember on one of those days I was coming out of Mr James's study, which was across from the doors to their part, just when Master Edmund was going up the big staircase. I know he saw me, but he never said a word, only bolted like a scared rabbit. It reminded me of when he was a boy. If he'd done something wrong, which was hardly ever, but nobody's perfect, are they? But if he'd upset something or been where he shouldn't – and that was usually because *Madam* had told him to – he wouldn't come near me for days. He was always a bit timid that way, Master Edmund. Didn't like trouble. *She'd* pretend she'd done nothing wrong, stare right back at you with eyes as hard as marbles, but not Master Edmund, he'd always run away from it. I'll never forget how unhappy he looked when I saw him that day.

I have never understood how Mr James come to make a mistake like that with those medicines. Perhaps he thought he was taking something else, although he'd only to read the label – and Mr James was the type who would always read a label. He was upset about Miss Georgina and Mr Booth, of course, and that was one thing I did wonder about, because Mr James did like everything to be perfect. And it must have made it that much worse, all the servants knowing about it.

The impertinence of the police was something I could not believe, the way they came snooping all over and asking questions. They got the whole place in an uproar, talking to the girls – well, I made sure none of them said anything they shouldn't, I wasn't having that, coming spying into respectable people's houses asking things which were none of their business. When they asked me about Miss Georgina and Mr Booth, I told them I didn't know nothing about it. It was the older man who asked me, not the other with him, the boy, or I'd have told him to wash his mouth out. Mr James wasn't cold in his grave and them saying those things. Well, he was barely in his grave at all, the way they insisted on messing him about before we were let to bury him.

Six o'clock in the morning, that's when the police came. I was getting dressed. As soon as I heard the car I went to my window, and I could just see the gravel on the drive and the foot of the steps, so I knew who it was. The minute I went out of my room, one of the maids came running up to me: 'Oh, Miss Pepper, the police are here! They've asked to come in!'

I told the girl, 'Bring them into the house before anyone sees them.' So she ran off – not that it would do any good, because the car was slap outside the house where anyone could see it that cared to look. I heard later that the police had been told to keep the arrest as quiet as possible, because it was all over the papers about Mr James being dead in suspicious circumstances. I suppose it was good of them, although their superiors might have reminded them to use the tradesmen's entrance while they were about it.

After the girl went off again, I just sat down for a moment to be by myself. I knew the police must have come for something important and you'd have thought my heart would be going nineteen to the dozen, but it wasn't. My hands were steady and when I got a sight of my face in the mirror it was set like a stone, so I knew I wouldn't give way, whatever happened. I went down and there were the policemen standing at the bottom of the front staircase. Four of them, three men and one woman, all in uniform except for one of the men. When I saw the woman policeman I thought: they've come to take Miss Georgina. Mind you, this woman, the way she was looking around, you'd have thought she was on a sixpenny tour of the house with a tea at the end. I stood at the top of the stairs and I said, 'My name is Pepper. I am the housekeeper. May I help you?'

The one without a uniform, I'd seen him before, his name was Mr Black and he was in charge. The others told me their names, too, but I don't recollect them. This Mr Black or Inspector Black or whatever his name was, he said, 'Is Mrs Gresham here? Mrs Georgina Gresham?'

'Mrs Gresham is asleep.'

'Please wake her up, Miss Pepper. I have a warrant for her arrest.' Even though I'd suspected it, when I heard those words everything about me went numb.

You might say it was funny, really, because then I said to him what policemen always say on the films: 'I think you had better come with me.'

I left them in my little room, all standing in a row with their dirty great feet on my nice blue rug. I shut the door tight and went into the kitchen and said to Mrs Seddon, 'I'm going up to wake Miss Georgina. If those coppers go snooping around, you send a girl up and let me know.' Then I went upstairs. I can't pretend my heart wasn't going then; in fact, I think I'd have gone over if I hadn't had hold of the banister. I took a tray for Miss Georgina because I thought I'd have to wake her up, but I found them both standing by the window in Master Edmund's room, looking down at the police car. I remember feeling surprised that Master Edmund was already dressed because it was so early. Miss Georgina was wearing a silk wrap. If they heard me come in, they never looked round. Their hands were resting together on the window-sill, hers over his – I could see the shine of her wedding ring in the sun.

For a minute I thought they didn't understand, they thought it was Master Edmund the police wanted, but then Miss Georgina said, 'Don't worry, Ada, I'll come down.' I thought: she's been expecting this.

When I went back downstairs, the police were sitting there, drinking tea as if they owned the place. I told them that Mrs Gresham was dressing and she'd be down when she was ready. Inspector Black was all for sending the policewoman up there, but I told him that wouldn't be necessary and he had enough decency not to press it. I noticed the woman looked disappointed. Hoping for a sniff around Miss Georgina's dressing-room, more than likely.

From the way Miss Georgina behaved, you'd have thought she was going to a garden party, not being charged with murder. She said to me, 'I want you to fetch me the black crêpe.' I knew the costume she meant, it was a Patou, very thin and floaty with a pale-pink sash for the waist and a ruffle at the shoulder, with a hat and gloves to match. It was beautiful, but it wasn't suitable for a dirty police station. I suppose she had an idea there'd be photographers – there is a snap, somewhere, of her going into the police station and she does look wonderful. If it wasn't for the fact of the woman policeman beside her, you'd have thought she was going to Buckingham Palace.

Poor Miss Jones was outside the door, crying her eyes out, but Miss Georgina made her do her hair three times over before she was satisfied. Then Miss Georgina got her hat adjusted how she liked it, and she turned round to me and she said, 'Do you remember your promise, Ada?' I thought of William when she said that, but I said yes all the same. Even though I wanted to be with William, I'd given Miss Georgina my word that I wouldn't leave her and when you give your word you can't go back from it.

Then Miss Georgina said to me, 'You can tell them I'm ready now. Just tell Mr Edmund to come in, will you, before you go?' When I left, she was puffing herself with perfume. Well, those policemen were fairly fidgeting about. Mr Black said they'd go and wait in the hall, and they barged straight past me without so much as a by-your-leave. I thought: Well, wherever you're going, I'm right behind, because I wasn't having him and his merry men cavorting all over the house. But they went right to the front doors and stood in front of them in a line. I looked at the woman and she looked like she was at the pictures waiting for the programme to start. I thought: She can't wait to get home and tell all the folks about this.

But when Miss Georgina came down it *was* like a film. Miss Georgina and Master Edmund came down the stairs together, arm in arm. I heard one of the policemen have a gasp, 'Aaaah . . .' like that. Miss Georgina put her hand out to Mr Black and said, 'Well, good-morning. Such an early hour!' I thought: Maybe they aren't allowed to do that, shake hands, because he didn't seem to want to take her hand, but then when Master Edmund put his hand out, Mr Black took it. The way Miss Georgina and Master Edmund greeted these policeman, they might have been a duke and duchess, and Mr Black looked so awkward, I'm sure he'd rather have died on the spot than say those criminal words to her that he had to say. I heard recently that he'd written a book about his time in the police, and all the famous murderers he'd arrested and so on. I don't know if he put Miss Georgina in the book – if he did, he more than likely painted himself to be the hero of the hour, but I was there and I can tell you he looked like a little boy that's been caught with a stolen apple up his jersey.

Miss Georgina said to them, 'Well, gentlemen, shall we go?' and after that Mr Black managed to say his little piece about arresting her for the suspicion of murdering Mr James and the rest of it. Then they took her away in the car. I stood on the steps and watched it go. Miss Georgina turned and waved. I thought it was for Master Edmund, because he'd been right behind me when we went down to the car, but when I turned round he was gone, so I suppose she must have been waving at me.

I wrote to William that night. I said I couldn't leave Miss Georgina in her trouble, however it fell out – which, of course, I didn't know when I wrote the letter, what was going to happen. I put that if things had turned out different I would have said 'yes' to him gladly and then I put that it would be for the best if we did not meet again. But what I put at the end – 'I love you and will think of you always' – I meant with all my heart.

I started writing that letter at ten o'clock that night and I didn't get finished until past three in the morning. It was only a little short thing and I dare say someone with education would have had it done in half the time, but it must be difficult even for a clever person to find the right words for a letter like that, and I hadn't written a letter since I used to send to Mother and Charlie in the old days. But I thought, it's not fair to keep William in the dark, I must finish this and get it sent.

I've still got the letter William wrote me in reply to mine. I keep it in my purse. Not with a ribbon or anything, but just folded up neatly. I should think it's a bit faded after twenty-odd years – I daren't open it up in case it comes apart. But I don't need to read it, I know it off by heart, what it says:

Dear Ada,

I agree it is for the best we do not meet again. It is not enough for me to be pals only with nothing more to hope. I love you more than I have ever loved any woman. There, now I've said it. Whatever happens you will always be in my heart. You are good, Ada, for your loyalty to Mrs Gresham and her brother as much as anything. Also because you forgave me for what I had done all those years ago when you didn't want it and you were a sport to say you would make a new start if this terrible thing had not happened. If ever things should change for you look me up because I swear I shall never marry any but you.

God bless you Ada.

William Ferguson

I would have been a good wife to him, I know I would.

EDMUND

Jimmy was supposed to be in Manchester. He'd booked a hotel room for the night, the police checked on that. Georgie would never have dared to do it if she'd known he was going to come back. Nobody knew Jimmy even had a key to the back door. Mrs Seddon said he'd told her not to bolt it in case Ada came back late. 'He'd gone out of his way to tell me not to,' was what she said in court. The front door was always bolted, of course, and Ada had gone to see her family . . . The business with the hotel room was odd, though. Because it was a small hotel, not his usual type of place at all. And he'd have worried about that, about the owner losing business because he didn't turn up. I wondered if he might have sent the hotel some money for the room, but they swore they hadn't received anything. That's what I can't understand, because it wasn't his way of doing things at all. It was a mystery how he'd got back as well, because Herbert didn't drive him and if he went on the train no one saw him, nor did any of the taxi drivers at the station. There was no question that he'd been to Manchester, because he'd attended a meeting there. None of the men he'd talked to thought there was anything odd in his behaviour and some of them were old acquaintances. Perhaps someone gave him a lift back to London – he could have driven himself, but if he'd borrowed a car that never came to light either.

It must have been one o'clock in the morning, half past, I don't know. I hadn't been long asleep, anyway. I was woken by the sound of Jimmy's footsteps in the corridor outside. When he opened the door of my bedroom I didn't see him as much as hear him, but I knew who was there. The room was pitch dark, then he opened the door and stood there in the light for just a second – a blink – I heard him breathe once, then he closed it again and the footsteps went away. I didn't move, didn't go after him, didn't beg him, forgive us, forgive *me* . . . I lay there for two hours and did not move one inch. And Georgie lay naked next to me, with the sheet thrown off and the skin on her back white like a pearl, fast asleep.

Georgie'd been difficult all day – she never said so, but she was missing Teddy, missing the things they did together. She mightn't have wanted him any more, but she was bored without him. She was so restless, I took her upstairs – we were in my bedroom, which was as usual, but then she wanted to stay. 'I don't *want* to go back to my room, Edmund.' Like a child. 'I want to stay here with you. Like we used to.' I told her she couldn't, but she wouldn't listen, told me she wanted me to read to her, so I did. *Blind Corner*, by Dornford Yates. I began to read and she went off to sleep almost immediately. I got out of the bed and into an armchair. I read until I'd finished the book and then I had nothing else to do, so I got back into the bed and tried to sleep, but I didn't do very well. I didn't like Georgie being there. I could never bear to be near her afterwards.

I tried to pretend I hadn't seen Jimmy, that he was part of a dream, but I knew he wasn't. My stomach was heaving and I wanted to get up and vomit, but I couldn't do it. I *couldn't move.* I couldn't even pull up the sheets to cover my head and that was what I wanted to do most of all – hide. Hide and never be seen again.

Would it have made a difference if we'd gone to Jimmy together, the two of us? I thought of that, us standing naked like Adam and Eve, with bare feet on the carpet while he stood in his hat and overcoat and looked at us. For some reason, I imagined he would tread on our feet and break them with his shoes, and that horrified me. I heard him go into the bathroom – not Georgie's, there was another one that he and I shared. I heard him vomit . . . That was a funny thing – Georgie's lawyer, Osbert Spencer, said to us, 'Don't mention *two* bathrooms, they'll think there's something wrong with you, all this washing and bathing. You must just call it *the* bathroom.' I didn't tell Spencer about hearing Jimmy in the bathroom, because I couldn't tell him why he was being ill. I said I'd heard nothing, seen nothing. At first I was all for telling him, but Georgie wouldn't hear of it and after a while I came to see it was too dangerous, too damning. She said, 'They'll never believe I didn't kill Jimmy if you tell the truth,' and she was right.

Jimmy stayed in the bathroom for a long time. I don't know if I nodded off or went into a trance, or what it was, but when I heard his feet in the corridor I sort of jumped back into myself and remembered what I was doing there, and what Georgie was doing. I heard Jimmy open the outer door and go on to the landing, and I didn't know where he'd gone to, but I thought: Now. I'll prepare myself now. I'll get dressed and work out what I must say to him. But I didn't do it. I lay on that bed and whimpered like a whipped child. I couldn't do it.

I was wondering if Jimmy had left the house, where he'd gone to and whether he'd come back. I suppose I thought he was going to come back because I was trying to prepare myself to talk to him, and eventually he did – I heard him go into his dressing-room and shut the door. It was getting light, so I got out of bed and stood by the window and smoked cigarettes. I didn't know if Georgie was shamming sleep, I thought perhaps she was, but I didn't go near her to find out. Afterwards, she said she wasn't and we had an argument, but I didn't really believe her until Spencer asked her about sleeping draughts and things, and it came out that she'd been taking three or four times the amount Dr Durrant had prescribed for her. Spencer asked her if she realised she was taking an abnormally high dose and she said, 'Well, it was a normal dose for me. I took it every night.' Old Durrant must have wondered why she kept asking for more, but he never was much of a doctor and in any case, Georgie had him wound round her little finger so tightly that he'd have given her a pipe of opium if she'd asked for it.

I suppose I guessed what Jimmy was doing. He must have gone into Georgie's bathroom to get the drugs, but I didn't hear him. That must have been because I was on the window side of the room, away from the door. But it was so quiet – the house, the garden, the road outside, everything was very quiet, very still. And Jimmy . . . Why didn't I try to stop him? Why didn't I talk to him, say that I'd leave, I'd go abroad, I'd never see either of them again, that it was my fault – say something, *anything*, to try to stop him. Haven't I thought about it every day since? But I don't know the answer, *I still don't know.* At the time, all I could think about was how none of it would have happened if I'd been allowed to die instead of Roland, because I went through life ruining it for other people, spoiling everything I touched . . . and while I was berating myself, there was a man dying in the next room and I had done nothing to prevent it.

Eventually, I heard a sort of thump, just one, coming from Jimmy's dressing-room. I thought Georgie must have heard that, because it was quite a loud crash – and after a few minutes I thought I'd better go and see what it was.

I think Jimmy was dead when I found him. I mean, I don't think there was any hope of getting him back. I suppose I didn't think too much about that, because if they'd brought him round and he'd become an imbecile or damaged himself in some way . . . one wouldn't want to live if one were in that sort of state, especially not a man like Jimmy. And that he *knew*, I suppose. About Georgie and me. Actually, there's no suppose about it. I couldn't get it out of my mind that he knew. It was in my mind every moment that I was in that room, waiting for something to happen. But it wasn't the whole thing – because I can't honestly say I was thinking about Georgie, either. There wasn't really any one thing; I wish I could say there was, then I might feel that I'd acted with some principle, not run around in a great sort of hare-brained panic, which was what I did.

Jimmy was lying on the floor in the middle of the room. I saw immediately that he must have been in the garden, because the bottoms of his trousers were wet and he had grass on his shoes. There was a table where he kept a tray with some whisky on it – he liked to drink whisky and water while he was getting dressed in the evening – and there was a decanter and a water jug . . . there was a note underneath the dressing-table and his pen. He must have fallen down while he was holding them. I think I went to him first, I looked at him or touched him or something, before I read the note.

It said, on the top of the paper, 'Edmund' and then:

I have always believed that I did my best when I had no advantage of birth or wealth, but it is not enough. I am at fault. I misjudged you because I considered you to be an honourable man and a gentleman, but you and she have broken every law of man and nature. I cannot bear to think of what you have done. If it were only Teddy Booth I could have excused it, but never this. I have taken 120 grains of Veronal. When I have completed this letter I shall take chloral hydrate to finish the job. I feel now as if I were a little drunk, but it is not unpleasant. I am not afraid. May God have mercy on you both.

He'd signed it with his full name, James Arthur Gresham. There was a postscript asking if I would see to some business – he'd given his word and wanted me to keep it. Then at the bottom he'd written: *There will be people who will say that I brought her to this, but what did I do to you?*

I put the note and the pen into the pocket of my dressing-gown and then I thought: Nobody must see the room like this, so I picked up the tray with the whisky and so on, and took it into the bathroom. There was a glass on it, a tumbler, which had some chalky stuff in it, like white powder. I thought that must be the Veronal, where it hadn't dissolved, so I rinsed it out and dried it with one of the towels, and then I rinsed and dried the water jug. I was bringing the tray back when I realised that it might look suspicious if anyone thought I had moved things about, so I took some gloves from the chest on the landing and put them on. I wasn't thinking very clearly. I don't know what I thought Dr Durrant would make of it, just that it was some awful mistake Jimmy had made, or that was what I hoped he'd think. I was worried that the servants would come and find Jimmy, and that they'd find me, and all sorts of things would be *thought*, and *said*, and . . . what appalled me most of all was the thought of anyone reading the note.

When I caught sight of Jimmy again, I felt that I couldn't bear to leave him lying on the floor – it seemed just such a – dreadful indignity, really, after everything that had gone before . . . so I tried to pick him up, but he was so heavy that I almost dropped him. That was something old Osbert Spencer made a great fuss about in court, because it was obvious that someone must have put Jimmy into the chair. I mean, I'd done my best but his clothing was rucked up from dragging him along the carpet, and Spencer kept arguing that Georgie couldn't have lifted Jimmy because he was so much larger that she wouldn't have been able to get him off the ground. Well, I *know* she couldn't, even if it was the insane strength of passion or the passionate strength of desperation or whatever the prosecution were trying to claim it was – Jimmy was six feet tall and he must have weighed sixteen stone at least; it was only because I knew there would be the most terrible crash if I dropped him that I managed to hang on to him at all. I bent over him and picked him up with my arms under his so that he was in a sort of sitting position with his back to me, resting against my knees. There was only one chair in Jimmy's dressing-room and I pulled him along backwards towards it with my arms clasped round his chest, which was jolly difficult, because he had a big, thick chest. Once I got him there I sort of wedged myself in between the chair and the wall, and tried to pull him up into it, but I couldn't reach properly, and Jimmy kept bumping against the chair and the chair kept bashing into my legs, and the shoulders of his jacket kept riding up round his ears and catching against the edge of the seat. In the end I stood in front of him and sort of hauled him up, so that he was sitting in the chair. I was bending over him, trying to adjust his clothing, when his head, *his entire head*, lolled towards me – it sort of swung and he looked straight at me. His eyeballs were so large and much rounder than when he was alive, like two eggs in waterglass . . . I wanted to close his eyes, but I didn't see how the lids could be made to fit over them . . . I couldn't bring myself to touch his eyes or his face. I tried to do it by shutting my own eyes, but standing so near him and not being able to see made it worse. Then, when I reached my hand towards where I thought his eyes were, his head moved again, it sort of bumped into my arm and I just had to stop – well, that was partly why I'd gone behind him to move him. I thought the chair might slide backwards and make marks on the wall, and somebody might guess . . . but more, well, not *more*, really the *reason* I did it – the point was that I didn't want to look into his face. I had sort of seen that his eyes were open when I bent down to him the first time, but he was half on his side, you see, and I couldn't see his face properly. I was worried that he would fall out of the chair, so I pulled it across the room and tried to wedge it under the dressing-table. The arms – the arms of the chair, that is – were too high to go underneath the table and I had to try to push the chair so that its arms were resting on the top of it. That was why the chair had to be tucked right underneath, so that his stomach could sort of hold him there – I thought he might slip down otherwise, but if his stomach was touching the edge of the table he'd be . . . well, he'd be safe.

I was getting my breath back when I noticed the cut flowers on the window-sill. Jimmy liked buttonholes, he wore one every day. He always went out and chose a flower for himself. He only ever picked one, but that day he'd taken five or six. As if he couldn't decide. Something about that did occur to me afterwards, when it was mentioned in court – that perhaps Jimmy went into the garden because he thought he'd seen something that couldn't be true, and he imagined that if he did something normal, something he did every day, he would come back to the house and find it wasn't so. But usually he picked only one flower, so the more he picked, the more he must have known that it *was* true, that there was no getting away from it. I suppose that sounds like one of those tin-pot psychologists, but it *is* easier to pretend, sometimes. Then you don't have to face up to whatever it is or have an argument about it, or do anything, really. I suppose I tucked the flower into Jimmy's buttonhole because I thought he would have wanted it.

I was about to open the door to leave Jimmy's room when I turned round – to make sure he was still there, I suppose. I could see the back of his head and shoulders in front of the leaded windows, with the lozenge shapes of glass and the first sunlight coming towards them, and as I was closing the door I suddenly caught sight of Jimmy's reflection in the glass, he seemed to be staring straight at me. When I went back to my room, and took off my dressing-gown and lay down again, I couldn't get his eyes out of my mind and I kept thinking: What if he moves, or slides down, or what if he isn't dead at all, what if he comes to? I suppose eventually I must have stirred or something, because Georgie turned over and opened her eyes, and said, 'What is it, Jimmy?'

I pushed her shoulder to awaken her. 'Wake up Georgie, wake *up*.'

'Oh, Jimmy, go away.'

'Jimmy's had an accident, Georgie.'

She just mumbled something, she wasn't properly conscious.

'Jimmy's dead, Georgie.'

'Manchester, not dead.'

I kept repeating this, shaking her, but she couldn't seem to wake up properly. After a while I started to understand what she was saying, but it was stupid things about thinking people were dead when they were really in Manchester. Well, then I lost my head – I shook her, I slapped her, I even threw a glass of water at her. She was actually quite groggy, but at the time I just thought she was being difficult, so I kept on and on until she sat up and started trying to fight me off.

'Jimmy really is dead, Georgie. We have to do something.'

'Did you try talking to him?'

I said, 'Well of course I did,' even though I hadn't, because there wasn't any need, but I suddenly realised that the servants would soon come up and I was desperate to put Georgie in the picture and get it all straightened out.

She kept saying, 'Oh, he can't be.'

So in the end I said, 'I'll show you.' She didn't want to come and see, and I had quite a struggle to make her, but in the end I got her out into the hall. There was a long time when we were both standing outside Jimmy's dressing-room door, arguing in whispers.

'This is completely absurd. He isn't even in the house.'

'He's in there!'

'He's in *Manchester*, Edmund.'

'Georgie, this isn't a game.'

'No, it's ridiculous.'

'Well, if it's so ridiculous, what are you afraid of? Why don't you just open the door?'

'I'm not afraid. I just don't want to. Stop shouting at me, Edmund. I want to go back to bed.'

'I'm not shouting. You're damn well going to open that door.'

She wouldn't, so in the end I grabbed hold of her hand and put it on the doorknob and turned it with my hand over hers. That hurt her and she gave a little scream, more of a yelp, really, and then I gave her a push and we both sort of collapsed into the room. The mind plays queer tricks and, for some reason, I expected Jimmy to be *facing* us in the chair, with the eyes wide open and the arms and legs strapped to the chair like an American execution. I said to Georgie, 'Whatever you do, don't touch anything.'

She was standing in the centre of the room, behind Jimmy. She was quite still, I mean she didn't go forward to him or touch him or anything, she just looked at the back of his head and then she said, 'He *is* dead, isn't he?'

'Yes. I think it was your sleeping medicine.'

She didn't ask me how I knew or anything; she just said, 'Let's get out of here.'

When we were back in my room, she said, 'He found out, didn't he?'

'Yes.' I showed her Jimmy's note.

'Burn it.'

'Do you think we should?' I don't know why I said that. Of course I knew we had to get rid of it immediately, but I just couldn't think straight.

'Burn it! Or do you want to show it to old Durrant?'

I said, 'It doesn't say your name.'

'For God's sake, Edmund, it doesn't need to. Who else could it be? Elspeth? Durrant will take one look at this and go straight to the police. Do you think that's what Jimmy wanted? For everyone to know? You idiot, do you think he'd want everyone to know why he killed himself?'

I said to her, 'Don't speak to me like that, don't call me an idiot,' but she just snatched Jimmy's letter out of my hand.

My cigarette lighter was on the mantelpiece and she picked it up and set fire to the paper. Then she said, 'Where are the medicine bottles?' When I said I hadn't seen any bottles in Jimmy's dressing-room, she said, 'Try the bloody bathroom, then.' I'd never heard her swear before and I was shocked. Not so much that she knew the word, because anyone can overhear a bad word, but that she used it with such familiarity, as if she'd said it before, or thought it. But at the same time I was quite ... well, quite *relieved*, if you want to know the truth, that she was taking over the situation. Acting like an older sister, not a younger one. When I didn't move, she went out to her own bathroom and came back with two empty medicine bottles and one of the little boxes they used for the Veronal powders. I hadn't seen them because I'd used the other bathroom when I rinsed the jug and glass. She said, 'I'm going to take these into my room and throw them into the wastepaper basket under my dressing-table.' The police found them later and of course they had Jimmy's fingerprints on them as well as Georgie's, and that caused another great fuss at the trial because we'd forgotten about the Veronal papers – the chemist wrapped up a certain amount of powder in a little paper and that was one dose – and they were still in the wastepaper basket in the other bathroom. I suppose I must have seen them when I'd rinsed the glass and jug, but it hadn't occurred to me that they were important. Osbert Spencer suggested that Jimmy had taken the powders and the sleeping draught in the bathroom and then gone into Georgie's bedroom and put the empty bottles and the box into her wastepaper basket, and she didn't hear him because of the sleeping powder *she'd* taken. Anyway, Spencer was delighted with the effect it produced, because it put the other chap in a corner and he tried to argue that Georgie knew that Jimmy'd taken the powders and didn't do anything about it, but the judge told him that it was a disgraceful and unchristian suggestion, or something like that, and of course that put them off the whole thing.

The newspapers had a field day when Georgina said she thought Jimmy'd taken the stuff by mistake. The humorists made a great thing out of the narcotics, jokes about how to have a perfectly harmonious marriage by being asleep all the time. But Georgie had a difficult time over the chloral hydrate, because even in the peppermint syrup she took, it still tastes pretty frightful, and nobody would swallow it of their own accord unless they absolutely had to, so it would be practically impossible to make a mistake. Even Georgie agreed about the taste and she was used to it. Then the prosecution lawyer, Anthony Keeble-Price, suggested to Georgie that she'd told Jimmy the syrup of chloral was some sort of tonic and that was how she'd got him to drink it, but before Georgie could deny it the judge jumped in and pretty well ordered him to shut up.

After Georgie'd thrown the bottles into the wastepaper basket, she said, 'Are we going to leave Jimmy for the servants to find?' I didn't know what to answer. I couldn't think what to do at all. Georgie kept glancing at the clock and saying, 'It's either you or the maids, Edmund.'

I said, 'What about you, why can't you be the one to find him?'

'Don't be stupid, Edmund.'

'He's your husband, Georgie, not mine.'

She said, 'That's why I can't be anywhere near when he's found, you fool!' Well, I didn't like that, calling me a fool, especially when she'd called me an idiot a few moments before, so I came back at her, and back and forth we went until I suddenly thought, my God, we're bickering like a pair of brats. I couldn't stop my hands shaking. I kept lighting cigarettes, thinking that would do the trick, but it didn't help. In the end I said I'd be the one to find Jimmy because it wouldn't fair to the maids.

Georgie said, 'I'll take another powder.' She meant the Veronal, because she had them hidden everywhere, like a squirrel with nuts. She said, 'Take one of my powders and pour it down the sink, and then leave the paper by your bed, then you can pretend that you took it. Say you couldn't sleep. You'll have to call Durrant and he might ask if you heard anything. You can tell him you had your old trouble and took something for it.' She meant from the war, because Durrant knew about that. I felt rotten lying about it, to Durrant and to the police. Small lies are always worse, I don't know why. Straining at a gnat and swallowing a camel, I suppose.

Georgie rearranged the bedclothes to look as if I had been sleeping on my own and went off to her room. I put the gloves back in the chest of drawers, then I got dressed and waited on the landing until the maid came down. The moment she saw me she knew there was something up and I told her not to let anyone go into any of our rooms until I'd spoken to the doctor. That was all I said. Then I telephoned Durrant and told him there'd been an accident. I was dreading talking to him, but it was far easier than I'd imagined. I told him I'd found Jimmy just before I telephoned. When he asked me about Georgie, I told him she was still asleep and that I hadn't liked to waken her in case I was wrong about Jimmy. Actually, that was rather a mistake. If Georgie had been there, awake, and if Durrant had seen her crying and all the rest of it, I'm sure he would have signed the death certificate without a second thought.

Durrant asked me if he could look in on Georgie – this was before he'd seen Jimmy's body – and I thought it was a bit queer, but I could hardly stop him. He trotted off to her room and when he came back he said it was best to leave her to sleep. If I'd been thinking straight, I'd have been surprised that Durrant wasn't more worried about Georgie, that *she* hadn't taken an overdose as well, but it came out at the trial that he'd just been handing out these powders and things to all his patients as if they were cigarettes, with only the vaguest idea of their strength. He retired after the trial – I think they pretty well told him he had to, but he must have been nearly seventy, so I don't suppose it was such a terrible blow. I'd thought he'd just put 'heart failure' or something on the certificate and that would be the end of it, but he refused to sign the wretched thing. He kept saying it was a long time since he'd attended Jimmy and asking about symptoms and all sorts of things, and I didn't have any answers for him. I tried to hint to him about suicide, thinking he'd be bound to do the decent thing and not report it, but that put him into a great pother and he insisted I telephone the police, otherwise he said he'd have to fetch them himself. He kept saying he had Georgie's reputation as well as his own to think of, and talking about scandal and the letter of the law – I should think he must have wished he'd just signed and shut up when he got into court and the lawyers tore him to pieces, but of course he didn't know it would go that far. None of us did.

Two policemen arrived and Durrant bustled downstairs and told them that Georgie was asleep and they must wait in the drawing-room. They had a perfectly ridiculous conversation – I wouldn't have believed it if I hadn't heard it myself and I think if I'd been in less of a state of shock I would have laughed. After all, Durrant had made all this song and dance about calling the police, and now he was telling them they couldn't see the body.

'We must see this gentleman, Sir, if he is deceased. You mentioned someone asleep, Sir, who might that be?'

'Mrs Gresham, the deceased's wife.' This was Durrant.

'Well, hadn't she better be told, Sir?'

'No, I don't want her disturbed.'

'Would this be on medical grounds, Sir?'

'I don't want her upset.'

'Well, Sir, she'll have to know sooner or later.'

And that started Durrant off on 'Allow me to be the best judge of that' and there was no stopping him.

The policemen obviously thought he was quite mad. One of them took me aside and said, 'Is there somebody deceased in the house, Sir, or not?'

'Oh, yes, upstairs, just as the doctor says.'

'We'll have to see for ourselves, Sir, if you don't mind.'

I thought Durrant was going to try to stop them going up the stairs by physical force, but he must have thought better of it.

Georgie stayed in her room while the policemen were upstairs. They told me that there would have to be a post-mortem examination and arranged for Jimmy's body to be taken away. They collected up quite a lot of things from Jimmy's study and the dressing-room, and took them. When I saw them examining the dressing-room, I suddenly realised that the doorknob had Georgie's finger-marks all over it. The prosecution lawyer, Anthony Keeble-Price, suggested she'd forgotten to wipe them off, because of course there was all this other palaver about the whisky. They couldn't understand why the decanter was empty, you see, because they analysed the contents of Jimmy's stomach and there wasn't any alcohol in it, or in the vomit, and one of the maids had said that she'd filled up the decanter during the day, so they assumed that someone must have drunk it. Keeble-Price said Georgie'd been in Jimmy's dressing-room with him, and *she'd* drunk the whisky and then washed the glass and the tray and everything so that no one would know. It never occurred to him that someone might be mad enough to pour good Scotch down the sink, but of course that was my own stupid fault. Actually, Old Spencer gave me quite a laugh with that point – he told the court that Georgie's fingerprints were bound to be on the dressing-room door, because 'those of you who rejoice in a felicitous state of matrimony will allow it quite natural for a wife to enter her husband's dressing-room at such times when his valet is not present'. Priceless! Knocked the jury completely for six – you could tell they didn't have the first clue what he was talking about.

The police managed to get rid of Dr Durrant in the end, and they went back to the drawing-room and sat there until Georgie came down. It was quite a wait they had, too: over an hour before she appeared. Durrant had left something for Georgie to take to pep her up a bit – Lord knows what it was, but it certainly made her eyes shine; she was fidgeting about in her chair and chattering away to these policemen as if she'd known them all her life. She wasn't herself at all, although they weren't to know that, and I think her behaviour made them suspicious, because she didn't seem in the least upset about Jimmy.

The week before Georgie's arrest was dreadful. I didn't know what to say to people in the office. I couldn't even tell them about the funeral, because the police wouldn't let us have Jimmy's body. Georgie and I knew very well what the results of the post-mortem would be, but I think we were still hoping for a miracle – that they'd find he'd had a heart attack or something. But there wasn't any doubt about it: apparently, choral hydrate has a very particular smell even when it's inside the stomach, and you can't mistake it for anything else. I don't know if it was Durrant's pep pills, but Georgie was very strange during that time. She wasn't behaving like a mad person, not talking to herself or anything, but she insisted on having every single newspaper delivered and she spent the whole day lying on her bed, looking for anything about James and cutting it out with her nail scissors. If she found a newspaper that hadn't run anything, she would tell Jones to return it to the shop and ask for the money back. When I came home in the evening she'd read me the cuttings, but it was as if she were reading a society column, not something about a man she'd been married to for nearly twenty years.

The servants brought up food on trays, but Georgie never ate it. I'd tell her to eat, but she wouldn't even pick up her knife and fork. She'd say, 'Oh, no, darling, I'll have a cigarette instead.' She'd never been particularly interested in smoking, but she'd take a cigarette from the box and I'd light it for her, and then she'd put it out almost immediately and ask for another five minutes later. I think she almost didn't care about what was going to happen, as long as she could lounge on the bed in her pyjamas, with newspapers spread out all over the room, clothes draped everywhere, sherry glasses, ashtrays, chaos – she was in her element. I begged her to let Jones in, or at least Ada, to tidy up the place, but she absolutely refused. She wouldn't even speak to them.

I asked Georgie at one point, 'Did you love Jimmy?'

She wouldn't give me a proper answer. 'Don't be boring, Edmund.'

I wasn't sure what to take from that, so I said, 'Why did you marry him?'

She laughed and said, 'Well, I couldn't marry you, could I?'

The night before the police came, she said, 'Can I come to your room, Edmund? It doesn't make any difference now.'

We both knew it must only be a matter of one or two days, so I said, 'Suppose they find us together?'

'Don't worry, darling, I'll be awake before they come.' So I let her. I don't think we slept much, just sat together and held hands.

It's very strange, how things happen. When they came and took her away, they said I wasn't allowed to see her until the following day and I just didn't know what to do. It should have been the worst day of my life and in a way it was, during the daylight hours, anyway. But in the evening something quite wonderful happened. I was in the dining-room – I'd fairly well given up eating and was smoking myself silly instead, when the door opened and in walked Louisa. We'd had the most terrible rain storm and she was soaking wet, but she looked absolutely beautiful. She said, 'I wouldn't let Ada tell you I'd arrived. I thought you wouldn't see me if you knew.' Well, I couldn't think of anything to say – I mean, there were all sorts of things I wanted to say. I wanted to take her in my arms and kiss her, but of course I couldn't do it so I put my jacket round her shoulders, and there she was, patting her hair with a towel, and she just looked up at me. She didn't speak, but her hair had gone into wisps where she was rubbing it dry and I suddenly stopped thinking about Georgie and the whole, awful *shambles* of it, and all I could think of was what a miracle it was she was there.

I said, 'Does Davy know you're here?'

She said, 'Davy's in Scotland. Nobody knows where I am except you.'

We went through into the drawing-room, and she kicked off her shoes and sat on one of the sofas and drank brandy. 'Edmund, I don't know what to say. What a dreadful mistake. I'm sure it can be sorted out, but how dreadful for Georgie . . .' Then she caught my eye and said, 'It *is* a mistake, isn't it?'

'Yes, I don't understand why it's happened.'

'I suppose the police have to accuse somebody in cases like this. People always want someone to be guilty, don't they? They can't seem to believe that accidents can happen . . . I'm glad I don't think like that, aren't you?'

'I suppose so. Louisa, may I ask you something?'

'Anything you like. You might be disappointed if you want next year's Derby winner, though.'

'Would you talk to me about Freddie?'

'Your brother Freddie?'

'I'm beginning to think I've just imagined having a brother, because nobody ever mentions him.'

I thought Louisa was going to change the subject, but she said, 'We used to call him Georgie's shadow. He was always following her around, repeating things she said.'

'I don't remember that . . . Louisa, what happened on the day he died?'

'Well, my father told us that one of the servants had killed him, a young girl. He said she was insane. I remember thinking that it must have been the girl who took us to see Freddie, because she was shouting and spitting and obviously quite mad. She came up to us and grabbed Georgie and dragged her away. We all followed, and she went round a corner and there was poor Freddie lying on the grass, face down. I didn't see properly. I saw some blood and then I couldn't bring myself to look after that. I was looking at Georgie's face all the time, because I didn't want to look at Freddie, and she never took her eyes off him. She just stared, she didn't even blink. She must have had the most dreadful nightmares.'

'Did you have nightmares?'

'Yes, a bit. We'd been playing hide-and-seek, and I used to dream about going to look for Freddie, and knowing I had to find him quickly before something terrible happened, and then finding him behind the hedge. I got over it, though. Children do. They forget things. Roland and I never talked about it. Father told us that we shouldn't and I don't think it occurred to either of us that we *could* talk about it, really.'

'But we're talking about it now, aren't we?'

'Yes, I suppose we are. You know, Edmund, I've often wondered – as an adult, I mean, not when I was a child – whether your father didn't blame Georgie for Freddie's death.'

'For causing it, do you mean?'

'No, not for that, but for not . . . looking after him. Making sure he stayed with us.'

'He can't have done. That was Nurse's job, not Georgie's.'

'I just thought perhaps your father said something to her and she rather took it to heart. After all, she was only eight years old.'

'Did Georgie tell you this?'

'Of course not! Would you tell something like that, if it were you?'

'Well, I might tell you, because I trust you.'

'Yes, but Georgie doesn't trust me. I don't think she trusts anybody, does she? Edmund, I'm just *guessing* and it's probably all nonsense, but didn't you ever think there must have been some particular reason for her and your father to be at loggerheads? Those things don't happen by accident. Georgie and your father, they were each as bad as the other. The type that gets an idea into his or her head and won't let go of it, and when they come up against anything that refutes that idea they just pretend it doesn't exist. Remember, Georgie was awfully isolated and if one has too much time to think about these sorts of things, one gets dreadfully sensitive and morbid.'

Then I asked her what I'd asked Georgie: 'Why did you marry Davy?'

It was rather funny, because she gave me almost the same answer. 'Well, you didn't ask me, did you?' At first I thought she must be making a joke, so I started laughing, but then I saw that she wasn't laughing, so I stopped. She said, 'I always hoped you might, but I could never quite believe that you would.'

'Why not?'

'Because you and Georgie seemed so glamorous to me, but so sort of . . . rare, like orchids or something, that you can't bring out into the open in case they die. I always felt so ordinary, I couldn't imagine why on earth you'd want to marry me.'

'If I'd asked you, would you have accepted?'

'Yes.'

We were like two statues, she standing and I sitting. I couldn't look at her and I had the feeling she wasn't looking at me either. Then she said, 'When Davy and I were married, I didn't love him in the way I loved you. But I knew I could love him and I thought: I'll do my best to make Davy happy – to make it a good marriage – and that's what I did.'

'Are you glad you married Davy?'

For minute, I thought she wasn't going to answer, that she was angry with me, but she said, 'Yes, we've been very happy.' Then she looked down at her feet and said, 'I still love you, Edmund.'

'And I love you.'

When I looked at her the look on her face was so like Roland's that I wanted to weep. I didn't, but I think I must have put my head in my hands, because Louisa sat down beside me and put her arm round my shoulder. 'Darling Edmund,' she said. 'I said I'd tell you anything and I have. But you do understand, don't you? We've got to be just the same, as if this conversation had never happened, and never talk about it, and perhaps, after a while, we'll start to believe that we imagined the whole thing.' I wonder if she does believe that, because she's never mentioned any of this again and neither have I. Perhaps she thinks I've forgotten it, but I've wanted to remind her of it many, many times. We did talk about Freddie and the other things, and the words she said . . . she can't pretend it didn't happen, because it did, it *did*. She said she loved me and I'll never forget that.

I remember that she stroked my forehead. I must have fallen asleep on the sofa, because when I woke up I was covered in a blanket and she was gone.

GEORGINA

Being arrested was the most peculiar sensation. The policemen were so wooden I felt that somebody had to keep up the conversation or we'd all petrify like a forest, but it was very difficult. I remember noticing some apparatus on one of the uniforms, a whistle of some sort, and saying, 'I expect that comes in useful, doesn't it?' We were all bouncing about in that ridiculous car and me doing all the talking. They just sat and stared at their big blue knees. I remember thinking to myself, what *can* I talk about, because after all, one didn't have very much in common with policemen, and then I remembered the cartoons in *Punch* about cooks and policemen, how they supposed that cooks were keen on policemen and always asking them in for cups of tea. It's probably all nonsense, but I suddenly thought: Wouldn't it be jolly for Ada to have a nice policeman to come to her kitchen once in a while – well, the 'no followers' rule was meant for the young ones, to stop them running off and getting married every five minutes, but hardly Ada – so I said to the policeman beside me, 'Did you see Ada? She's my housekeeper.' I made a great thing of how well she looked after us. I even told him she was a good cook – may God forgive me – but he didn't bother to answer. I wasn't expecting him to say 'Barkiss is willin', but the stupid man just sat there like a lump.

I had the impression that nobody quite knew what to do with me at the police station and after a lot of dithering they sat me down in a nasty little room with the lady policeman, at least I suppose that's what she was – I had no idea such things existed until I met her. I tried to talk to her, but she was no better than the men. It's a funny sort of job for a woman to have, but perhaps she couldn't get a husband. Not surprising if she showed as little spark as she did with me; after all, men do like to know that one is conscious – for the purposes of conversation, if nothing else. Except Jimmy. I think I unnerved him when I was awake. Still, I thought the police-lady might have married a policeman. They could have had a police dog to take for walks and drive about with a police horse, and the whole affair would be a glorious parade of blue serge and silver mountings, splendid for the baby's pram. Then Mr and Mrs Policeman could sit together in the evening, side by side with their big feet in mustard baths, and the dog as well, all four feet. And it seemed so funny, the idea of the three of them in a line like that, that I started laughing, and the wretched woman said 'there, there' and insisted I drink a cup of her horrid tea. But she wasn't too bad, I suppose, apart from the fact that no woman prepared to wear that hideous uniform could have one iota of dress sense.

Like the wardress at the prison. We used to play card games; simple ones like gin rummy mostly. She didn't know anything worth playing and of course there was no money involved. I always won. I cheated. I think she spotted it, but she didn't say anything – perhaps she thought she was keeping me happy. Which I suppose she was, in a way. Playing cards with her was certainly better than talking to all those bloody lawyers. Trying to trip you up all the time – I used to say to them, 'You're supposed to be on my side.' Questions, questions, round and round in circles, never satisfied ... they pretend to be concerned with the truth, but it's all impertinence. My lawyer was a good one, though. He said to me, 'Whatever happens, you must deny any relationship with Mr Booth. If you admit to that you'll be as good as telling them you killed your husband.' He meant that the jury were people with sordid minds. Which was quite true, I could tell that just by looking at them. I've seen the same expression often enough, usually on Ada's face. More and more, recently. Ada can't help having a sordid mind and of course it's much worse now she's old. Being a spinster naturally doesn't help. Ada is exactly the kind of person who would believe that a woman who'd committed adultery was automatically a murderess. In fact, that's probably exactly what she *does* believe.

Really, I do resent Ada, even when she's out of sight downstairs she still manages to come *broadsiding* into one's thoughts. But it was lovely to see Teddy again, although, frankly, one could have wished for happier circumstances. When I saw him in the witness box, I wanted to rush over and kiss him. Of course he was *magnificent*, a perfect gentleman. I knew he would be. No gentleman would mention a lady's name in public the way they wanted Teddy to – and clearly the judge understood that. Well, it wasn't as if Teddy had been having an affair with some little shop-girl. I used to look at his hands when he was in the witness box and remember him touching me, and then I wouldn't have to listen to all the stupid questions they kept asking . . . Teddy used to bend over me with his lips puckered like a child's and his eyes tight shut and say 'kissy?'. He always had very sweet breath, in spite of his cigars. I suppose it was all the champagne he drank. Dear Teddy. Nice to think of him in heaven, if there is such a place. Teddy's heaven would be unlimited bubbles, racing cars and lots of gorgeous tarts with no diseases afterwards, and he deserves every moment of it.

But it was a wretched business, the whole thing. I've forgotten most of the details, but I will say this: I have never believed *for one single moment* that I did anything wrong. And

I never believed that I had anything to hide, either, except that society said I did. It has always angered me that I have had to hide my true emotions because of narrow-minded people who don't know what love is. They made me conceal my feelings for Edmund as if I were a criminal, a sexual pervert. But I'm not. Because *I* know. I know what love is.

EDMUND

It was a delight to know that one was loved in return, but dreadful, too, was the regret that I could have been married to Louisa for so many years if only I had asked. But one can't let oneself dwell on that sort of thing, or rather, one tries not to. At first, I was in a turmoil, I couldn't think of anything else but Louisa, even Georgie and the trial. But then there came a certain acceptance and that was rather a relief, in a way. Because you can't keep on thinking and wishing ... Davy Kellway died last year and I suppose anyone would think 'Why not?'. But he was a good, decent man and Louisa was his wife for years and years. One can't just go elbowing one's way in; too much like dancing on the poor fellow's grave. That's not to say that I wouldn't very much like ... but it's too late, far too late. What use would I be to her now?

I did consider condemning myself to save Georgie – that was all to do with Louisa, I think, a sort of feeling of heroism came over me – but I could never work out how to go about it. There was a great muddle in my head about what would happen if I confessed, because then Louisa would believe that I really had killed Jimmy and I couldn't work out how I could possibly explain it all without the police thinking I was quite mad ... These things would occupy my mind for hours and hours, but it was ridiculous. If I'd told the truth I would have simply dragged Georgie down with me and made the whole thing far worse for everybody. Because then Louisa would have had to know the real truth. In the end, it always came down to the fact that I couldn't bear her to fund out – because then there would never be any hope at all.

Georgie'd been so calm when Jimmy died, burning the note and all the rest of it, but when she was being held before the trial she just seemed to go haywire. I don't suppose for a moment that being in prison was a pleasant experience – you'd think that anyone in Georgie's situation would be doing their damnedest to get themselves *out*, wouldn't you? But she was behaving as if she couldn't wait to get the rope around her neck. She drove her lawyers mad – never told the same story two days running. She'd say something, then contradict it and they'd say, 'But you've just signed a statement saying this other thing,' and she'd say, 'Well, you can tear it up, can't you?' I couldn't get any sense out of her either.

She's always had little pet words and phrases, saying things backwards, making anagrams and that sort of thing, and she likes to use them in our conversation. It's never bothered me, but while she was in prison she did it all the time, almost as if she was speaking a foreign language. It was very frustrating, because very often one simply could not grasp what she was saying. I thought: surely she must *want* me to understand, but she wouldn't make herself clear. A couple of times when I saw her, Mr Gannon, her solicitor, was present, and she kept leaning over and whispering into my ear, all of it gibberish. I suppose it was better than saying it aloud, but she treated Gannon as though he were the gamekeeper or something – when she wasn't ignoring him altogether. It did cross my mind several times that she might be going dotty. One day I asked her: 'All these words you keep saying to me, what do they mean?' and she said, 'Whatever I want them to.' I think that Gannon and Spencer thought she was dotty as well, because they kept telling her that she mustn't go into the witness box.

They asked me to persuade her, but she said, 'Nonsense, I'll just *tell* them.'

'That's all very well,' I said to her. 'But *what* are you going to tell them?'

'Let's see . . . well, Your Honour, I was lying in bed with my brother Edmund, doing the most unspeakable things, which Your Honour would never countenance in a month of Sundays . . .'

'For God's sake, keep your voice down. You've got to get your story straight.'

'You needn't worry, Edmund, I'll keep you out of it.'

'Georgie, they could hang you. Is that what you want?'

'No, of course it isn't. Now do shut up, you're being very tiresome.'

She kept insisting she would speak in court and in the end they had to let her. Which was just as well, as it turned out, because the judge was very taken with her. But I could quite understand why they thought it would be a disaster if she gave evidence. She'd christened the two of them Gammon and Spinach and she used to sing *With a roly, poly, gammon and spinach* . . . in front of them, quite loudly. I must say she really did sound mad when she sang, because she's dreadfully cracked and she can never hit the right note.

A lot of Spencer's work in court was straightforward bullying and I was amazed that the judge let him get away with some of it, to be honest. Chambermaids, barmen, that sort of person, they don't have much education and old Spencer had them all running round in circles in no time. With some of the younger men they would put on a certain air – my father would have called it 'Jack's as good as his master' – but it soon came off when the questions started flying. There was one poor little thing, a waitress, I think, from one of the big sea-front hotels, and she said, 'Oh, Sir, won't you stop asking questions? I don't know whether I'm coming or going!' That caused a great laugh and I think it was even reported by some of the newspapers. But old Spencer had pretty much told me – well, he *did* tell me – that if the adultery could be proved, Georgie would hang. Because that was the thinking, you see. Natural enough, I suppose. But it was queer, because the judge didn't seem to want to believe it either – I mean, the other side put forward all these people from hotels and restaurants saying they'd seen Georgie and Booth together, and common sense would tell you that they couldn't all be short-sighted or mistaken. Spencer made it appear as if they were, of course, and I don't know anything about the law, but it looked to me as if the judge was doing his best to help.

When I came into the court to say my piece I was as nervous as the devil, but I got along easily enough. Felt a bit of a fool when the judge offered me a chair – I told him I was perfectly fine to stand, but it made him fuss worse than ever, somehow. I heard afterwards that he wasn't in the war – flat feet or something – and he'd developed a neurosis about it: that he wasn't as good as the chaps who were, that sort of thing. They called Louisa as a witness too, but I didn't hear her. I hadn't seen her since that night, you see, and I didn't want the first time to be when she was stuck up there answering questions in front of all those people. Because there were queues every day for the seats, people fighting to get into the court, men from the press everywhere . . . I even heard a rumour that somebody was taking in a camera, hidden in his hat or coat, and he was going to make a fortune selling the pictures to the newspapers. Never saw any pictures, though, but that was a typical thing to hear because everyone was in such a ferment about it.

I met Louisa after she'd given her evidence and we went and sat in a tea-shop somewhere. She was very indignant about the questions they'd put to her; she really thought it was a terrible injustice that all these intimate questions should be asked. I remember she said, 'Why do people make up these dreadful stories, Edmund? They kept asking me if Georgina was having an affair with Edward Booth – if I'd seen anything, heard anything. How can people be allowed to say these things?' Louisa was so *blazing* about it, so angry for Georgie, that she was being accused of something despicable – I felt too ashamed to tell her it was true. Then she saw something on my face, there must have been some sign . . . I couldn't help it. Not enough of the old whitewash on the wall, I suppose. I knew I'd let the cat out of the bag because she suddenly stopped and said in quite a different voice, 'I know I'm lucky to have such a happy marriage, Edmund.' She said it so gently. She was telling me she knew. Then she said, 'But it makes no difference.'

'Her lawyer thinks she'll be found guilty if she admits the adultery. He thinks the jury won't make a distinction.'

'Yes. Yes, I can see that.' Then she said, 'Perhaps this is cowardice, Edmund, but I'm glad you didn't tell me beforehand. I shouldn't have liked to commit perjury.'

When it was all over, Louisa found a place far from London where Georgie could slip away until the fuss had died down. Georgie went there almost as soon as the trial finished and I followed a few days later. I was – well, I suppose you could say I felt relieved, but there was an unpleasant feeling that one had got away with it, somehow. I can't pretend otherwise. 'Thou shalt not get caught' – people always say that's the eleventh commandment, don't they? But no matter how much I told myself that Georgie was innocent, or that I was innocent, underneath it came a feeling one couldn't shift: that we weren't and somehow all those people in the court knew it.

When Georgie came out after the verdict, they were so angry that I thought they would force their way past the policemen and tear the three of us – Georgie, Louisa and me – to pieces. There must have been men there, but it's only the women I remember. Clawing like harpies, shouting 'Bitch!' and 'Murderess!'. Louisa was standing in the middle of it all, holding Georgie's arm and helping her into the car with Spencer. I was just behind them. I lost my footing getting in and one of the women grabbed my sleeve. I saw her face only for a moment – the top set of her false teeth was hanging loose from the gums and her hat had slipped down over one eye – then the policeman picked me up and helped me into the car with the others and we sat there, pinned together in the back seat, and nobody said anything while the driver nudged his way through the crowd ... And I thought: *They know.* Somehow, they know.

It wasn't over, that was the trouble. It wasn't finished. Jimmy deserved better than a lot of lies. Those people didn't know him, but they knew that what had been done wasn't justice. The day before I left for Suffolk I went into Jimmy's old club to fetch some letters and one or two bits and pieces, and while I was there I ran into Teddy Booth. It was in the lobby and I was standing in such a position that I saw him before he saw me. He was turning over some letters on the porter's desk, and when he heard me call out he raised his head and looked round to see who it was. When he saw me, his face – his expression – completely changed. He governed it almost immediately, but although he was civil enough when he spoke, it was that depth of revulsion – because that's what it was, absolute revulsion – and I knew that he knew about us.

I thanked him for what he'd said in court and he muttered something in reply. He may have asked me how I was or how Georgie was, I don't remember. I could see there was no point in pretence so I said, 'What will you do?'

'Nothing.'

'Will you tell anyone?'

'No. That won't help Jimmy, poor bastard.'

I felt as though I'd been drenched with ice water. I tried to speak, I didn't know what I was saying, nonsense probably, but he cut me off. He grabbed my arm and took me outside. At first I hardly heard him, he was spitting the words out so fast. 'Jimmy wrote me a letter. The week before. Oh, you needn't worry on that score, Lomax, I've burned it. He told me he had a suspicion, he didn't know what would happen, but he had to find out if it were true. He asked me to protect Georgie, said he wanted me to know he didn't hold me at fault. But I'll tell you something, Edmund, something for nothing. Jimmy didn't have to blame me – I blame myself.' I wanted to say something, not to defend myself – how could I do that? I think I tried to thank him again, but he said, 'That's enough.' He let go of my arm and went back into the club.

I went up to Suffolk the next day – I hadn't got the letters, so I'd wired to have them sent on. I couldn't get Booth's words out of my mind. I wasn't worried that he would tell anybody what he knew, because I was sure he wouldn't. It was the experience of seeing ourselves through his eyes that was so dreadful. Every time I thought of his face I almost vomited. Because that brought it home to me: whatever happened between Georgie and Teddy Booth, he was a good, decent man and I knew that to everyone like him, to *Louisa*, what we'd done had made us outcasts.

Louisa had found us a good big house in Suffolk and hired a couple of the local women to do for us. The garden was a long stretch of land overlooking an estuary. No boats, because it was too choked with reeds. It was next door to a rather beautiful little church – whitewashed walls, timber beams, very simple, but quiet, with a churchyard full of flowers. I used to go and sit on a bench in there when there wasn't a service. You could see right across the estuary – barely a house or barn in sight, nothing but miles and miles of water and reeds. I spent a lot of time sitting there. I used to try to pretend that Louisa was with me in the house, that she was going to come out and sit down next to me, just as if she'd been there all the time. If I could pretend that, I could pretend that none of it had ever happened, but I could never make it last very long.

Georgie stayed in bed most of the time. She seemed quite happy. We played cards and solved the crossword puzzles, and laughed about books and did all the things that we've always done, the things she likes. She wanted the newspapers, the gramophone that Louisa brought us, all the ordinary things, and as long as she had those she was quite happy. I remember she joked that people would be shocked if she wrote her memoirs, but she didn't mention Jimmy or the trial. She talked about Booth, though, how fond she was of him. I think she may have written to him, but he didn't reply. I didn't tell her we'd met.

There was a man I knew, Wilfred Strauss. We were at school together and he lived in a village near the house where we were staying, but I hadn't seen him for years. An acquaintance had told me that Strauss had become a recluse, but he sent an invitation that we should go to tea with him on a certain day. I thought Georgie would refuse, but she told me she'd written to him and accepted. It turned out that he was very well thought of in the neighbourhood and because he was a bachelor all the local ladies wanted to look after him. I think he must have been the only person in England who hadn't heard about the trial. At first I thought he was simply being polite, but it soon became clear that he wasn't interested in the papers or the wireless, or anything except his hobby, which was taxidermy.

We sat in his study, which was crammed with stuffed

animals of various shapes and sizes – everything from a llama with a monkey on its back to a glass case full of sparrows – and had a marvellous tea, just like the ones I remember from visits to other boys' houses during my school-days. I don't think I have ever seen so many different types of cake on a single table – all of them baked by these ladies. I remembered Strauss quite well from school – thin and rather shy, the sort of chap who gets called peaky and dosed a lot. He'd grown quite portly – too much cake, I should think. He ate it with his fingers and kept asking us if we wouldn't like another slice. Afterwards he took us round his house and pointed out all the things he'd stuffed. They were very well done – there was one in particular, a lioness, positioned with her head looking out from behind a door, as if she were about to spring. Strauss said he'd done it eleven years before and his housekeeper was still terrified of it. I remember he talked a lot about a taxidermist called Potter who used to make tableaux with small animals and dress them up in fancy hats and so forth. Strauss showed us one he was re-creating: guinea pigs playing cricket. He'd made stumps and pads for them, and he'd had half the women in the village stitching away at miniature striped jackets and caps with tiny badges on them.

Georgie was very elated on the way home. Strauss had offered his car, but she insisted we walk, to my great surprise, because she never walks anywhere if she can help it, she's too fond of motoring. As soon as we were out of earshot, she started roaring with laughter. 'Guinea pigs! Wasn't that the funniest thing you've ever seen in all your life?'

I couldn't quite see what she was getting at, so I said, 'Well, it's nice for a chap to have a hobby like that.'

'But those little coats and hats! Oh, Edmund, weren't they cunning?'

I didn't like the sound in her voice, because I knew that

once she got excited like that it might last for days, so I tried to calm her down, but she wasn't having any of it. 'Oh, darling, I'm so happy, I could stay here for ever. And wasn't it kind of Louisa to find us such a perfect little house? Don't you think it's wonderful, all this? Don't you, Edmund?'

'Yes, lovely. Can we go home now?'

'Wait, I want to pick some flowers. I'll pick some for you, shall I? Wild flowers? Would you like that, Edmund?'

'Let's go home, Georgie.'

'All right, stick-in-the-mud. Here you are.' She started trying to shove a great bunch of flowers into my buttonhole. 'We'll always be together now, won't we, Edmund?'

All her grasses and things were staining my jacket. I felt as if someone had poured lead into my stomach. 'Leave it be, Georgie.'

'Don't you see, this was meant to happen.'

'No, I'm afraid I don't see.'

'It was meant to be like this. I did love Jimmy, but I can't be too sorry, darling, because now I'm here with you.'

'I don't think you should talk about Jimmy like that, Georgie. Come on, let's get home.'

'We'll go home, Edmund, if you like. But that's what you have to understand, darling. There's nothing either of us can do to change it.'

That evening, I was sitting on my bench in the churchyard watching the sunset over the estuary. I thought about what Georgie said, 'There's nothing either of us can do to change it,' and it seemed to me that that was the whole problem. Because all my life, since I was a child, I've been in a fog, a great big pea souper. I can't see where I'm going – I can't do anything – I can't change anything. All my life. I was no good in the army, no good at my work, no good at anything. Useless, completely and utterly useless. I think I felt more lonely sitting on that bench than at any other time in my life. There was no one I could talk to – even Louisa wouldn't have understood. If I'd gone to her and said, 'I'm useless,' she would have lied to me, even Louisa; she'd have told me it wasn't true. Because you'd have to say that, wouldn't you?

I wanted to smoke, but when I put my hand in my overcoat pocket for my cigarette case there was something big and lumpy in there instead. I fished this thing out to look at it – it was one of the guinea pigs in cricketing flannels from the tableau. Georgie'd taken it. She'd stolen a bloody *stuffed guinea pig.* I suppose some people might have thought that was funny – perhaps it *was* funny – but to me it suddenly seemed like absolutely the last straw. I got up and walked out into the water and flung this thing away from me as far as I could into the estuary. I thought, I'll go after it. I'll go out there and the water will swallow me up, and that'll be the end of it. I felt so alone, so . . . closed off from the rest of the world, somehow, as if I were already dead, sealed up in a chamber with this fog all around me . . .

I don't know why I stopped. I think it was the reeds catching round my legs. I looked down and saw that my trousers were sodden, my overcoat was trailing in the water. I sort of came out of it a bit then and thought about Louisa, and what she would think . . . then I went back to the house.

ADA

I never went near the trial. I didn't want to hear Miss Georgina's and Mr James's private business told in front of every Tom, Dick and Harry. Mrs Seddon had to give evidence, but it was only about who was in the house and what Mr James said about locking the doors, and she said they were respectful to her, which was something. She told me that the gallery was stuffed with every journalist and nosy parker you could think of, with nothing better to do than mind somebody else's business.

Young Mr Gresham that inherited the house, Mr Leo, he didn't keep it long. He never lived there, just put it up for sale, lock, stock and barrel. Couldn't wait to get it off his hands, but there weren't too many wanted a big place like that – even if it hadn't had its name all over the papers – although I don't doubt there were lots that wanted to get a look inside it because of what they'd read. I missed the space, when we moved in here, and most of all I missed the light. When I first came here, I went down to the basement, and it seemed so dark and poky – I thought: Well, this is where you'll be stopping for the rest of your days, Ada, and I tell you I felt so miserable I could have cried. But you can get used to anything in time and at least we weren't bombed out like some poor souls.

Hope House was eventually sold to a school and as far as I know it's still there. I thought Miss Georgina would be upset to be turned out of her home, but she didn't seem to mind it and neither did Master Edmund. The night before those policemen came was the last night Miss Georgina ever spent at Hope House. Mr Leo said she wasn't to come back ever again and anyway, Miss Louisa had arranged for her and Mr Edmund to go into the country for a rest. Mr Leo paid off all the staff, all but me and Miss Jones, and we had a job and a half on our hands trying to sort everything out, I can tell you. Miss Jones had to be let go because Miss Georgina and Master Edmund barely had enough to pay my wage, let alone any other. Since the war there's not been even that, but you've got to take as you find, haven't you? And I've got my little bit that I've saved up over the years, so we're not ready for the poorhouse yet.

Miss Georgina did come back to Hope House the day Miss Jones was packing up her clothes. She kept interfering, pulling things out of boxes and leaving them lying about, saying she didn't want them, then saying she did, then saying she had to try them on to be quite sure . . . I was frantic with worry, there was so much to do, but Miss Jones was so patient, it was a miracle. When she'd finally got finished, Miss Georgina made a great play of calling the two of us together and she said to her, 'Now, there's something I want you to have, I've been saving it for you.' Then she cast around and saw that everything was packed, so she went to the nearest crate and started pulling things out, and she couldn't find what she wanted so she went to the next one, and the next . . . I don't know how Miss Jones stood it, watching all her work turned upside down like that. Finally, Miss Georgina came up with this old fox fur. It was the mangiest thing you've ever seen in your life, with great big bare patches, and honestly, you wouldn't have used it to line a cat's basket – it was only there because she never threw anything away. And she was going to give this to Miss Jones, who had been her maid for nearly seventeen years! I said, 'You're not going to give that to Jones, are you, Miss Georgina?'

She said, 'Why ever not?' As if I was the one who was mean. She held it out to Miss Jones like it was the crown jewels she was giving her.

Miss Jones said, 'Thank you, Madam.' How she managed to keep a straight face I'll never know, with Miss Georgina looking at her as if she was expecting a curtsey or something.

Well, the minute she'd gone, we *roared.* The room looked as if there'd been an earthquake, Miss Jones had this disgusting old fox thing wound round her neck and the two of us were holding on to each other else we'd have fallen down from laughing. I said to her, 'I'd better help you pack up again.'

She held out the fox and said, 'You can start with this. I'd hate Mrs Gresham to miss it.' Well, I thought I was going to burst, I laughed so much. Miss Jones did pack that old fur, as well, and Miss Georgina must have seen it in the cupboard when we got to Thurloe Street, but she never said a word. That's why I was so surprised when Miss Georgina gave me all what she'd worn in court. That's a tale in itself, mind you. I was sure Miss Georgina would want her best clothes for the court, but she didn't ask for a single thing. Instead, she asked Miss Louisa to choose for her and Miss Louisa was to ask her own dressmaker to sew the things. I was very surprised, because Miss Georgina was so fussy about her clothes: everything had to come from Paris, right down to the foundation garments, and she was always making nasty remarks about Miss Louisa's dress sense. Well, as I said, they weren't anything like Miss Georgina's usual outfits, but they were good clothes. I'd be wearing them now if I could fit into them, but Miss Georgina's always been as slim as a reed. They take up all my wardrobe, much more room than my clothes that I wear every day, but I've kept them nice.

You know, they never asked me to go with them to Thurloe Street, they just acted as if they expected it and I suppose I did, too. Apart from the clothes and the odd bit of furniture and carpet, Miss Georgina didn't take nothing out of Hope House more than she'd brought into it. Of course, none of the pieces fit, they're far too big for this little house, but what could we do? There wasn't the money to buy new and anyway it's all rubbish what you get now, there's no quality like there used to be. We had a dreadful job cutting down the carpets, too. The one that was in the dining-room at Hope House, the middle part of it is in Miss Georgina's front room now and the outside was cut into strips to go up the stairs. It was a shame to do that to a good carpet, but we didn't have any choice. It was Mr Herbert who did that. He'd been given his notice along with all of them, only he said he'd stay and help with the moving for Master Edmund's sake and he wouldn't take anything for it. I don't know what I'd have done without him and Miss Jones, I'd never have managed it on my own. But I hadn't time to brood over what happened, I had all the moving and then I had enough to keep me occupied. I had to do the cooking again for one thing and find a woman to do the rough. It took me three months to find someone even half-way decent. She's long gone now, of course, no money to pay her.

Soon after we were settled in, Miss Jones wrote to tell me that she and Mr Herbert were going to be married. I thought: What a pair of dark horses, because I never knew they were courting. I suppose I did feel a little bit jealous, if I'm honest. It was funny, I'd always thought of Miss Jones as young, because she wasn't twenty when I first knew her. But there she was, going on forty and getting married to Mr Herbert, who was one of the finest men you could ever hope to meet.

When the war broke out, Master Edmund was ever so keen on it. I went off to buy the material for the black-out and he came along with me, and then insisted on clambering all over the furniture and trying to rig it up. When the raids started he used to take the bottles – all the gin and whisky – he used to take them off the table and line them all up along the skirting board. He said that way they'd be safe if the house was hit. But he and Miss Georgina wouldn't have been safe because they insisted on sleeping upstairs. That was *her* doing, of course. She loved every minute of it. She used to go out looking at the bombed houses and watching them putting out the fires . . . and she'd bring things home – a tortoiseshell comb, an apostle spoon, a scarf that came up lovely when it was washed . . . They were little things, like you'd pick up a pebble off a beach. I suppose it was stealing, really, but with the house burst open by a bomb and everything scattered on the ground, it didn't seem like that. Once she picked up a lovely mirror in a silver frame. I don't know why it wasn't smashed, the bomb must have fallen in a funny way is all I can think. But it made her happy, finding those little things like that, and she used to put them in a big cardboard box under her bed. She never had no use for them, she just wanted to have them. Now I come to think of it, they must be still there.

That was before my sister Winnie died, when I still had contact with my family. Winnie got bombed out and her second daughter, Edna, she was evacuated with her three. The youngest can't have been more than six months. Edna said it was dreadful, this long train journey with nothing to eat, and no one had the first clue what to do with them when they got there. Edna was always my favourite, but I've lost touch with her since Winnie's death. I can't ask them here. It's no place for young people, this house. But it's a shame, really, because when you're my age, you want to see the young ones and Edna's are all I've got. Otherwise, what have I got to look back on, except all what I've said? I suppose you could say it was exciting with the newspapers and all that, not many people have had the life I've had, but it's hardly the same as a husband and children, is it? Grandchildren, too, I'd have had by this time, if I'd married. I could have been a help there, looking after them. That's what I should be doing at my age, enjoying my grandchildren and instead I'm stuck down here with nothing. I might as well have been born a dog, the way Miss Georgina's got me at her beck and call. 'Fetch, Ada!' Yes, that's what I'm like, a dog. It's not the work, I've never minded that. I'd have worked my fingers to the bone for my family, but I didn't get the chance.

I never thought I deserved more than the next person, but I did want a family, just what it's normal for a woman to want, natural, and there was William, he was asking me to marry him, but Miss Georgina would never have let me – not that she ever thought anyone would want to marry me. People like Miss Georgina think the whole world's their servant, they can do just as they please and not spare a thought for anyone else. But I stopped her little game once before, didn't I, when I told Mr James about Mr Booth, and she knows it was me who did that all right. I stopped her before and I'd do it again, too. Believe you me, if it comes to that, I *will* do it again – and it might. Because I've been thinking about a lot of things in the past few weeks – I may be old, but my brain still works well enough . . . and I've been making a little plan.

It's queer how you go through your life with certain things fixed in your mind: you should do this, you shouldn't do that. Well, it's almost like a belief, really, a way of thinking you get yourself into. Then one day you find you don't believe it at all, but it's just like a habit you've got of thinking that's how you should behave. Of course, there's good habits and bad, I wouldn't deny that, and normally I'd be the first to say let sleeping dogs lie, but I'm damned if I won't give this one a poke and see if he barks. After all, I'm an old woman now and I'll be dead for long enough, that's for certain. It comes down to what my friend Ellen said all those years ago, about having a choice. Because I never had a choice, Miss Georgina never let me have one. And when all's said and done, I'm a human being too, just as much as she is, and now I say that's what I should have. A choice.

PART TWO

83 Thurloe Street, SW
August 1955

GEORGINA

I'll pour my own drink tonight. Edmund usually pours my drink, but tonight I'll do it myself. One for Edmund as well. With my cocktail, wearing my most beautiful evening dress, sitting in my favourite chair, I'm quite ready. This always was my better profile. Photographs, paintings, everything, always this profile. Portrait of a lady. Portrait of a murderess. Portrait of an old woman drinking gin.

How extraordinary that it should all have begun with Roland. Stupid, handsome Roland. I wonder if he knew that Edmund was in love with him? I suppose Roland might have been a pansy, because he was certainly far too handsome to be anybody's husband. Perhaps he and Edmund did buggery to each other, because that's what they do, isn't it, pansies? But then things always get so confused in wartime, nobody knows where they are.

When you love someone you want to know everything, don't you? Everything about them. And now I do. I suppose I should be grateful to Louisa, really. The subject came up quite by chance when she was here yesterday. She'd come to make sheep's eyes at Edmund, as usual. I must say that quite the funniest thing about the whole episode was the way Louisa thought that *I* was the one who'd sent that wretched handkerchief to Roland. I confess I was puzzled for a moment when she mentioned finding it in Roland's things when they came back from France, but as soon as she said it was a handkerchief with writing on it, I knew exactly what she meant. 'To My True Knight'. Poor old Louisa. I almost laughed when I saw the mixture of sympathy and eagerness on her face – the furrowed brow, the speaking eyes – like a dog that wants to lick your hand. So pathetically easy to imagine what a ridiculous fairy-tale she'd made up all those years ago . . . that I was in love with Roland . . . that I'd married Jimmy because Roland didn't want me . . . how I'd had to hide my grief when he was killed . . . I almost started laughing, but then I realised what must have really – what really happened: Edmund and Roland. Together.

I had to tell Louisa everything. If the circumstances were different, I might have kept silent, but she wanted to take Edmund away from me and I couldn't allow that. Besides, I've been sparing her feelings for long enough, and why should I? She's been biding her time ever since Davy died last year. *Let no man put asunder.* Except that women are the ones you have to watch, not men. But I'm far too clever for her. Besides, I haven't come this far to give up Edmund to a woman who looks like a failed attempt at a French poodle.

Well, she's gone now and I don't suppose she'll be coming back. Women like Louisa make a fetish out of understanding people, but they know absolutely nothing. The silent sympathy, wanting to please, to be liked, to be loved – but with all that love and sympathy she couldn't understand Edmund and Roland, could she? But I can. Because Edmund and I are the same. How could we ever be parted? I can forgive him for Roland because I understand him. Forgiving him is the easiest thing in the world.

Another little drink wouldn't do us any harm, as they say. I don't want us to lie in a grave and rot like poor little Freddie. Scatter our ashes to the wind and that'll be that.

I'm not going to say any more. If you want any more you can sing it yourself.

Chin-chin.

ADA

Supper's only cold bits tonight: bit of cold meat. I wish it was something better, but I burned my arm a few weeks back, it's come up in a great blister and I've been frightened to use the oven ever since. But no matter what's on the table, Miss Georgina always has the silver out. Although you probably wouldn't know it *was* silver, the state it's in nowadays.

I think I'll have a glass of sherry. Just a little one won't hurt and besides, I've got to have a bit of a celebration. Better put a comb through my hair first. Might even look in the mirror, seeing as it's a special occasion. Haven't looked in the glass since I don't know when. Might surprise myself. Been doing a lot of that recently, I have, surprising myself. I'll surprise a few other people, when they hear what I've been up to, as well. Because do you know what I did? I wrote a letter. Not to just anybody, but to a certain person. Can you guess who that person was? Not the Queen or Mr Churchill, but someone important to me, very important – but I can't keep it to myself for ever, not for one more minute, in fact. I wrote to William Ferguson. I'd had it in my mind to do for some time – I'm more than just a pretty face, you know – but I was worried that it wasn't what you should do, write to a man. My dear mother would have said that it was what fast girls did – not that she could write much more than her name – but times change and girls do all sorts since the war, don't they? And if

I'm not old enough now to know my own mind then I never will be, that's what I say.

It wasn't a love letter or anything like that, it was just a note, really. *You may be surprised to hear from me after so many years, but since my last, I find myself in different circumstances from my former. A meeting would be very agreeable to me if you would care to.* William must have replied the same day he received it, because Master Edmund brought his letter down two days after I'd sent mine. He said he was glad to hear from me and he asked me if I still liked a walk in the park – I'll have to tell him my legs aren't up to it now, but it doesn't matter, because he said in the letter that he's got his own car, imagine!

I shouldn't get too excited. At my time of life it's not decent. But now I know I might have *something* if I'm granted another couple of years. Because why would William answer my letter if it wasn't meant to be? And I'll tell you something for nothing – if he asks me this time I'll say yes straight away. I'm going to tell him about the pickles as well, repeating on me. I nearly wrote it in my letter but then I thought: You can't put a thing like that in a letter. But I am going to tell him that was why I didn't say yes straight away the last time, not because I didn't want to. That's the kind of thing you need to know about someone if you're going to marry them, that pickles don't agree . . .

I know, I'll have one of Miss Georgina's chocolates to go with the sherry. Just the one. It can't hurt, diabetes or no diabetes. This box is supposed to be pink, but you'd never know it from the lid. Been sitting in the sun too long. I thought as much when she gave them to me. And they've all gone and melted inside the box. She must have been given these as a present and quite a few years ago, too, by the look of them. Still, I'm not one to bear a grudge and anyway, we're past all that now. But I will say this: Miss Georgina's stopped me once from doing what I should, but she'll not stop me again. I won't give her the chance. Because William and I are *meant*, as I said. What I've done this evening, that's for others to judge whether it's right or wrong, not me. But I'll tell you this: if I went and left Miss Georgina, she'd find some other poor soul to torment, same as she's done to me, same as she's done to her own brother if the truth were known. When I say 'torment', I don't mean like the devil with the old toasting fork that they used to tell us about in church – although Miss Georgina could teach the devil a thing or two if she wanted, I'm sure of that.

And it's not just myself I'm thinking of. There's Master Edmund and Miss Louisa too, because she's a widow, now, since Lord Kellway died last year. So you see, you've got one that can stop four being happy and that doesn't seem right to me. But don't go saying I've gone mad. I've been thinking it over for a couple of weeks now and I say a fair exchange is no robbery. Because what's Miss Georgina had of me? My life, that's what she's had. Now, that may not seem much to some, but it's the only life I've got or ever shall get if it comes to that.

It's simple, really. It's my pills I take for my diabetes. The doctor gave me a new sort. He said to me, 'Don't go taking too many of these, Miss Pepper, or you'll drop off to sleep and we'll never wake you up again.' I told him I'd lost them. The whole lot. Said I dropped them down a drain in the street, but I never, I've got them safe in my bag. There's no taste so's you'd notice and since sugar's been off the ration I've been putting a lot more into Miss Georgina's cocoa. It was an accident the first time, putting in two spoons instead of just the one, but then I thought: Well, there's an idea, so I've been piling it in until the cocoa's like syrup and the cup still comes down empty on the old dumb waiter. There's enough sugar left in the bag for one more cup. I've crushed the pills, I wrapped them up in paper and brought the rolling pin down on them. Made my hands hurt, doing that, I had to run them under the cold tap until they felt better. Now I'll just put the cocoa on the dumb waiter and send it up . . . Gone!

So you see I'm not mad. I've worked it all out as careful as anything. It'll be very peaceful, just like falling asleep, really, and then – well, perhaps I'll put on the brooch Miss Louisa gave me. I meant to save it for William, but it won't make any difference if I wear it now. I've got it in one of the biscuit tins. A burglar wouldn't think to look there. And my white gloves, I knew I'd put them by for something . . . This is a proper celebration. Shame there's no one to share it with, really. I shan't tell William about any of this, mind you. He always was a little bit proud of himself and I don't want him getting ideas . . .

It's funny how your memory works, really, or perhaps it's just the sherry, but I suddenly remembered something Charlie and me said years ago, something I'd forgotten I'd remembered. Or remembered I'd forgotten, I don't know which. It was when we were quite small. We were sitting on a wall somewhere – which was unusual in itself, come to think of it, because Bertie was usually off playing with the other boys. But that day we were together and he said to me, 'What would you like to see most in the world?' Well, I couldn't think of anything, so I said the Queen – Queen Victoria that was – I said I'd like to have a sight of her. 'Course I never did. But perhaps I'll see this queen. I should like to see her, because she's lovely, Queen Elizabeth, ever so beautiful. Perhaps I'll go with William. We'll go together to see the queen. 'Your Majesty, may I introduce Mr and Mrs William Ferguson. Ordinary folk, but you won't find loyaler subjects in all of England.'

What's that? Great loud bang, nearly knocked me over.

Honestly, they'll have the plaster down off the ceiling if they're not careful. What do they think they're doing with loud bangs at this time of night? I'll have to go and see to it, whatever it is. Can't have been a bus, not unless it's run off the road and into the house. Oh, that would be dreadful, I hope it isn't that. Well, the sooner I get upstairs, the sooner I'll find out. Come on, Legs, take me – up – the – stairs – just – once – more – so – we – can – see – what's – at – the – top. Little rest now. Get breath back. Feel dizzy – that must be the sherry doing that. *Lips that touch liquor shall never touch mine.* Dear, oh dear. Well, I hope Miss Georgina finds some peace. She's never had none in this life, that I do know. Not from herself or anyone else. Off we go again, Legs, nearly there now. Just catch my breath and then – nasty stiff old door handle, come on, open up . . . Here we go – now we'll see what all this racket's in aid of. What? What are you doing? I don't understand – what are you doing? Oh, no, no – I . . . William, oh, William, Wuh

EDMUND

Georgie was pouring a cup of cocoa between the floor-boards when I came in. That bright smile. 'I didn't mean you to see, darling. It was sweet of you to think of it, but I've never liked cocoa. I don't know what Ada does to it, it looks more like that brown paint every day. Do you know the paint I mean? The plain one they use for walls?'

It's all a game to her. Nothing's more important than a bloody crossword puzzle. Nothing means anything except whatever word she's chasing. 'Distemper.'

'That's the one.'

She wasn't surprised when she saw me carrying the gun. 'You heard it, didn't you, Edmund? What I said to Louisa?'

I heard every word of it. I was standing right outside the sitting-room door. Eavesdropping, I suppose. I was going to go in – to see Louisa, because I was upstairs when she arrived – but then I heard them talking about Roland, about when he died. Louisa said, 'But it was so much worse for you when poor Freddie was killed.'

'I was a child. I barely remember Freddie.'

'I mean, at least there was a good reason for Roland's death. He wouldn't have wanted anything different.'

'No, I don't suppose he would.'

Then I heard Louisa say, 'I'm sorry, Georgina, that was thoughtless of me. Does it still hurt to think of Roland?' Georgie didn't answer and she said, 'I know, Georgina. I've known ever since I found that handkerchief you sent him. I recognised the writing. I thought you were so brave. You must have been desperately unhappy and yet you never said a word. Oh, you don't need to worry, I've never told a soul. When I found out, I wanted to talk to you about it so much. Edmund said it was him, but I understood why you didn't want to see me . . .'

Georgina started laughing. 'You thought I was in love with *Roland*?'

'I realised when I found the handkerchief. It was with his things. I kept trying to write you a letter, but I couldn't think how to say any of it, and I was worried that James might read it and that there would be a terrible—'

'What handkerchief?'

'Surely you remember? It said "To My True Knight". In red ink. You'd written it.'

Until that moment I had no idea what Louisa was going to say, but as soon as she started talking about it I knew it was the favour and I knew that Georgie would realise, too, and when she did, she would tell – because it was me, not Georgie but me, *I* had given Roland Georgie's present – 'To My True Knight' – Georgie would guess everything, she's clever and she knows everything, and she would hate me and want to punish me, and she would tell Louisa and . . . I stood there, outside the door, and I realised all those things, quick as a flash, one after the other. It was like being punched. I knew I must get away from the door before Louisa came out, but I couldn't seem to move. I could hear Georgina talking, but I couldn't take in the words. I heard her say something about Roland, then she – then I heard her say, 'Don't you understand, Louisa? Edmund and I have been lovers since the war.'

There were footsteps coming towards the door, they were too quick, I couldn't get away, couldn't get to the stairs in time. Louisa saw me standing there in the dark passage like some sort of criminal. I went towards her, I didn't really know what I was doing, but I got myself in front of her, I suppose with some idea of trying to explain myself. I wanted to speak to her, but my mouth couldn't seem to let the sounds come out. Then I tried to move my hand towards her to touch her, but I had somehow got myself jammed – I was stuck like a cheap sort of mechanical toy. Louisa was moving towards me very fast with her head down and I could see she wasn't going to stop, so I tried to move again, this time so that she could come past, but I couldn't. It was as if all my muscles had locked together; I didn't have any strength to make my legs work, and I was standing between Louisa and the front door. I tried to say her name, but all that came out was a rasping noise. She wouldn't look up, she was pawing at me to get past, sort of swiping me with her hands, and then she suddenly gave me a shove and I fell sideways on to the hall table. By the time I'd righted myself she'd gone.

I stood there holding on to the edge of the table for some time, I've no idea how long. I know at one point I tried to move, but my legs didn't seem to be working very well and I only succeeded in knocking a lot of newspapers on to the floor, so I thought I'd better hold fire for a while.

It mended eventually, whatever it was, and let me get upstairs. I got hold of the gun. I hid it under the chest of drawers the day we came here. Georgie didn't know. What they call a side-arm. Put six rounds in. To blow my head off, I suppose. Sat on the bed for a while, holding it ... *I shall be whiter than the whitewash on the wall.* No bloody whitewash left on the wall now. Not one bloody brushful. Couldn't bear the thought – without Louisa. Can't let Georgie take Louisa. Can put up with many things, but not that. Can't put up with it. Hope. That's what it is. Chap's got to have hope. No hope without Louisa. Might as well go straight on the scrap heap.

Decided to go downstairs with the gun. Not angry, quite calm in fact. Arms and legs working again, in good order. Sounds coming out of the mouth. Practised a bit of talking in the mirror: 'Hello, this is Edmund Lomax speaking to you in English.'

I thought I would kill her, you see, but her pouring cocoa between the floor-boards and talking about distemper threw me off a bit. She made me a drink. Gin. Strong one. Said I needed it. I didn't need it – drank it to please her, that was all. Always done everything to please her. What she wanted. Not her knight, though. Not anybody's knight. Wanted to be Louisa's, but wasn't good enough. Never good enough.

Georgie wanted me to kill her, you see. To shoot her. I didn't realise at first. She said, 'I knew you would have a gun somewhere. Have you got bullets or shells or whatever they're called?'

I said, 'There's not much use in a gun if you haven't got bullets, is there?'

She said, 'Well, is it loaded?' She wasn't at all frightened, more excited, as if it was an adventure. 'You're the man of the family, Edmund. You have responsibilities.' I asked her what on earth she was talking about and she told me to sit down. We had the drinks then, while she talked. I don't know if it was the gin, or what it was, but everything just started slipping away from me, I couldn't get a proper grasp of things . . . When I entered the room I thought I wanted to kill her, but then she made me so confused, I couldn't think. I didn't want to, I wanted to put the gun down, just to . . . oh, I don't know. I don't know what I wanted. But then Georgie said, 'I didn't want to have to tell you this, Edmund, but I killed Freddie.'

'You didn't kill him. A stranger killed him, a madman.'

'I killed him, Edmund. He was making too much noise. Always following me around. "Dordir, Dordir," in that silly way of his, demanding attention. Making a noise. "Little boys are allowed to make a noise, Miss Georgina. Little girls must play quietly."'

'No, it was a stranger. Just somebody who was there. They killed him. It was an accident. They killed him by accident, then they ran away.'

'I hit him with a stone.'

She kept saying that *she'd* killed Freddie. What I said about an accident, I didn't know if it was true or not, it was the first thing that entered my head, because I couldn't believe . . .

But she insisted. She kept telling me, 'I threw the stone into the privy afterwards. I killed him, Edmund.'

'No.'

'I did it, Edmund. You know I did. Haven't you always known it?'

Have I always known it? I can't remember. I don't *think* I've always known it, but perhaps that's wrong. A thing like that, you'd remember whether you knew it or not, wouldn't you?

Georgie said, 'I killed your brother, Edmund. Don't I deserve to die?' Deserve to die . . . I don't know if she deserved to die. I don't even know if she was telling the truth. She said I've got responsibilities, but how am I supposed to know what to do? She's always told me what to do. She could have been making it up – I don't know, I can't remember anything about it. Georgie said, 'Be careful, Edmund. Don't spoil my dress. Madame Tussaud's will want it.' Then, 'Goodbye, Edmund. I love you. Kiss me, I want to die with a kiss on my lips.' So I kissed her and she made me – she took hold of the gun and made me put it into her mouth, and then she started retching and coughing so I took it out, but she made me put it back –

her eyes were staring, looking at me, making me do it. She's always always telling me what to do . . . And I did it. *I did it.*

I suppose I must have forgotten about Ada. She'd obviously heard the shot and she came up to see . . . But she startled me, popping round the door like that. I didn't mean to shoot her, it was just a reaction, a . . . reflex. Poor Ada. I suppose most of her life has been spent with us one way or the other. Where would she go when we didn't need her any more? What would happen to her? Perhaps it was for the best, really; she couldn't do much any more. Still, not much reward for a lifetime of service, was it? But at least you don't have to come up here and find us, poor old girl. At least I've spared you that.

Too tired to stand up any more. Have to slide down the wall – like *so* – easier to be on floor. Put the gun between my knees . . . Nice to sit down here in the doorway between Georgina and Ada. My two guardsmen. I thought I would die at Passchendaele. Should have died. I suppose one ought to be grateful, but I've made such a mess of everything. People leave notes, don't they? Jimmy did. Not that there's any paper down here apart from old newspapers . . . Got no pen. Can't get up again. That rhymes. *Got no pen, can't get up again.* Never get up again now. Besides, who would I write to? Not Louisa, not now. 'I'm sorry.' That's what they usually write, isn't it, suicides? But I'm not sorry. I'm glad. I've been waiting for this for a long time. Such a long, long time . . .